It's Not You It's Me

Allison Rushby

First edition May 2004

IT'S NOT YOU IT'S ME

A Red Dress Ink novel

ISBN 0-373-25058-4

www.RedDressInk.com

Printed in U.S.A.

ALLISON RUSHBY

Having failed at becoming a ballerina with pierced ears (her childhood dream), Allison Rushby instead began a writing career as a journalism student at the University of Queensland in Brisbane, Australia. Within a few months she had slunk sideways into studying Russian. By the end of her degree she had learned two very important things: that she didn't want to be a journalist; and that there are hundreds of types of vodka (and they're all pretty good).

A number of years spent freelancing for numerous wedding magazines ('Getting on with your draconian mother-in-law made simple!', 'A 400-guest reception for $2.95 per head!') almost sent her crazy. After much whining about how hard it would be, she began her first novel. That is, her husband (then boyfriend) told her to shut up, sit down and get typing (there may, or may not, have been threats of severing digits with rusty scalpels if she didn't, but it's okay, he's a doctor).

These days, Allison writes full-time, mostly with her cat, Violet, on her lap. Oh, and she keeps up her education by sampling new kinds of vodka on a regular basis.

You can read more about Allison at www.allisonrushby.com.

It's Not You It's Me

ACKNOWLEDGMENTS

Firstly, I'd like to praise the Goddesses for managing to put Karin Stoecker in the right place at the right time, and Tess for e-mailing to tell me that she was. It's nice to know that good things *do* come out of gossip!

Thanks to Karin, Sam Bell and Margaret Marbury, along with the gals of the RDI NYC team, for showing me a good time worldwide. Strangely enough, all the restaurants I went to served excellent gelati and I was left wondering if my dessert reputation had preceded me.

:-) to all my Web-site buddies who read this novel in e-serial form and had the good manners to beg for each new installment.

Danken Sie Gott for Heidi and Thomas who (I hope I got that right!) speak German. Also to Jeff Zalkind of www.worldofcrap.com fame for his "Learn to Swear in German!" page, which came in very handy because Heidi and Thomas aren't rude-on-command kind of people.

Nibble, nibble to the literate guinea pigs. Again.

But, mostly, hurrah for David. For just hanging in there.

Chapter One

I've got approximately forty minutes to spare in the airport lounge, even after I've done the obligatory pick up and put down everything in the newsagent thing, and the 'Ooohhh it's lovely, but I can't afford it, duty-free or not' *faux* shop. With nothing else left to poke and prod, I find the nearest café and order a skinny latte. I'm sitting, stirring the sugar into my napkin-ringed glass on autopilot, when I hear the announcement reverberate around the airport.

'Could passenger Mr Jasper Ash please notify the nearest Qantas desk of his whereabouts?' the voice booms. 'Mr Jasper Ash—please go directly to the nearest Qantas desk.'

Do not pass go, do not collect $200, I think absentmindedly.

And then the name they're calling sinks in.

Jasper Ash.

I stand up suddenly, to see if I can spot him. I can't. Of course I can't. It's a big airport, and from the sound of that announcement he's probably not here anyway. The other people in the café look at me as I frantically search the faces walking past. When I sit back down again I realise why they're staring—jumping up so fast, I've spilled most of my coffee in my saucer and it's run over and formed a puddle on the table.

Jasper Ash.

Now there's a flashback.

'Jasper Ash,' I say the name to myself quietly, as if mouthing the words will somehow make this all seem more real.

It's a name I haven't said, or heard anyone else say, for some time. Mainly because it's a name that doesn't get a lot of use any more. Not now that he's got a new one, that is. A new name. A new name for a new life.

I wonder for a moment whether it's actually even him— the Jasper Ash I know. But then have to admit to myself that it probably is. It isn't exactly a common name. And it's pretty likely he'd travel under it—being his real name, it'd be the one on his passport. It's not unlikely he'd be in an airport, either. I'm sure he does a lot of travelling these days.

A waitress comes over to wipe down my table for me, and I order another skinny latte as most of the old one's now retreating to the kitchen in her soggy sponge. While I'm waiting for it to arrive, I can't help but think back to the days of Jasper Ash.

We met—it must be almost three years ago now—because he was looking for a new place to live. He was going steadily crazy where he was at the time. The guys he'd been living with—all engineering students—were too noisy for him and constantly gave him ten kinds of crap about studying voice and piano at the Conservatorium. He told me once, later on, that when he read my ad in the classifieds of the Saturday papers he couldn't believe his luck. A cheap share on trendy, hip and young Magnolia Avenue, complete with a river view? Right near the best shops, the best restaurants and within walking distance of the Conservatorium? He'd thought it was simply too good to be true.

Still, Jasper being Jasper, he didn't ring early about the room, and it would've been almost three o'clock in the afternoon when he turned up on my doorstep already over half an hour late. I was actually surprised to see that he'd made it to the door. Half the people who'd made appointments to check out the room that day hadn't even turned up. Well, that's probably not quite true. Most likely they'd turned up, parked, seen the place and driven away at high speed. I'd expected that, though, because 36 Magnolia Avenue—Magnolia Lodge, to its residents—was a little, um, different from the rest of Magnolia Avenue.

Different. I laugh to myself with a small snort now, making the people seated at the few tables around me in the café look over again. Magnolia Lodge, *different*. That's the understatement of the new millennium.

The thing was, the rest of Magnolia Avenue consisted of trendy little townhouses with big wooden decks, cosy braziers, remote garages and low-maintenance courtyards. Scattered in between these were dinky little cafés and shops that only ever sold one kind of thing—designer products for pampered pets, frozen life-on-the-go takeaway gourmet meals, five hundred kinds of scented candles, and so on.

Well, 'and so on' kind of stopped at Magnolia Lodge. Magnolia Lodge was tucked up right at the end of the street, hidden in the corner as if it were a decrepit old organ that was being rejected by the rest of the street's sprightly young body. The fact of the matter was number 36 was not so trendy, not so hip and *definitely* not so young. It was actually more like a pensioner palace—a thirty-apartment block full of old people and…

…me.

The token young person.

Well, at least it was a politically correct apartment block.

I could see the 'this wasn't what I was expecting', mouth hanging open, shocked surprise written all over Jasper's face when I opened my front door. At another time I probably would have had a laugh about it and asked him if he was trying to catch flies or something, but the truth was I'd just about had it with finding someone to rent the spare room in my apartment for some extra cash. This was the third Saturday that I'd been ushering people around the place. And those were the polite ones—the ones who hadn't done a runner when they finally found the apartment block behind all the shrubbery.

'Hi, I'm Charlie—Charlie Notting.' I stuck my hand out.

He shook it. A good shake that made me lift my eyebrows. It wasn't like most of the soggy Weetabix handshakes I'd been getting in this doorway lately. 'Jasper Ash,' he said.

I invited him in and offered him a drink, which he declined. Instead, he just stood in the middle of the living room and looked around.

'Not what you were expecting, hey?' I got right down to it.

'Never—'

'Never even knew it was here.' I finished off the sentence I'd heard from just about anyone who'd ever knocked on my front door. I tried not to sound too defensive as I said it.

He nodded.

'Nobody does.' I sighed then, wondering just how many more times I could do this before someone's blood ended up on the carpet and I lost my bond money. 'Would you really like to see the place, or are you just being polite?'

He turned and looked at me then, and I felt bad. I hadn't meant to snap, but I'd just about got to the end of the line with this whole showing people around thing. This was my home. I liked it. And having several people every Saturday for three weeks in a row slag it off wasn't my idea of a good time.

I think Jasper might have got what I was really saying by the tone of my voice, because he shook his head then. 'Don't get me wrong. It's nice—the apartment. Just didn't know the street went up this far.'

I started to warm to him a bit when he said that. This guy—Jasper—he was perhaps a bit nicer than the other people I'd shown through. He seemed sincere, anyway—as if he really *did* think the apartment was nice—which was a start. I took a deep breath in and tried to quell my nasty side. 'Come on, I'll give you the grand tour.'

We did the whole thing. The kitchen, the bedrooms, the two bathrooms, even the garage, despite the fact that Jasper didn't have a car. Eventually we headed back inside and stood on the balcony overlooking the garden and, beyond that, the river.

'Wow. Really is a river view, isn't it? It's magnificent.'

'Yep.'

'What's that?' He pointed at something down at the end of the garden.

'Oh, that's the shed. It used to be a boat shed, but the people who live here are mostly too old to be messing about in boats now, so they let me use it instead.'

'What for?'

'I'm a sculptor—that's what I do. When I'm not waitressing to pay the bills and trying to finish off my degree, that is.'

'You're a slash person too, huh? Probably a good sign.'

I gave him a look. A slash person? 'What's that supposed to mean?' I hoped he didn't have a machete stuck down his pants.

He laughed. 'Sorry. Didn't mean to scare you. Just that everyone our age seems to be a slash person these days. Waiter-slash-actor, waiter-slash-writer, waiter-slash-artist. I'm a music tutor-slash-songwriter myself. A waiter-slash-sculptor-slash-uni student, yeah? That's great. Never met one of those.'

I had to laugh when Jasper had finished explaining this to me, because it was true. Everyone *did* seem to be a 'slash person', as he called it, these days.

Personally, I was trying to cut my slashes down and just be a waiter-slash-sculptor by finishing off my last subject at uni—the last few credit points before they would finally give me my BA in Fine Arts. Finally. I'd stuffed around here and there, and left all the subjects I didn't fancy but had to do till last. While I should have graduated last semester, there was one subject—a Modern History one—that I couldn't quite seem to pass. Mostly because of the vast number of dates the subject required me to store in my brain. There was just something about dates and my brain that didn't click. Anyway, this was my second attempt.

I was about to tell Jasper as much when there was a knock on the door. I went over to find that it was Mrs Mc-Cready, who wanted to let me know they were about to have high tea and a game of croquet on the lawn in a moment or two.

'Wonderful,' I said to her. 'I've got a lovely tin of lavender shortbread that I've been saving. I'll bring it down with me.'

When I closed the door and turned to head back to the

balcony, Jasper had moved and was now standing facing me. 'Lavender shortbread?'

I stopped in my tracks, right there in the middle of the living room, as I realised that my quelling-the-nasty-side thing obviously wasn't permanent. It didn't seem to matter how well we'd been getting along, talking about slash persons. All it took was this one little comment and a tiny smirk from Jasper to bring the past weekends rushing back at me, pushing me over the edge into shrew territory. I put my hands on my hips then and let it rip.

'You know, I like it here. It's a bloody great apartment for the price, and the people here are really nice. So what if they're old? They care about each other, and that's more than I can say for any of the apartments I've lived in before this.' I paused for a breath. 'God, I could have died in one of those places and no one would have known until the smell wafted out or someone's cat coughed up my eyeballs. If you had any guts you'd come downstairs with me and actually *have* some lavender shortbread and maybe *play* a game of croquet. It wouldn't kill you.'

Jasper just smiled an amused smile. He leaned back on the balcony, calm and composed. As if he owned it, really. 'No idea what you're talking about. Just never heard of *lavender* shortbread before, that's all.'

I took my hands off my hips, uncertain. 'Oh.'

'I'll play a game of croquet. Have some of that lavender shortbread too, if you're offering.'

There was a pause. I cleared my throat. Cleared it again. 'OK, then. Let's, um, go.' And I grabbed the tin out of the kitchen, trying to avoid his gaze as I passed by. Then, together, we trundled off downstairs.

Down in the garden, Mr Nelson was setting up the trestle table and the ladies of the Lodge were hovering around

him, waiting to put their darling little china plates of miniature sandwiches and butterfly cakes onto it.

'Here, I'll give you a hand with that.'

Jasper, to my surprise, went straight over to help Mr Nelson out. When he was done, he introduced himself. I put
my tin of shortbread on the now erected table and introduced him round to everyone else. Mrs Holland, who made
the best cucumber sandwiches—buttered, without crusts,
the secret was to use *real* butter, not the low fat, olive oil,
canola-based stuff that seemed to be all you could get in
the shops nowadays—Mrs Kennedy, who made the best
iced tea, Mr Hughes, who made the best Victoria sandwich,
and the two Miss Tenningtons—identical twin sisters—
who weren't the greatest cooks, but were always able to provide the best gossip in the whole building. We overlooked
the fact that they made half of it up. It was still good gossip.

Introductions over, Jasper and I made ourselves comfortable in two low-slung deckchairs to watch the first
game of croquet. We had to have those chairs—everyone
else claimed their bones were too old to get out of them.
When Jasper had watched long enough to work out what
was going on, we played a game ourselves, highly unsuccessfully—the two Miss Tenningtons creamed us with their
years of experience—but we had a great time anyway.

As we played, I got to have a better look at Jasper. I
hadn't really had a good chance before, during the tour of
the apartment. And then, of course, after the lavender shortbread incident there'd been a lot of deliberate non-eye contact. But now I saw he was taller than I'd first thought. Very
tall. Maybe six-foot-four? Thin too—but not in the too-
skinny 'my mother never fed me' way—and very dark, with
almost black hair and equally dark eyes.

The one thing I really noticed, however, was his manner. My God, but he was lovely. He was *charming*, in that fifties kind of fashion which you see only infrequently these days, in women or men. Not the kind of fake 'let me open the door for you, my dear' sleazy charm that makes hardcore feminists want to pull their armpit hair out in frustration and leaves the rest of us wishing we'd had the good sense to grow some so we could do the same, but the kind of charm that makes everyone around the person who exudes it feel good about themselves.

It's a gift, that kind of charm. And it was a gift that Jasper was using in full force that day. He was laying it on thick—flirting shamelessly with the Miss Tenningtons, who tittered around coquettishly, loving every minute of it and vying against each other in the way only identical twins probably can for his attention. It occurred to me that with his looks and his manner he should have been Irish. Or a film star. One of the old ones. The proper ones, like Jimmy Stewart.

I stopped myself then, realising I was letting my imagination get the better of me. What was I going on about?

When the game was finished, Jasper and I sank back into our deckchairs with some iced tea and a plate heaped full of tiny cucumber sandwiches, a few butterfly cakes and some of the lavender shortbread, which was proving to be quite a hit.

'So?' I eventually said to him, mouth full of butterfly cake. 'What do you think?'

'They're the best.' He held up half of the butterfly cake he was eating. 'This place, though, it's a bit strange.'

'What do you mean, exactly?'

'Er, croquet on the lawn? Butterfly cakes? Cucumber sandwiches? Bit like being in the middle of a Miss Marple film, isn't it?'

I understood what he meant then. All too well. I'd had the same thoughts myself for the first few weeks after I'd moved in. 'Don't worry, sooner or later you'll hear Mr and Mrs Ruben in apartment 21 screaming at each other and throwing the crystal around and you'll take the Miss Marple thing back. I did.'

'Ah. So these are just the civilised people?'

I nodded and laughed as I dusted some icing sugar off one side of my mouth. 'Pretty much. They've all got their secrets, though, just like everyone.' I leaned in towards him then. 'Mr Hughes, for example, has been having a rendezvous or two with Hilda Tennington. I've caught her sneaking out of his apartment a few times now.'

'Really? Hilda? Sly old dog.'

'Apparently he needs his eye drops put in for him.' I nodded as conspiratorially as I could before I leaned back out and started talking normally again. 'What I really meant to ask you about was the room.'

'Oh. The room. I'll take it, if that's all right. Long as you can promise me I won't be the one who's murdered at the start of the midday movie.'

'I think I can promise that.'

'My piano? That'll be OK too?'

'It's fine with me. It'll be nice.'

'What about everyone else? They mind?'

I looked around at them all. Somehow, I didn't think so. 'Jasper, if I know them as well as I think I do, they'll probably be knocking down the door to have sing-alongs. You'd better learn how to play "A Nightingale Sang in Berkeley Square" before you move in. It's their collective favourite.'

'Easy enough. Then I'll take it.' He stuck out his hand for me to shake to seal the deal. 'But only if you call me Jas.'

Chapter Two

So, Jas it was.

And after the ladies had made him polish off the few left-overs on the table we waddled back upstairs. I made sure we were out of earshot of anyone else before I told him the one and only condition of his moving in.

He could only stay till the end of the year.

I explained that it wasn't personal or anything. None of us—the whole fifty-two, three cats and two illegal dogs—who lived in the building would be here this time next year. Because, in approximately eleven and a half months' time, Magnolia Lodge was going to be demolished to make way for a swanky new apartment complex. One hundred apartments, a pool and a gym. One hundred apartments that you couldn't swing a cat in, but would look like all the other hundreds of apartments and townhouses in the rest of the street.

Jas said this was fine, that he'd be finished uni by then and was planning on moving to Sydney when he was done.

He moved most of his stuff in that night.

Over the next six months or so, we got on brilliantly. Even better than I'd thought we would. Our lifestyles suited each other, for a start. When we weren't at our crappy jobs—waitressing at a café for me, piano-tutoring at a kids' music school for Jas—or at our separate unis, we were busy at our 'real' work.

I'd be sweating away down in the boat shed, welding together my latest piece of sculpture, or making my way to the dump to search for interesting pieces of scrap metal to use for my next. I was thinking about holding an exhibition in the middle of the next year. Meanwhile, Jas would be tinkering away at the piano, songwriting. Sometimes, if the wind carried to the boat shed just right, I could hear him playing the same bar of music over and over again, adding a piece, subtracting a piece, the song getting longer, in fact *becoming* a song, as the days passed. Our work was similar in an adding, subtracting, trying things out way that eventually led to an end product after a lot of sweat and a bit of good luck.

When we needed some time off we'd head to the local swimming pool, have a barbecue in the nearby park, or just take a walk. Once I took him to Byron Bay for a week, to visit my mother. He was blown away. Not a great surprise, because most people were by my mother and the things that surrounded her: by her house, which was wooden and built over five levels down a hill to make the most of the view; and by her own sculpture, which dominated every room and the front courtyard of the house and was made entirely of sandstone—not like my metal productions at all (to tease me she would call me 'junkie Charlie' because of my frequent scavenging trips). But mostly by her, with her booming voice and large-enough-for-a-whole-group-of-people personality.

The real surprise was the fact that she liked him back. Suffice to say that Mum didn't get on with all that many people. She either liked them or she didn't, and usually she'd tell them her verdict within the first five minutes of meeting them. Sometimes it could be quite embarrassing.

She told me on the phone, a few days after we left, that Jas would be very famous one day. She could tell by his aura. When I relayed this to him, Jas thought it was the funniest thing he'd ever heard, but he still called her back pretty smartly to see if, hopefully, she had any other nice big fibs to tell him.

Community life at Magnolia Lodge went along swimmingly too. Right from the moment he started flirting with the Miss Tenningtons on the lawn, Jas was a hit with the elders of the building. The funny thing was, after a few months of our living together, a rumour seemed to have passed around that we were married. We became officially Jasper-and-Charlotte to the people we knew fairly well, or 'the nice young married couple in apartment 10' to the people we knew only in passing.

One day, when we came home, there was an invitation under our door to my own wedding shower, organised by Mrs Kennedy in apartment 14. I went over, invitation in hand, to explain that we weren't really married, but when she opened the door Mrs Kennedy and the three other ladies who were there planning the party were so excited I didn't have the heart to tell them the truth.

It was a recipe shower, as it turned out, and I still have all the recipes in the scrapbook they gave me today. I don't use the Miss Tenningtons' mutton one very much—never, in fact—but the caramel fudge one from Mrs Holland comes in quite handy on rainy Sundays.

Jas and I became even more involved in building life after

our fake marriage. We played croquet every second Saturday, and even started going to bingo on the second Tuesday night of each month. After our first night at bingo we made a pact.

We would draw the line at bowls.

Bowls, we decided, would be taking it too far. Apart from the white uniform being expensive, and a little more than unflattering, we agreed that it was probably best to save something for our *own* retirement.

As we got to know the people in the building better, little treats started to turn up on our doorstep. Lemon butter. Lime butter. Passionfruit butter.

There was a lot of butter.

Pumpkin scones, fruit scones and plain scones were also popular.

We'd do little things in return. Change lightbulbs. Open tough jars. Things like that. Whatever we could, really. But while things were tottering along beautifully with everyone else, it was at this time, around the six-month mark, that Jas started to act a little oddly.

I'd always thought it was strange that he never brought any friends back to the apartment. In fact, a few weeks after he'd moved in I'd noticed this and thought that maybe he was worried that it wouldn't be OK with me. So I mentioned it, asked if he wanted to have a housewarming or something and invite all his friends along. He just shook his head. He was busy, he said. With his work. Now, I knew that he didn't get on with his family very well, that they didn't agree with what he was doing— studying music—but there must be people he socialised with, and why he didn't want them in the apartment was a mystery.

As for me, I had people over by the dozen. My mother,

my aunt Kath, friends from work, the odd love interest—whoever.

I didn't give up on the friends thing with Jas, though. I would ask again, every so often, just in case he changed his mind. Or, that is, I kept asking until things went a bit strange. Because all of a sudden Jas started bringing people home. Every weekend. Always different ones.

And all girls.

The first time, I didn't think much of it. I got up on a Saturday morning, half dressed, and went into the kitchen to find some tall blonde girl there I didn't know. I knew Jas had been out the night before with some people from uni, but I didn't know he'd brought someone home. I said hi, made a hasty cup of tea and scooted back to my room with the paper. When I emerged an hour or so later she was gone, and Jas didn't seem to want to say anything about it.

The next week, it was the same.

There was a girl there Saturday morning.

And a different girl there Sunday morning.

All blonde and all tall. Well, maybe there was one bordering on brunette and one you might have called strawberry blonde…but always a different girl.

The weekend after that there weren't any girls. Not here, anyway, because Jas didn't even bother to come home.

Things went on like this for weeks. Girls arrived, then disappeared mysteriously early in the morning of the next day. For the short periods of time it was just us in the apartment Jas hid in his room, working furiously. He avoided me. He avoided everyone. He stopped going to croquet, he stopped going to bingo, he even looked as if he'd stopped eating, he got so thin. The ladies pressed new recipes on me, fattening recipes for lasagne and roasts and bread and butter pudding with butterscotch sauce.

I went through stages. At first I was worried—this wasn't like Jas, not like the Jas I knew, anyway. Why was he suddenly so withdrawn when we'd been getting along so well? I tried to talk to him, but he dodged the questions, avoided me, simply didn't come home. It carried on and on in the same way. The girls kept coming and would leave around midday. I'd stay holed up in my room until they left.

It was embarrassing, having to go out into the kitchen when there was a 99.9 per cent chance there'd be a half-naked girl in there who always looked too good for that time of the morning. And generally with a smile that even lemon-scented Jif and the scratchy side of the kitchen sponge wouldn't be able to wipe off her face.

I just didn't feel comfortable.

After weeks and weeks of this, I started to get a bit shitty. I was sick and tired of being a prisoner in my own room every weekend morning. And things had heated up. Girls came over during the week. And when, one Saturday, a few of my CDs went missing, I moved up from shitty to simply furious. I didn't talk to Jas for the rest of the week and decided that if things kept up like this he was out.

But things didn't stay like that at all. Because after that Saturday the girl thing stopped just as abruptly as it had started. Jas didn't go out with the friends from uni any more, either. The friends I'd never met.

During the week that it all came to a halt Jas took me out for dinner and apologised awkwardly. He said he'd been stressed, that he'd gone a bit crazy, hadn't known what he was doing, but now knew he'd been acting like an idiot. He promised it wouldn't happen again.

I didn't know where to look. I mumbled something in reply and that was that. After that evening we didn't talk about it again. And a few weeks later things returned to al-most normal between us.

For a while, anyway. Because as time passed I started to realise something about myself. A thing that came as a bit of a shock.

I knew I'd overreacted a touch about Jas having all the girls over—and I'd felt as guilty as hell when I'd found the 'missing' CDs under my bed a few weeks after Jas had hit the emergency stop button on the chick conveyer belt. In fact, I'd worried and fretted and carried on about the girl thing so much I was behind on my sculpting. Uni was suf-fering too. I'd already had one extension on an assignment I couldn't seem to get started, and it didn't look like as if it was going to be handed in any time soon. I'd simply spent hour after hour during those weeks sitting in the boat shed doing nothing. Staring at the walls. Staring at the floor. Star-ing at the ceiling.

And I was still doing it. The staring thing. Especially if I could hear the piano.

It wasn't just that, either. There was the weekend thing too. The thing where I'd wake up at five-thirty or so every Saturday and Sunday morning like clockwork and lie there, wondering if there was a girl in Jas's room. Praying that there wouldn't be and being overjoyed when it was true.

I kept on like this for months.

And by the end of the year, just a few weeks before we were due to move out, I was so far behind on my work I realised I was never going to catch up in time to hold my exhibition. Not that I even wanted to any more. Because I'd been slowly realising that there was something wrong with it all. Something not quite right.

I couldn't relate to what I was doing, where I was going with my sculpture—couldn't get involved. Up at the apartment I'd hear Jas working away, completely absorbed in his songwriting, frustrating me with every note he played on the piano. I would have given anything, *anything* to be able to block out the world around me like Jas and my mother seemed to be able to do for hours at a time.

Things had only got worse on the uni front as well. I'd received a conceded pass on my assignment, and was now trying to convince myself that the saying 'third time lucky' might just be true, because it certainly didn't seem as if I was going to pass on this, my second, attempt. It was the worst of times. And then, as if all of the above wasn't enough to be getting on with, I worked something out.

I'd been sitting there in the boat shed, doing little or nothing as per usual—unless you could call kicking around the bits of scrap metal on the floor doing something— when it came to me. I could hear Jas playing and singing. A new piece I hadn't heard before, or couldn't remember. It was perfect, whatever it was, and I knew he must have written it himself. It suited his voice, which I noticed instantly, because a lot of things other people wrote didn't. He had a strange voice, low and raspy. Very distinctive.

Halfway through his song I became startled and coughed. I'd forgotten something. To breathe, in fact. And I needed to desperately. I felt something strange and brought one hand up to my chest. My heart was going thumpa-thumpa-thump. That's when it came to me.

I was completely, desperately, totally, devotedly, idiotically in love with Jasper Ash.

I was in love with Jas.

Why I hadn't realised it before was beyond me. It was so obvious.

The feelings I'd found so hard to control when he'd had

girl after girl over for the night. The waking up early every weekend morning. The sitting and listening when I should have been working. The…oh, everything.

It was cringeworthy.

So that's what I did. I sat for a bit longer. But this time, instead of staring at the walls, staring at the floor, staring at the ceiling, I cringed. Long and hard. And when I was done I wondered just what I was going to do about this. This…love thing. The L thing. It didn't take me long to realise there wasn't much I *could* do.

It was pointless.

In two weeks' time, Jas and I would be packing our belongings into boxes. In three weeks' time we'd be moving out. Jas to Sydney and me to my mother's place in Byron Bay. And there wasn't any way I could change that. Not my plans anyway, because my mother needed me. She was sick. And I was going to go and look after her.

There wasn't any way Jas could change his plans to move to Sydney either, because he'd made this great contact. Some guy in the music industry who might be able to get him started in the business. So that was that. To say anything now would be pointless.

Futile.

Basically, an all-round waste of time.

Chapter Three

So, I shut up about it. I hid my feelings.

Oh, probably not very well. I have to say that much. I was probably as transparent as the thinnest of thin rice paper. I probably mooned around the apartment like a lovesick cow. But Jas didn't seem to notice, or if he did he didn't say anything, and things continued as usual.

Until our third last day together.

We'd been fairly busy up until then. Of course everyone in the building had to leave, so we'd spent the last few weeks running around and helping out with the odd spot of packing. Wrapping up endless china cups and knick-knacks for the arthritic Miss Tenningtons—why old ladies always seem to own about a hundred china cups and saucers in rose patterns that never match is beyond me—and waving people off as their families came and transported them to, usually, nursing homes.

By our third last day together, our third last day in the apartment, just about everyone we were close to had gone.

There was only a handful of people left in the entire building. It was quiet. Too quiet. Even the building seemed to know it was coming to the end of its days, because the day before the lift had stuck between floors—thankfully, there was no one in it—and had refused to budge for twelve hours. It had taken five workmen to get it started again.

It was almost midnight when I got home on that third last day. I'd just finished my last shift at my crappy waitressing job, and though I should have been ecstatic I wasn't. The day before I'd been notified that I had officially failed my Modern History subject. Again. I had a million boxes to pack. I had to move. My mother was sick. All my friends from my days at Magnolia Lodge were being packed off to nursing homes around the country that they didn't want to go to. My sculpture had died a slow and painful death. Life wasn't exactly great.

When I got up to the apartment and opened the door I was surprised to find it was dark inside, even though Jas had said he'd definitely be up late packing. Just as I was about to turn the light on there was a noise—a chair scraping against the balcony tiles. I dropped my hand from the light switch and looked out to see Jas stand up.

'Hey,' I called out, wary, a part of me already sensing something was wrong.

'Come and take a seat,' Jas said.

I crossed the floor, dropping my bag and keys on the dining table on the way.

'What's up?' I tried to read Jas's expression as I sat down in the iron chair he'd pulled out for me. Before he could answer, something distracted me. I sniffed. Sniffed again. Spotted the small plastic bag on the balcony ledge, then the papers and the lighter. 'Is that...?'

Jas made a face. 'Was. Sorry.'

My eyebrows lifted. I hadn't seen Jas smoke before. 'What's going on?'

'Don't know how to tell you this, Charlie…'

'What? What is it?' I started to get scared. 'Is it Mum?'

'No. No, nothing like that. It's Mr Nelson.'

'Mr Nelson? What's wrong with him?'

Jas paused. 'He died this afternoon, Charlie.'

The information didn't really register at first. I'd waved at Mr Nelson that morning as he stood on his balcony, and only a few days ago I'd run over to his apartment to give him an old toiletries bag I didn't need any more. He'd mentioned he needed one. And Jas—Jas had been over there all the time. He and Mr Nelson got on like a house on fire— they were always up to something. Usually no good. Their favourite pastime was swapping dirty jokes. Preferably dirty jokes about blondes. What was it with blondes?

'It was a stroke.'

I didn't say anything. There wasn't anything to say. No protests to make. I simply stared up at him blankly, then back down again at the balcony floor.

Jas kneeled down in front of me and put his hands on my knees. 'Can I get you something? A drink? Water?'

I tried to say no, but nothing came out.

'Charlie?'

I shook my head, unable to meet his eyes.

Jas stood up and pulled out another of the chairs to sit beside me.

And then we sat.

We sat there for ages on that balcony. Just sat. Saying nothing. Watching the shadows move around on the lawn and the ferries travel up and down the river.

At about twelve-thirty a.m. I got up. 'I'm going to have a shower,' I said.

I showered until I'd used all the hot water up. Then I stood there for a bit longer as the water got colder and colder, until it was freezing, almost punishing myself. I don't know why. Now, I think maybe the sensation of the too-cold water made me feel something other than the numbness I'd felt since I'd walked through the door and heard the news.

When I finally emerged from the bathroom, Jas wasn't on the balcony any more. I walked into the kitchen to see if he was there, which he wasn't, then went back to the bathroom, still drying off my hair. 'Jas?'

'In here.' The voice came from his bedroom.

I hung my towel over the bathroom door before going over and pushing his door open slightly. He was lying on the bed. Face up. 'You OK?'

'Yeah. Just tired.'

I went in and lay down beside him on my stomach, my chin resting on my hands.

It was then that we talked about Mr Nelson. I can't remember exactly what we spoke about, but I remember we talked for hours. In the end, not just about him, about…everything.

And I must have fallen asleep right where I was, because I remember waking up halfway through the night and looking for my bedside clock to check the time. This confused me because, of course, not being in my bedroom, it wasn't there. I must have woken Jas up then, because he rolled over and his arm landed on top of me. Now we were both on our sides.

Kind of close.

Actually, from my point of view, more like kind of *achingly* close.

I stayed as still as I could. I didn't move in case he moved. I didn't dare.

Then, slowly, it dawned on me that I wasn't going to be able to control myself. Or my arm, anyway. Because my arm, independent of my sanity, started to snake up and under his arm and over his back. And with a little levering we were closer still. Close enough to…

…kiss.

Which is what I started to do to him. Very softly at first, so soft that he didn't even wake up. But that didn't last very long. Because, like I said before, I couldn't control myself. I couldn't help it. It just…happened.

As I leaned in even closer, my heart was thumpa-thumping again, like it had done in the boat shed all those weeks ago, and I remember this strange feeling washing over me. Half of me was petrified of what Jas would do when he woke up, the other half was so excited I didn't think I would be able to wait until he did. It was *excruciating*.

And then he woke up.

His eyes flicked partly open and his body jerked, startled. I knew then that this was it. Whatever happened next was how it was. How he really felt. There was a sickening moment as Jas started to pull away…

But then he leaned in. Even closer. And he started to kiss me back.

It was—well, even now I can't explain it. I've never been kissed like that before, or again. I don't think I ever wanted anything that badly, so for it to actually happen—I wasn't even sure I was really awake. The one thing I could tell, though, was that he wanted it to happen too. Because the moment he'd opened his eyes and realised what was going on he'd seemed relieved for a split second. As if he'd been waiting. Biding his time the same as I had.

We kissed for what seemed like for ever. Until I decided it wasn't enough.

Still painfully nervous, I inched my way on top of him. And I mean inched. I was so scared. Scared that this bliss would stop at any moment. But we kept kissing. And I kept inching. Finally I was there. At the summit. I had climbed Mount Everest. If I'd had a flag, I would've stuck it in.

Charlie was here.

I became gamer then, spurred on by my victory. I ran my hands underneath his T-shirt and then, in one swift movement, pulled it over his head. His chest was just beautiful. And, yes, I know everything I'm saying is so cliché and next I'll probably be using awful words like 'glistening love cavern', 'glowing milky-white orbs' and 'throbbing, pulsating manhood', but that's how it was. I mean, after all the lusting I'd been doing over the past month or so, Jas could have had a full third nipple and I would have waxed lyrical about its lickability or something.

And, oh God, as if things weren't good enough already, he then ran his hands up over my thighs and onto my hips, pushing my white cotton nightie up in the process.

I thought I would die.

But not before I'd remembered my manners and thanked my fairy godmother for giving me the foresight to shave my legs that morning and not to wear my rotten old men's pyjamas with the easy-access fly panel that was, well, a bit rude at times.

He rested his hands on my hips then, on top of my undies, and I prayed, prayed, prayed as hard as I could, to the goddess Hussy, that he would just rip them off. But he didn't. His hands slid down again onto my thighs.

I started to get impatient then. Why don't men ever know there's a time for foreplay and a time to get straight down to business? I'll never understand it. I didn't want to get bossy, though, so I decided to get even gamer instead. I wiggled my hips down, down his body, until…

Eureka!

I found what I wanted. What I *needed*. And, my, it was glorious. Truly glorious—there are, after all, benefits to a guy being six-foot-four. It was everything I'd been dreaming of in that boat shed and more. So, Charlie, I told myself. This is it. Really it. Not that silly flag stuff on Mount Everest, but country-conquering territory.

Slowly, slowly, I snuck my hand into his boxers. I wanted so badly just to grab it, but I didn't. I like to think I'm a lady! Instead, I prolonged the agony. I ran my hand over his hip and down onto his leg. Over his stomach and…oh, everywhere. Everywhere but. And when I couldn't wait any longer I went for it. But then something went wrong.

I stopped, confused. It was, um, shrinking. And, frankly, that wasn't something on my agenda. It wasn't something that was supposed to happen.

Oh, fuck.

'Charlie—don't.' Jas had frozen. 'Just get off me,' he added, scrambling up, pulling my hand out of his boxers.

I moved just as fast off the top of him and onto the other side of the bed.

And inside my head I swore and swore and swore.

The one thing I was grateful for was that it was dark in the bedroom, like the balcony had been before. This was a good thing, because for that awful, quiet moment before anything was said I knew that I just never wanted to see Jas again. I wanted the bed to engulf me. For me to sink right in, where no one would ever find me. To never have to hear what he was about to say.

I waited, all the time just dying inside. Withering away. And those words kept repeating and repeating themselves in my head. *Charlie—don't. Get off me. Charlie—don't. Get off me.*

At first, sitting on the other side of the bed, Jas didn't say anything. Then he sort of groaned, and that was it. But it was a telling groan. Or at least I thought it was. A 'how embarrassing, my flatmate's just jumped me' kind of groan. *Charlie—don't. Get off me. Charlie—don't. Get off me.*

And then it started. 'Charlie, I…'

Charlie—don't. Get off me. Charlie—don't. Get off me. I couldn't bear it any longer. 'Just say it. And quickly.'

He stopped. Ran both his hands through his hair. 'Don't know what to say…'

'How about "you're repulsive, Charlie"? Oh, too late. You already covered that. No words required.'

He reached over somewhere beside the bed then. I watched his hand.

Oh, no. No!

The light turned on.

As if it wasn't bad enough just to hear what he was going to say, I had to hear it in the light. Where every expression could be read. Where he'd be able to see each word stab right through my heart. And it was so bright, that light. Worse even than the lights in dressing rooms when you're trying on swimsuits after a sucking-coffee-through-double-choc-coated-Tim-Tams/triple-helping-of-sticky-date-pudding Winter.

'How can you say that? That you're repulsive?' He looked at me as if I was crazy.

'You obviously think so.'

He stretched his hand out to touch me on the arm.

'Don't.' I pulled away.

'You know that's not what I meant. It's not you. Not you at all. It's me.'

I laughed then. Really laughed. 'That's original. It's not you, it's me. I've never heard that one before.'

He swung his legs over the side of the bed so that his back was to me. 'No, I mean it. It *is* me.' There was a lengthy pause. 'I just can't.'

'Yeah. Right. With me, you mean. What you mean is, it's me. Not you. Me. *Me!*' The fact that he couldn't just admit the truth drove me past crazy.

'I…' He ran his hands through his hair again. Hard. I flinched, wondering how much hair he'd just pulled out. 'Just can't. Not now. Not with you.'

I sat there, winded by those final three words. Final in every sense. *Not with you.* So it was me. And there it was, out in the open. Strangely enough, it didn't make me feel any better. 'But all those girls…' I thought to myself, then realised the words had actually come out of my mouth. I shut it tight, but couldn't shut out my remembering their oh-so-similar morning smiles. Their different faces. Names. Amanda. Rachel. Kirsty. Sophie. Rebecca. Theresa. What was so different about them? I became acutely aware of the bed beneath me. The bed in which, not so long ago, they'd all…

Ugh.

Something inside me started to bubble after this. I sat there for a bit longer as it churned away in my stomach. And then I worked out what it was. It was anger. It was easier to be angry than to feel embarrassed—less painful. Soon enough, it worked its way out. 'Well, I'm sorry I'm not good enough,' I spat, hitting the mattress with one hand.

He turned again. 'Charlie, don't be stupid.'

'Stupid? What's so stupid about it? One minute you're sleeping with every girl in sight and the next minute you're throwing me off. What am I supposed to think?'

Jas stood up. 'Wish I could explain it to you, but I can't.'

'What's there to explain?' I was acting like an idiot and I knew it, but I felt that if I stopped fighting, even for a moment, I'd just break down and cry—and I couldn't, *wouldn't*, do that. Not here, anyway.

I got up off the bed and snorted inelegantly. 'I guess I'm just not blonde enough for you.' Jas had started to say something, but I held my hand out to stop him. 'Don't say it. Just don't talk to me. I don't want to hear it.' My voice was getting louder and louder by the minute. I turned and left the room, slamming the door behind me.

Chapter four

I don't think I slept at all that night.

It didn't seem to matter what I tried to think about, that one moment in time kept running itself through my head again and again. The awful moment when I knew it had all gone wrong. The moment when the, um…tower crumbled and fell, for want of a better way of putting it.

What I didn't understand, though, was that I'd been sure he was interested. At the start, that is. After all, he was the one who'd pulled in—he'd *kept* kissing me. So why pull away later instead of as soon as he'd got a chance? It just didn't make any sense. And the more I thought about it, the more convoluted the whole thing got. So convoluted that it gave me a headache, and at five a.m. I had to get up and take some paracetamol. Which must have worked, because the headache was gone when I woke up again at eleven-thirty.

I lay there for fifteen minutes or so, just listening, to see if I could hear Jas in the apartment, hoping that he wouldn't be around so I could get up and go down the hall safely to the bathroom. I didn't hear anything. And when my bladder couldn't stand the stress one minute longer I got up. As I went down the hallway I had a quick scan around. He wasn't there.

But things had changed.

After my trip to the bathroom I took a closer look. Most of Jas's stuff that had been packed away earlier in the week was gone. I went down the hallway to his bedroom and opened the door. All that was left was his bed and some clothes. I closed the door smartly—the last thing in the world I wanted to see right now was that bed—and made my way to the living room.

There was a note beside the phone.

Charlie
As you've probably already noticed, I've moved most of my stuff out. I'll come back and pick the rest up around one. Not sure if you'll be there or not, but you know you can always get me on my mobile if you want to talk. Either way, I'll give you a call at your mum's in the next few weeks. I don't want this to be the end of us.
J.

I don't want this to be the end of us. I re-read it, holding the note in my right hand.

Ha! Us!

What 'us'? There was no 'us'. There was only me, lusting after Jas, and Jas who wasn't returning the favour. Unrequited love. There's nothing *quite* so embarrassing. I did the cringing thing again, thinking about it.

And what made me feel even worse was that I'd seen a friend go through it once. Unrequited love, that is. I'd watched her make a fool of herself for months on end over some guy. Seeing everyone else watch the proceedings like a spectator sport had been equally as bad as the point when the guy had finally turned her down and she was heartbroken.

Exactly how Jas must have been feeling about me. Utterly embarrassed for me. Udderly, I thought, as I remembered the lovesick cow once more.

I checked the clock on the wall. Just past midday. I had to get out of the apartment. And fast.

I had the quickest shower of my life, dressed in anything I could find and ran to the bus stop. I didn't care where I went, didn't care what I did, just so long as I wasn't there when Jas came back. I didn't want to be around to see that embarrassment of his when he came through the front door.

I went to the movies and saw something. I can't remember what it was, just that it was bad and something I never would have seen if I'd had any real choice about it—which I didn't. The fact was, it was on, it was a two-hour time-filler, and that was all I cared about. After that I bought a shirt I didn't like nor want, and definitely couldn't afford, then picked up some groceries that I didn't need. At five p.m. the shops closed, and as I couldn't bear to see another film I wasn't remotely interested in I caught the bus home.

Jas wasn't there, and everything—every last possession that was his—was gone.

I went into his room and just stood there. I couldn't even smell him. It was as if he'd never been there at all. As if he'd never existed. I walked around the room slowly, running one hand against the wall, taking everything in. I stopped when I came to something rough.

Oh, nice.

The bed-head. Jas's metal bed-head had made a mark on

the wall. No prizes for guessing how that had happened. And who it *hadn't* been with.

I turned and left the room, wondering why I'd gone in there in the first place. It had been a stupid thing to allow myself to do. I had to keep busy, to try and forget about what had happened.

I made my way to the kitchen, stopping by the phone on the way to turn the answering machine off. And then, when I had, I thought better of it and switched it back on again to screen any calls.

In the kitchen, I was surprised to find another note from Jas. Well, not another note. The same note as before, with a sentence or two scribbled onto the bottom. He'd added:

Hoped you'd be here so we could talk. Will call.
J.

He did call. Several times, in fact. But I didn't call back. And funnily enough it wasn't me, but my aunt Kath who saw him next, three months later. We were both staying at my mum's, looking after her while she was unwell. Watching a rare spot of TV one evening, she suddenly hollered, 'Charlie—Charlie, come here, quick.'

I rushed into the living room. 'What?'

She just pointed at the TV 'Isn't that, um, what's-his-face? Your flatmate? The guy you were living with?'

After a good few minutes of wide-eyed staring at the TV my brain kicked back in. I was surprised she'd even spotted him. Because it was Jas, all right. But at the same time it wasn't Jas. It was someone called…Zamiel. Apparently named after one of the original fallen angels—not to be confused with the original *Charlie's Angels*, of course.

He was wearing a full black leather bodysuit held together with what looked like safety pins, along with thigh-high boots and a whip. He'd been made-up with a whitened face, lots of kohl eyeliner and blood-red lipstick. His hair, black as black, was doing things that hair simply can't do by itself, and it was so hideously razored I just *knew* some celebrity hairdresser had been paid a very large wad of money to get the desired effect.

I flinched seeing it. Him. The closest I can come to describing it would be Edward Scissorhands meets Liz Hurley's famous Versace dress on acid.

I sank slowly down onto the floor and watched the rest of the programme. It was one of those half-hour current affairs shows that like to expose mechanics who are ripping the general public off, banks who are ripping the general public off and, every so often, run another story as well. Naturally, they'd gone to town on this baby.

It seemed that Jas—sorry, *Zamiel*—was the lead singer in some band called Spawn. The presenter seemed to be under the impression that everyone knew about Spawn, so I presumed they'd been in the media for a while now and, being so busy looking after Mum, I just hadn't heard about them. Apparently the group was promoting some less than desirable things, like devil worship. There was lots of lovely information specifically about Zamiel too. Like *Playboy*, they'd arranged these things into two categories—his likes and dislikes.

Likes: eating live animals, sleeping in his custom-designed coffin, seducing young boys.

Dislikes: organised religion, old people, vegetarians, Britney Spears.

But then they got to the biggie. Zamiel as the new homosexual pin-up boy. And his new boyfriend. A very, very famous actor.

Cue footage of very, very famous actor sticking his tongue down Zamiel's throat.

Cue presenter saying how disgusting it all was and that society was obviously falling apart at the seams.

End of story.

'Oh,' Kath said, and I jumped a bit. I'd been so engrossed in watching the TV I'd forgotten she was even there. 'Oh,' she said again. 'And I thought he was such a nice boy. I guess I'd better go check on your mother.'

And then she left me by myself. But I was never really alone, was I? Not when I had my acute embarrassment to keep me company. It was back again now, in full force. Jas was *gay*. He *was gay*. *He was gay*.

And then, inch by inch, the redness crept its way up my neck and took over my face as I realised what it was I'd done. He was gay. And I, Charlie, had jumped him and then screamed a million things at him to cover up my embarrassment at being rejected. When really what he had been trying to do was tell me something.

He was gay.

Oh, God.

I put my head in my hands then and stared blankly at the TV. There was a sitcom on and I suddenly wished that all my problems could be solved in the final five minutes of every half-hour too. A tall blonde had chosen that precise moment to walk into the kitchen on the show and I was suddenly reminded of something. Those girls. Over that month. In the Magnolia Lodge kitchen. The ones with the smiles. What about them? That was the one piece of the puzzle that didn't fit.

I sat and thought about it for ages. I tried to work back through the whole thing. Tried to see it from an impartial point of view, rather than that of the lovesick cow.

Moo.

First there were no girls. There weren't even any friends. Then, for a short period of time, there were lots of friends and lots of girls. Then there were no friends and no girls again. So most of the time there were no friends and no girls. It just didn't make sense. But maybe…

Maybe that was the whole point? That it *didn't* make sense. Perhaps that was where I was going wrong in trying to sort this all out. After all, he was at uni, he dressed nicely and he'd bought us both tickets to *The Sound of Music*. Oh, no. That was it. No wonder it didn't make sense to me. It hadn't even made sense to him. Because that was what he'd been doing—he'd been working it all out, the sexuality thing. Like you're supposed to do at uni. And now he'd worked it out. He was gay.

Charlie, my girl, you're a genius.

Just three months and a very embarrassing incident in Jas's bedroom too late.

I really couldn't call Jas back after that, and when he phoned again, around a month later, it was at a bad time. Mum had been really sick for a few days and had finally let Kath and I take her to the hospital. She hated the hospital, so we tried to stay with her for as many hours of the day as the staff would let us. To make matters worse, it was hard for me, being at Mum's—seeing her sculpture and realising I was getting nothing done. Going nowhere fast. Then there was skipping around the subject of uni every time someone asked when my results were coming out.

I was preoccupied.

And by the time Mum was home again I'd conveniently lost Jas's number. So I didn't call him back that time either. Yes, I know it's a poor excuse, but I had other things on my mind. Mum, taking care of the house, catching up on sleep…plenty of things that seemed far more important at the time.

Life went on without Jas, until eventually it was time for me to move back out of my mum's and get on with my life. It felt like an eternity since the days of Magnolia Lodge, but in reality it had only been six months. Six months since I'd seen Jas. Well, that's not entirely true, because since the night that Kath and I had seen him on TV, Zamiel was suddenly everywhere. The media had gone Spawn mad, and I couldn't turn on the TV or buy a newspaper or magazine without some piece of scandal in it about him.

Packing my bags, I came across Jas's phone number—in my undies drawer, of all places. I held it in my hand for a few seconds, entertaining the thought of picking up the phone and actually calling him. Having a laugh like the old days. Giving him some well-deserved grief about his long hair and leatherwear. But only for a few seconds. Then I shoved the piece of paper in my jeans pocket—out of sight, out of mind.

I found it again the next day, when I was in the kitchen. Once more I held it in my hand. I think I might have even reached out for the phone this time. But if I did I wrenched my hand back smartly and then busied myself pouring a tall glass of water, because the next thing I remember is taking the glass outside with me to sit in Mum's sculpture court-yard.

As it happened, I chose to sit on Jas's favourite piece of hers—a full-size table and four chairs. Some people thought it was weird when they saw it, but what they didn't know was that it was *our* kitchen table and *our* chairs. Mum's and mine before I'd moved out of home the first time. I'd watched her photograph it from every angle one day when it was at its messiest, complete with the Sunday paper, left-over bits of crusty bread, a tub of butter, a jar of honey, the chairs we'd been sitting in pulled out and left at angles. And that was the sculpture, the scene frozen in time.

I smoothed the phone number out on the table, eyed it until I'd finished my glass of water, and then systematically tore it into the smallest shreds I could. As I tore I went about convincing myself that everything really was different now. Not just between the two of us, because of what had happened at the apartment, but truly everything. The small world we'd built together was no more, just like the apartment block we'd lived in. There was no point in calling him. I wasn't part of his new life and I didn't want to look like a desperate groupie, wanting to be remembered now he was famous.

It would be almost another year and a half before I saw Jas in person again.

Chapter five

'Flight 624. Flight 624 to London via Singapore is now boarding. At this time we would like to ask that first and business class passengers, and passengers in rows 50 and higher please board first. Other rows will be called shortly.'

I stop thinking about Jas and Magnolia Lodge and wake up to myself. That's me. My flight. I check my boarding pass, see that I'm in row 55, and get up hurriedly to board. As I leave I notice my coffee. I haven't drunk a drop of that second cup.

I wait in line to swipe my boarding pass and collect my headphones, wait my turn for the flight attendant to tell me which side of the plane I'm on, wait for people to stow their bags. Finally I make it to my seat. An aisle seat, just like I'd asked for...but right next to the toilets.

Well, I think, I didn't see that coming.

And, even better, I've been lumped with the oldest plane in the world. No personal TV screen for me, and the nearest communal one is miles away.

When I'm settled in, I check the in-flight magazine to see what movies I'll be missing out on. Seen it, seen it, seen it and don't want to see it anyway, so I'm fine. I try not to move on to thinking about the other downsides to flying on the oldest plane in the world—the fact that it might not stay in the sky. I ditch the in-flight magazine then, and memorise the safety card.

When I'm done, I crane my neck, looking out of the window to see if I can spot the viewing lounge, wondering if Kath and her husband Mark and my two favourite people in the world—their newborn twins, Annie and Daisy—have stayed to watch the plane leave. I'd offered to catch a cab out to the airport, but Kath had insisted that they take me—they were hunting for an excuse to go on their first big outing as a family and I was it. I squint, scanning the airport windows. They might still be here. I don't think they'll be rushing home after all the effort it had taken to get to the airport in the first place.

In order to see me off they'd had to get up early and practise assembling and disassembling what we'd come to call the mega-stroller of death and destruction. They'd been trying to reach the record time of a five-minute set-up, but so far couldn't break the seven-minute barrier.

Frankly, crossing the carpeted airport floor, we'd looked as if the five of us were about to make a trek through the Himalayas rather than one of us was flying to London.

I still had to step back in wonder every time I saw that stroller. You couldn't even call it a *stroller*, in my opinion. I went shopping with Kath and Mark to buy the thing and quickly became stroller-flabbergasted. First of all, there were whole shops devoted to the things. Just to strollers! Then there was the choice these shops offered. There were strollers for running and strollers for shopping, and even strollers with little flags that you pulled along behind your mountain bike.

The one Kath and Mark finally decided on was the biggest smash-'em-up-derby stroller of them all. Hence the name—the mega-stroller of death and destruction. The mega—for short—was a double seater that, like eighties limos, seemed to go on for ever, with a tray down at the bottom that you could carry things in—like three weeks' worth of groceries, if you had to—and all kinds of things that flipped in and out. It probably even had indicators and side mirrors that I hadn't discovered yet.

I bought them a bumper sticker for it—'This *is* my other car'.

Still, there obviously wasn't enough room for everything in that stroller, because as we'd made our way towards Immigration, Mark had had to stop every so often to pick up the bits and pieces he was losing off the contraption as he went. A teddy bear here, a Teletubby there. Annie and Daisy had simply gurgled happily.

'Here we are,' Mark had said, pulling up the stroller in front of my stop. I'd given Kath a hug then. And Mark a hug. And Annie and Daisy a kiss. And then another kiss. And then another one.

I was going to miss the twins terribly. I'd prepared myself for it because I knew I'd got all too used to having them around for the last four weeks. The whole four weeks of Annie and Daisy's lives. Not having them as my sun—the thing my eating and sleeping and just about everything revolved around every day—was going to feel strange. Very strange indeed.

I gave them both one last kiss. 'I'm going to miss you guys,' I said, taking one each of their tiny hands.

'Ring me when I'm up at four a.m. feeding them and I'll swap places with you,' Kath groaned.

I looked up at her and laughed. She didn't mean it. But then I took another glance. Noticed the bags underneath her eyes. OK, so she might mean it a little bit.

'I've got to go,' I said, giving Kath and Mark one quick, last hug. 'Thanks so much. For everything...'

'Stop it,' Mark said. 'We should be thanking *you*. You've been a huge help this month.'

'Go on.' Kath urged me over to the Immigration queue. 'Have a good time. Enjoy yourself. And don't think about...things. Just have fun.

'And call us as soon as you get off the plane,' she added as an afterthought.

'OK, I will.' I turned around and headed off. I didn't look at the twins again, or I knew, just knew, they'd give me one of their silly googly smiles and I'd end up kissing them for ever. Such a sucker.

But that's the way aunts are supposed to be, isn't it? Well, honorary aunts, anyway. I'm really a cousin, but because of my age, and the amount I hang around them, I've been promoted to the glorious rank and title of Auntie Charlie. Or Auntie Charlotte, if they're going to be a picky pair and insist on the name I was lumped with—after my grandmother—which I'm sure they won't.

Because cool Auntie Charlie will make sure of that.

I'm planning on being the bad auntie, you see. The one who lets them have double ice-cream cones and takes them to get their ears pierced when they're staying on holiday even though they're not supposed to get them done till they're thirteen. The popular auntie.

I did the bag in the X-ray machine thing, then made my way through uneventfully to line up and have my passport stamped. Don't turn back. Don't turn back, I told myself.

So of course I turned back. Looked for the four of them. Saw them. Waved. They waved back. I waved a bit more, then turned back again to take a step forward as someone left the queue.

And that was it. When I turned around again I couldn't see them any more.

Instantly I felt a pang of loss for a family that wasn't really my own, but who treated me just as if I were.

Like this trip, for instance. A present from Kath and Mark. And, I guess, sort of from my mum. A present that I'd only received last night. They'd sat me down after dinner and given me the envelope.

'For you.' Kath had passed it to me without any great aplomb. Almost as if it were just a piece of mail I'd overlooked. 'You don't have any plans for the weekend, do you?' she'd said.

I'd taken the envelope from her. 'No—why?'

'Open it and see.'

I'd opened it up…and then I'd almost died.

It was a plane ticket. And an itinerary. For me. For tomorrow.

Mark was standing beside Kath when I looked up again. I opened my mouth to begin to say something to them, but nothing came out. I tried again, opening and shutting it, my tongue suddenly feeling ten times larger than usual. Kath gave me a glass of water and, after drinking it in its entirety, I was able to speak again. Not much, however.

'But, why?' was all I could come out with.

So they told me. The trip was just something they thought I deserved. Something they'd heard me talk about—something they'd been thinking would be good for me for a while and were waiting for me to get around to. But I hadn't. So they had. It wasn't much—not a big trip, they said, and they'd left the ticket home open, so I could stay on if I felt like it. They added that if I was wise I'd take it and run, as there wasn't going to be much sleep going on in the house for probably quite some time.

Not much—not a big trip. I couldn't believe they'd said that. Here they were, just having had not one baby but *two*, and they were paying large sums of money over to travel agents…for me. I had to come right out and say it. I was going to pay for it. I'd give them the money back. I'd meant to book something myself, but kept putting it off.

And that was when Kath spoke up, cutting me off. 'It's, um, from your mum, Charlie,' she said. 'She gave me some money for incidentals. Things you might need but that you might not know you need, if that makes any sense.'

The three of us had simply looked at each other, blinking, for a bit. Until, that was, Kath's eyes slid over to Mark and she sighed. 'And now it's probably time for Mark to apologise for the trip he chose.'

Mark had got a very sheepish air about him then. 'I thought you were meant to be having fun. And this looked like fun. To me, anyway.'

I checked the itinerary more closely. London and an open ticket back. Fantastic—just as I thought I'd read. Oh, but there was a tour attached. Wait…

To Oktoberfest?

Kath shrugged. 'I'm afraid it's non-refundable. I hope you like beer. And sauerkraut. And big fat sausages. For five days.' She poked Mark with one finger as she said each sentence.

Now, I'm what I call a sad vegetarian—as in, the kind of person who lusts after large pieces of steak but can't eat meat directly after seeing actual live cows, lambs, pigs, chickens et cetera. I'd seen a truck full of chickens whizz past me on the highway not long before this, and a feather had landed on the windscreen. So I knew I was going to be vegetarian for at least a week or so. Or until someone offered me a plate of something that just looked far too good to pass up.

So, anyway, the sausage thing. It didn't sound very appealing. And as for beer—I don't drink the stuff. Never have. Oh, I've tried a few times, but I just don't seem to like it.

But I waved my hands as if I couldn't believe what they were saying. No, no. The trip was great. It'd be fun. Educational. I might even learn to *like* beer. And big fat sausages. And, um, sauerkraut.

Bleh.

Plus, it wouldn't be all artery-hardening activities like sausage-eating. I'd get to see heaps of other things. Munich, for example. And the ticket home was open. I could do whatever I wanted. It'd be better than great.

And as I picked up the ticket and itinerary and turned them over in my hands, I realised that Kath and Mark knew me better than I knew myself. It didn't matter where it was—around the corner would have been fine. I just needed to get away. To do something different. And if I had some fun along the way—well, that wouldn't be such a bad thing, would it?

Of course not.

'Miss, can you fasten your seat belt, please?' The flight attendant is standing over my seat staring at me as if I'm a loon. By the look on her face I think she might have asked me more than once already. Hastily, I grab the two ends of my seat belt and buckle up. When I'm done, I have one last crane of my neck to check for Kath and Mark and the twins before I concede defeat.

Left with nothing else to do, I get my book out of my backpack and read right up until they begin the safety demonstration. When that starts I put my book down on my lap and listen carefully. I even get the safety card out of the seat pocket and read that too.

Like I said before, the oldest plane in the world…

I'm watching attentively as the flight attendant shows us how to fasten and unfasten our seat belts when I hear it. This *clunk*…

And something lands on my lap.

I drop my safety card on the floor in fright.

I'm stunned for a moment, unsure of what's happened. But when I look down, there's a videotape in my lap. Instinctively I reach my hand up to my head as I realise that one side of it hurts. As I feel around, I notice there's a little lump on it. No, hang on, a mid-sized lump. Wait a second—quite a big lump, actually. Quite a big lump, which is starting to throb.

'Hey, are you OK?' the guy in the seat beside me asks.

I turn to him. No, I want to say. No, I'm not. I've got a lump on my head. Not a little lump, not a mid-sized lump, but quite a big lump, actually. But I can't get the words out. Instead, I bring my hand down off my head to see if there's any blood.

There's not. This is probably a good sign.

The flight attendant comes and crouches down beside me. She picks the safety card up off the floor and puts it back in the seat pocket in front of me. 'I'm so sorry. It's never done that before.'

I look at her blankly and she picks the videotape out of

my lap and holds it up. 'It's the safety video. It ejected out of the VCR stored above you. Is your head OK?'

I keep looking at her. 'I've got a lump.'

She feels the side of my head. 'Oohhh, you do too. Does it hurt? Do you have a headache? Should I see if we have a doctor?'

Too many questions. 'It doesn't hurt much,' I say, before I realise what the implications of what I've just said could mean in today's litigious society, and add a little disclaimer, 'Yet'.

She pauses, thinking. 'Well, maybe we should move you up to the front, just so we can keep a better eye on you. We're about to take off, so I'll have to leave you for a minute or two, but I'll come right back, OK? Don't go anywhere, now.' She walks down towards the front of the plane.

As I watch her go, I wonder where she thinks I'd run off to. I mean, I'm on a plane, here. I don't have too many options.

True to her word, she comes back as soon as we've levelled off. She gives me her arm to help me get up. 'Jessica will keep an eye on you up front. Just tell her if your head starts to hurt, all right? Now, do you have anything overhead?' She gestures at the lockers.

I shake my head, no, and she turns and starts walking back up to the front of the plane. I follow.

We keep going. And going. And going.

Then, suddenly, as she parts the swishy curtain that divides the have and the have-nots, the clean and the unwashed, I realise she's putting me in business class. Excellent. But, no—wait. We keep going. We pass another swishy curtain. And we enter…first class.

Ta-da!

I look around me in awe. Toto, I don't think we're in economy any more.

The people in the few seats around the doorway turn and stare at us. Under their gaze, I try to look as if my head really hurts now. As if it hurts in a first-class-this-seat-reclines-*all*-the-way-back kind of hurt.

There are about five people in first class, and—I count them—about twenty seats. What a waste.

Another flight attendant—Jessica, I presume—comes over. Yes, it is Jessica. I read her name-tag as she gets closer and note she speaks French and German and Japanese, which I'm sure would come in very handy if I did too. The flight attendant who's been with me till now, Lisa—the economy-model flight attendant who speaks nothing but plain old English—leaves.

'Just take a seat here,' Jessica says, directing me into a seat behind a man and sitting me down. 'And do tell me if you start to feel sick or you get a headache, won't you?'

I nod.

'Would you like a biscuit and some apple juice? Everyone's just had a snack.'

I nod again, never one to say no to a biscuit. Or apple juice. And certainly never one to say no to *first class* biscuits or *first class* apple juice that I can eat in my *fully reclined* seat, watching my own *cable TV* all while I'm on my *personal phone* if I so feel like it.

'Yes, please,' I say politely.

Jessica turns around and leaves. I watch her go with interest. I've never seen a first class flight attendant before. I inspect her closely. I may never get another chance to see one in captivity. She has really expensive stockings on. I can tell. Because they look nice. All shimmery. And very unlike anything I've ever worn waitressing that usually came three in a packet and were holey by the time I left the apartment.

I'm impressed, to say the least.

And, after a good inspection, I have to admit that first class is fantastic. Everything about it is—well, first class. The flight attendants, for example, like Jessica—they're better-looking *and* they speak four languages *and* wear expensive stockings. Even Jessica's red lipstick is first class, I think, as I watch her lean down and talk to another passenger.

I realise then that she's a Woman. I've always wanted to be one of those. Yep, I know—I guess the breasts and all the other equipment give you instant qualification into the club, but that's just to be a woman. The kind without the capital 'W'. What I'm talking about is a Woman. With the outfits and the shoes and the smell. The kind of Woman who sashays instead of walks. The kind of Woman men trample each other over in order to get to her first and light her cigarette. A Woman like Marilyn Monroe or Jane Russell in *Gentlemen Prefer Blondes.*

A *vavoom, boom, boom* kind of Woman.

And, yes, I realise that you can't go out till five p.m. when you're a *vavoom, boom, boom* kind of Woman, because you have to spend all day getting ready, but what the hell? It's a great look. I catch another glimpse of Jessica as she smiles her perfect red-lipsticked smile at another passenger, making me wonder if her lipstick is a magic lipstick that's reapplying itself every five minutes—a magic lipstick that's resistant to leaving even a smidgen on her glossy white teeth. Maybe she's done that trick—the Vaseline on the teeth thing that they do in the beauty pageants.

Or maybe I'm taking it all a bit too far now? Either way, I'm distracted—distracted away from Womanly things by material things.

By my seat, actually. Because, I think—wriggling my satisfied behind around a bit—it is *sooo* comfy. It's really more like a lounge chair. I snuggle back and fold my hands neatly on my lap, wishing I'd worn something a bit classier than my old denim jacket, black stretch pants and grey felt Birkenstocks.

Like the pale pink pashmina the woman a few rows up is wearing.

I almost laugh out loud then. Me in a pale pink pashmina? How long would that stay pristine and pale? Well, I know the answer to that—until right before the apple juice and the biscuit arrived, that's when. I'm not a pashmina kind of girl anyway. Mark brought me one back from overseas once and I accidentally put it in the wash. It was more like a short, gnarled scarf after that.

I spot the arm of the guy in front of me as I think this. He's wearing a denim jacket quite like mine, which makes me feel a bit better—because I figure he's actually paying to be here. At a cost of approximately $7,000 one way or $11,000 return, if I remember the figures on the whiteboard of my local travel agency correctly. It's even a pretty old and daggy denim jacket he's wearing, which makes me wonder for a second or two—but then I tell myself it's probably meant to be that way, it's been professionally beaten up and most likely cost ten to fifteen times the price I paid for my one, which I think came from Bettina Liano and was already way out of my budget.

I lean forward a bit to see if I can read the label on the bottom of his jacket. It's sticking out over the side of his chair. There's a patch there with some writing on it that seems vaguely familiar, and if I just…

There's a clearing of a throat above me, which makes me glance up. It's Jessica. With my biscuit and apple juice. On a plate. A real plate! And in a glass. A real glass! I'm sure my eyes are completely round by now, and I probably look very much like a character in a Japanese cartoon.

I smile at her. She doesn't smile back.

Uh-oh. Bye-bye Woman; hello economy-class-passenger-eating-Rottweiler, I think.

'If you're going to disturb the other passengers, I'm afraid I'll have to move you back to—' She starts to lecture me, but stops when the guy in front turns around.

'Oh my God,' I say a little too loudly as I recognise him.

He just stares.

'That's it,' Jessica hisses under her breath, and I get the distinct feeling she's going to throw me out of first class.

The guy keeps right on staring at me.

It's Jas.

Chapter Six

And without his make-up, long black hair, leather body-suit and whip, he's a lot easier to recognise.

I think he might even be wearing the same denim jacket he had when we were living together.

Beside us, Jessica is still making annoyed first class flight attendant noises.

'It's OK,' Jas says, standing up next to her. 'We know each other.'

'Oh.' She doesn't look particularly pleased with this, as if we've broken the rules somehow—me coming from *economy* and all—and moves her attention to smoothing her skirt with one hand for a moment.

Somehow, I feel it would be an appropriate moment to break into a rousing, economy meets first class 'breaking down the barriers' rendition of Paul McCartney and Stevie Wonder's 'Ebony and Ivory', but I can't quite bring myself to do it.

'Right. I'll leave this here, then, shall I?' She puts down

the tray with the biscuit and apple juice onto another seat's table and stalks off.

I stand up too. Awkwardly, not sure how Jas is going to react. After all, you hear stars complaining about it all the time—people claiming they went to high school with them etc. Confused, I mumble, half looking at the floor, 'I heard them calling for you. At the airport.'

He makes a face. 'Late. Still.'

This makes me smile and I raise my eyes to meet his. 'As usual.'

There's a pause then, as if neither of us knows what to do next. I'm about to sit back down, thinking I'm making a nuisance of myself, when Jas makes a move.

'What am I waiting for?' he says, and steps forward to give me a kiss on the check and a hug. I hug him back. He smells shockingly familiar. But the hug feels right and puts me at ease.

'Come on. Sit with me,' he says.

And this time I don't need to worry about the convenience of an aisle seat. You could put on a production of *Cats* between the rows up here if you wanted to. I make myself comfortable beside the window and Jas passes me my biscuit and apple juice. I pull out my tray-rest. 'Somehow I don't think they're getting homemade wild fig and wattle-seed biscuits back there.' I nod my head in the direction of economy and tell Jas the story of the wayward videotape and how I ended up here with the famous people.

When I'm done, he feels my head for the lump.

'Ow!' I yelp as he finds it.

'Sorry. It's pretty big. Sure you're all right?'

'I'm certainly a lot better now,' I say, holding up the biscuit and taking a big bite. With my other hand I feel the lump one more time as Jas watches me. I can't help noticing he looks exactly the same as he used to.

'Charles. Your hair.'

My hand still on my head, I pat what's left of my hair, knowing precisely what he's talking about. We used to have this joke. We'd been swimming one day, a few months after he'd moved in, and I'd pulled my wet hair back into a ponytail to get it out of the way when we were done. Jas had fallen about laughing when he'd seen the end result. It was my ears. They were—well, of the sticky-out variety, which is why I kept my hair medium to long and down. Always. Thus, the second nickname—Charles.

I realise my face must have fallen a bit when he mentioned it again because Jas touches me on the arm. 'No. It's great. Just different, that's all.'

I shrug. 'I'm growing it. I had to have it short. It was damaged.'

'Damaged?'

'Um, over-processed, actually.' I roll my eyes and take another bite of biscuit. 'It was the only option. Hair extensions cost a fortune, you know.'

'Tell me about it.' He shakes his black hair at me.

I realise then that he probably *does* know. 'You've had yours cut too,' I say. It's a lot shorter than I've seen it in all the magazines and on TV.

He nods and picks a bit of hair off his jacket. 'Only this morning. Hated it. That's why I was late.'

I notice something then—hair lying on Jas's right shoulder, the one next to me. Without thinking, I reach over and dust it off. 'It's all over you! I don't know how you could get on plane after a haircut. I always have to rush straight home and jump in the shower.' It's only as I reach the end of my sentence that I catch on to what I'm doing. Slowly,

I pull my hand away and look up to meet Jas's eyes. He's staring at me again. 'Sorry, I can't believe I just did that.'

His eyes don't move and I get that feeling again. The one where I wish I could just sink down and disappear. This time into my plush first class seat.

But then something unexpected happens. Jas laughs. 'Hair might be different, but you haven't changed a bit, have you?' he says, starting to laugh even harder.

This makes me pause. 'What's that supposed to mean?' He laughs away. 'Hey!'

'Sorry. Just funny seeing you again, that's all.'

I raise my eyebrows at this one. 'Funny seeing me?' I halt for a moment before I decide it's OK to go for it. After all, it's going to have to come up some time, isn't it? 'Funny seeing me?' I repeat. 'It's been pretty funny seeing you in all your get-up, that's for sure.'

Jas moans. 'Ah, man. Knew that'd have to come up sooner or later.'

'Really? Did you? And here I was, almost forgetting the fact that you've been tramping around for approximately two years posing as a devil worshipper, eating live animals and seducing young boys.'

'A guy needs a hobby.'

I snort delicately so that apple juice doesn't fly out of my nose—who says I don't belong in first class? I could handle that pale pink pashmina. 'No, really, tell me the whole story.'

So he does.

And it goes pretty much the way I'd imagined it. Jas had gone to Sydney and met up with his contact in the industry at exactly the right time. One of the big record companies was putting together a 'let's go for maximum shock value and freak the public out' kind of band, and he'd gone along and auditioned. Apparently they liked his 'look'—tall, dark, pale, thin. But not so much that they decided to leave him how he was. Instead, he was signed up and kitted out in a full black leather bodysuit. A few weeks, a stylist, publicist and hairdresser later, he was Zamiel and Spawn was on the road. Apparently it was just a bonus that he could actually *sing*.

'I couldn't believe it the first time I saw you on TV.' I've listened to the story open-mouthed.

'Not surprised.'

'But it's great, isn't it? It's what you always wanted?'

Jas pauses. 'No. What I always wanted to be was a song-writer. You know that.'

'But you write Spawn's songs, don't you?'

'Course,' he laughs. Then, looking around furtively, 'No,' he whispers.

'Oh.' There doesn't seem to be much more to say to that, so I move on. 'So why the trip to London? Are you going to see your, um, boyfriend?' I mumble the last word.

'Boyfriend? What are you on about?'

'You know.'

'Yeah?'

I say the actor's name.

Jas laughs. 'You're kidding me, Charlie. You, of all people. You don't actually believe all that stuff?'

'Well...'

'Come on—tell me that you think I worship the devil, that I eat live animals, that I got town planning to change my house number to 666.'

'I never said I thought it was *all* true.'

'You think I'm going out with piglet-face?'

'Piglet-face!' I laugh, then cover my mouth with my hand. It's not very nice, but he's right. The actor does have a bit of a piglet-face. He is a bit of a *Babe*.

'It's his nose.' Jasper puts one finger on the tip of his nose and pushes upwards.

It's highly realistic. I laugh a bit louder.

Standing a few rows in front, Jessica gives me a dirty look and instantly I remember the Eleventh Commandment—there shalt be no rowdiness in first class. I cover my mouth with my hand again.

'You really think I'd go out with him? You crazy? I do have *some* taste, you know. Wouldn't go out with a guy like him.'

'He had his tongue down your throat on TV one night. Or do you let just anyone do that now?' I regret the words as soon as they come out of my mouth, as they remind me of That Night, our last night in the apartment together, but Jas doesn't seem to notice.

'That? All him. No idea he was going to do it. Amazing what you can make something seem like when you cut it down to ten seconds of footage.'

'What do you mean?' I'm confused.

'What really happened—he grabbed me, mauled me as I was coming out of some club. Wasn't expecting it. Didn't even know he was there until after it all went down. Guess I knew he had a bit of a *thing* for Zamiel, but I didn't think he'd actually pull a stunt like that. Used up a whole perfectly good bottle of Listerine that night. Think he'd just eaten Indian for dinner or something.'

I make a face at this. 'So you're not going to see him?'

'Cross the road *not* to see him.'

I wait expectantly for further explanation about his trip, but I don't think it's coming. 'Well…?' I try, wondering if he's being deliberately evasive.

'Right. Sorry. Nothing exciting. Just a break, I guess you'd call it. Holiday.'

I nod. Fair enough. Everyone takes holidays, don't they? Even fallen angels.

We both rest our heads back on our seats at the same time.

'What about you?' Jas says then. 'How's your mum going now? All better?'

Silence.

'She's dead, Jas.'

His head lifts up slowly as I turn mine. The horror is already in full force. 'Shit. Charlie, I'm sorry. Should've…'

'It's OK.' I've known about it for some time, after all. I just didn't need to be reminded. Like Kath had said at the airport, 'Don't think about…things.' And this was one of them. One of the doozies.

'When?'

'Ages ago. The January after we left the apartment.'

'But that was only a few months. Thought she was just sick?'

'It took us a long time to convince her to see a doctor. By then it was only a matter of weeks.'

'Cancer?'

I shake my head. 'No, not at all. It was a blood thing. A clotting thing. Technical. Things might have been a lot better if she'd just seen someone earlier. You know what she was like. She thought waving around a few sticks of incense would do the trick.'

Jas pauses. 'Remember that week we spent at Byron with her?'

I nod.

'Remember how she made me try that old pottery wheel? Always thought that looked so easy, but when I tried it, it felt like my hands were being ripped over gravel. She was one tough lady. And her sculpture. That courtyard. Blew me away first time I saw it.'

I nod again.

Jas lifts his head up. 'Gave you a call about that time—January. A few times before and after that too. Why didn't you call back?'

'I know. I'm sorry. It was bad of me. I was busy with Mum and then, I don't know...' I look away.

'Don't worry. Doesn't matter.'

It does matter, but I don't know how to explain it.

'Tell me what you've been doing since then,' Jas says.

I think about it. 'It's not very exciting compared to you.'

'You'd be surprised. Everyone thinks my job's ultra-glamorous. Isn't at all, really.'

I shoot him a look. Oh, sure. After all, what could be more glamorous than the life of a rock star?

'Seriously,' Jas protests. 'Spend most of my time travelling just like this.' He runs his hand over his jacket. 'Dressed in 1998 couture. Very good year in my opinion. So tell all. I'm waiting.'

I pick up the last few biscuit crumbs on my finger and pop them in my mouth before I begin. I explain how I was kept quite busy after Mum died, settling her affairs, selling her house and buying myself a tiny cottage in Byron Bay.

'And your mum's sculpture?' Jas asks.

'I, um, only kept a few pieces.' I flinch when I say this, thinking of her work in someone else's house, but the fact was I'd needed the money to pay for medical treatment. I hadn't had much choice.

'The table and chairs? You kept them, didn't you?' Jas says quickly.

I shake my head. 'I sold them. To a gallery.'

'Oh.' I can see the disappointment lying behind Jas's eyes. 'And your own exhibition? How'd that go? Was one of the reasons I called. Wanted to come.'

I busy myself drinking the last bit of apple juice. 'That, um, sort of fell through.'

'Fell through?' Jas frowns. I pretend not to notice.

'It just wasn't the right time.'

'But you're working?'

'*Working*, working? Or sculpting, working?' What is this, an interrogation?

'Either.'

'I haven't been able to. Not since after…' I don't finish the sentence, not wanting to go there. 'I've been sketching a bit. Now and then.' More then than now, truth be told.

'Sketching?' Jas knows this is what I do before I actually start a piece and that I obviously haven't been sculpting much lately. Which is true. I haven't.

'At least you've got your degree now. That must be a bonus.'

Silence again.

Jas looks at me as if I'm joking. 'You *do* have your degree now? You must have finally passed that subject. It's been two years, Charlie.'

More silence. Telling silence.

But I have to say something. Explain it somehow. 'It was just that it was all a bit much…'

Jas butts in then. 'Jesus. Sorry. I'm doing it again. Course it was hard after your mum died.'

And, as this is partly the truth, I leave it at that.

Chapter Seven

We talk and talk and talk. Through lunch, through dinner, through supper. The food, of course, is *très magnifique*—see, I'm even talking like a first classer now! We talk non-stop through the hour wait in Singapore, which we spend at a café. We even talk through 'lights out', when we're back on the plane again. Eventually everyone gets sick of us and Jessica has to give us the official Quieten down, please. Her lipstick, I note, is still in place. Tattooed?

We talk—well, whisper, all the way to London.

And by the time we get off the plane and are waiting for our bags at Carousel 9, our voices are starting to go. I can't help but notice that, even with the luxuries of first class—the little hot towels, the comfy cotton in-flight socks, the slices of lemon in our tea—we still look pretty much like everyone else jostling around for the best place to wait for their bags. Like the living dead. But at least after an icepack or two, fetched grudgingly by Jessica, the lump on my head's almost gone. That's something.

Jas's luggage comes out quickly, and as he picks it up I see it's got an orange 'priority' tag on it. The beat-up black bag isn't what I'm expecting him to have.

'No Louis Vuitton travelling case?' I say as he wheels his bag over. 'Or is that still coming?'

He drops it down beside me. 'You have some very warped ideas of what my life is like.'

I glance at him, still keeping one eye on the carousel. 'I'm not the one who gets around in limos wearing six-inch thick make-up and thigh-high leather boots, remember?'

'Make-up? That's different. Louis Vuitton beauty case should be coming out any minute.'

'Ha-ha.'

'What's your bag like?' Jas asks.

'It's a blue wheelie one. The same as every second person will have because they just bought it on sale at the same place I did.'

'Should be easy to find.'

I turn away from the carousel for a moment. 'It shouldn't come out for a while yet. It's packed away in the seventh layer of hell. That's just below the sixth layer of hell, where I was sitting before the divine videotape clunked me on the head and I landed in heaven.'

Jas sighs. 'Come on. Economy's not that bad.'

I give him a look. 'Do you even remember it?'

He shrugs.

'Close your eyes for a moment,' I say.

He gives me the look back.

'No, I mean it.' I reach up and cover his eyes with one of my hands. 'Now, try and remember what economy's like.'

'I've only been on domestic flights in economy.'

'What a problem. OK, then. Imagine that. Imagine being on a flight between Sydney and Melbourne or something.'

'Uh-huh. Got it.'

'Great. Now, seat a big, fat, smelly man beside you on one side, who constantly hogs the armrest, and a reluctant female flyer with chronic airsickness on the other. Add a movie you've already seen and hated and a touch of cramp and sleeplessness and multiply it all by approximately twenty-two hours.' Then I take my hand away.

'Ah.'

'Now tell me it's not that bad, considering you're supposed to be on *holiday*.'

'Get your point.'

'Thank you.' I do a mock curtsey. 'I do what I can for the rich and famous.'

I turn my attention back to the carousel, which has started spewing out the economy bags, most of which are something like mine. I'm suddenly thankful for the fluorescent pink ribbon Mark, a seasoned traveller, tied to the handle late last night, as I can now see it attached to my bag, trundling down the carousel.

'There it is,' I say to Jas, and take a step forward to jostle my way to the front of the crowd in order to retrieve it. At least it's here, I think to myself as I see it. I've heard stories about bags going on holiday to Bermuda without their owners.

Jas stops me then. 'It's OK. I'll get it.'

'My hero,' I say, pointing out the pink ribbon.

I watch as he grabs the handle and goes to pull it off the carousel. But as he does there's a confused look and a harder pull before he's able to set it down on the ground and lug it towards me.

'What've you got in there?'

'Clothes. Half of which I won't wear because I'm a terrible packer. It's something I've come to live with. Doesn't seem to matter where I go or for how long.'

'Better you than me.'

I smile, glancing at his jacket. Something tells me he's not going to be doing much shopping in London. As for me…

I can't make any such promises, budget or no budget.

Bags in hand, we stand around a bit now, knowing that this is the end of the road, but neither of us wanting to make the first move to go. I think about asking Jas if he wants to meet up again for dinner tonight, but then decide against it. He'll have other things to do. Famous people things. He's probably staying at the Savoy, or the Ritz or something, and the closest I'll get to those hotels is if the kleptomaniac in me feels the urge to steal a pack of matches.

'I guess…'

'Well…'

Jas puts his bag down and gives me a hug. 'Have a great time,' he says. 'With your sausages and sauerkraut.'

I make a face. 'I'm planning on keeping my stomach a sausage and sauerkraut-free zone. You have a wonderful holiday. It sounds like you need it.'

Jas makes a face as well. 'Yeah. I'll try.' He hands me something then. A business card. 'So you can call me. Mobile works here.'

'Thanks,' I say. But somehow I don't think I will. I'd just look…desperate. As if I was only interested in him now that he's famous. After all, I didn't return his calls for the last two years, why else would I start now? 'So, um—bye, then.' I go to turn, but Jas lunges forward and bends down to my height. He puts one hand on each of my shoulders and gives me a kiss on the cheek.

'It was great seeing you again, Charlie.'

I swallow.

He steps back now and smiles quickly. 'Call this time, yeah?'

I nod. 'Um, OK. Thanks.' I hold the card up. Then I turn for real, waving with my free hand. I head off in the direction of some nearby phones, remembering my promise to give Kath and Mark a call as soon as I got to the airport.

They really worry about me.

Kath picks up the phone on the second ring. 'Charlie?' she sounds frantic.

OK, so maybe they worry a bit too much.

'Yep, it's me. I got here just fine. On first class, I might add.'

'First class?'

I explain the videotape scenario to Kath and then my chance meeting with Jas, aka Zamiel.

'And how was that?'

'Strange. He seems exactly the same. I thought he'd be really different now, but it was just like old times.'

'Did he eat any live animals?'

I laugh. 'Yep, they had them in a cage so he could just go up and pick them out when he felt like it. And there was a spittoon on the floor he could spit the bones and fur into as well.'

There's a pause on the other end of the line.

I laugh. 'Come on, Kath, you know that's not true,' I say, but feel a bit guilty remembering that I sort of, kind of, just a little bit might have believed it myself not so long ago. Media brainwashing, of course.

I ask about the twins and Kath tells me all the news. Who ate the most—Daisy—who tried to speak—yes, at four weeks; she is obviously *very* intelligent—Annie—who pooed the most—Daisy. Then she asks what I'm going to do next.

'I'm going to catch the Tube to the hotel, and then I might have a bit of a walk around,' I say.

'Charlie, you should have a rest. You must be exhausted.'

'I'm fine. Stop worrying!' But I smile as I say it. Really, it's nice to have someone who frets about you.

She makes me promise twice that I'll call her in the next few days before we both hang up. As I replace the receiver, I take a look around to get my bearings. I'd seen a sign for the Tube before—past the carousels, I think. Ah, there it is. I make my way over towards it, reading the signs all around as I wheel my bag. It's only when I finally look down that I see him…

Jas. Sitting on his bag. Right where I left him fifteen minutes ago.

He doesn't notice me until I'm standing right in front of him. When he still doesn't look up, I start tapping one toe to get his attention.

'Ah,' he says, spotting me.

'What are you still doing here?'

He freezes and looks decidedly as if he wishes he was small enough to hide behind his bag.

No chance.

'I…er. Deciding where to go.'

I stop tapping now. 'What do you mean? Don't you have any plans?'

Jas shakes his head.

'Are you out of cash or something?'

Jas stands up and pulls out his wallet. 'Don't know, actually.' He opens it up. There are two US dollars, but no useful money. 'I've got a few cards…'

This I've already noted, wide-eyed. 'Few' isn't quite the

word. Jas has the whole set in there—as if he's collecting them. Amex, VISA, MasterCard, Diners. And no cash. Who does he think he is? The Queen?

He puts his wallet away then, and looks at me like the last puppy at the pound. 'What I mean is, I don't have anything to *do*.'

I stand in silence, surprised. Very surprised. I guess I'd been half expecting him to ditch me before we disembarked the plane and I'd be left to watch him push the paparazzi aside as he made his way through Heathrow, dived into some waiting limo purring at a designated pick-up point and sped off to a sixties rock-star-style night of debauchery at some exclusive hotel, where all the big names had been sitting around for hours waiting for him to arrive and do the first line of the night on his specially requested black granite coffee table.

Phew.

I give him the once-over now. Old denim jacket. Beat-up bag. Black hair stuck to his white T-shirt. Puppy eyes. The guy's a mess.

'What?' Jas eventually protests.

'Well, what do you want to do? You can't hang around here for ever.'

He glances around a bit before he shrugs. I can tell he's decidedly unimpressed with his surroundings. Here I am, chomping at the bit to get out and rediscover London, and Jas is coldly inspecting Heathrow as if it's just somewhere to be when he's not somewhere else. 'You really don't have anything to do?' I ask again.

He shakes his head one more time.

I tip my head to one side and size him up. 'Fine. Why don't you come with me, then?'

He starts at this. 'What? On your trip?'

I nod. 'If they've got a spare place, I don't see why you couldn't.'

'But…'

'But what?'

He sags back down to sit on his bag. 'Couldn't.'

'Why not?'

'You're just being polite.'

I laugh then. 'When have I ever been polite to you, sad sack?'

Jas sighs. 'That's true.' He looks up and smiles. 'You really don't mind?'

'As long as Zamiel's not coming, why should I mind?'

There's a short silence while Jas sizes *me* up. Then he smiles again. 'Left Zamiel at home. He's a complete arsehole. Takes all the packing space.'

'I guess we'd better ring the tour company and find out if it's even possible or not. No point thinking about it if it isn't, is there?' I find the number on my itinerary and check to see if I've got change for the phone. I don't. 'I'll have to get some coins.'

Jas shakes his head. 'Hang on. Got my mobile here somewhere.' He sticks his hand in his back pocket and comes out with something about the size of one of his many credit cards.

I can't believe my eyes. 'That's a phone?' I've never seen one so small. It must have cost an absolute fortune.

'Yep.' He hands it to me after turning it on. 'Don't look like that. It's just a phone. Works exactly the same way.'

Just as I take it, it starts beeping. 'I didn't break it.' I freeze, cradling it in my palm. 'It wasn't me.' But then I see why it's beeping. Jas has messages. Fifteen messages. 'Mr Popularity.' I hand the phone back. I watch as he scrolls through the numbers, deleting each one. 'Aren't you going to listen to them?' I ask.

'No.' Delete, delete, delete.

'OK,' I say slowly. When he's done, Jas goes to pass the phone back to me, but I tell him he can call. Somehow I don't think my insurance would cover me dropping a phone so small. I read out the tour company's number while Jas dials.

We're lucky. There are three spare seats left on the tour. And, after reading all the numbers off his VISA card, one of them is Jas's. He keeps talking after that, discussing details, and after a while starts to frown. He raises his index finger. 'Ah, there's a problem,' he says. 'No single rooms left. There's people sharing, though, so it should be OK.'

I pause for a moment, thinking sharing a room with strangers wouldn't exactly be my idea of fun. Who knows what kind of axe murderer you'd end up sleeping with? I wave my hand to get Jas's attention and he asks the woman on the other end of the line to give him a second. 'Don't do that. Just ask if I can get a twin instead of a double. We could share then, rather than putting you with someone you don't know.'

He frowns. 'No. It's OK, I'll…'

'Have I ever been polite to you?' I ask him for the second time today. 'Don't be silly. Of course we can share.'

'Really? You're not just saying that?'

I roll my eyes. 'It's not like we haven't shared before.'

'Thanks.' He raises the phone again and asks the woman if we can change my room to a twin. We can. And that's it. All set. Details finalised. Jas turns the phone off again.

'So, roomie, what *were* you going to do with the rest of today?' I ask Jas.

'Er, probably a movie and peanuts and vodka from the mini-bar.' He looks ashamed of himself, but then perks up. 'But Oktoberfest! This is going to be great. Can even pick up where we left off.'

I freeze, remembering the last time we shared a room. 'What?'

'With the beer coaching.'

'Oh, right,' I breathe a sigh of relief, realising what he's on about. 'OK. I'm game. Good old number three.' I hold three fingers up. 'How could I forget?' Back in the old days, Jas had coached me in three things:

1. Olives
2. Anchovies
3. Beer

They were his specialties—he practically existed on beer and pizza back then. I'd never liked any of them, but in just a few short months after he'd moved in Jas had had me eating big fat olives stuffed with feta and pesto straight from the fridge and ordering extra anchovies on my pizza and Caesar salads. Beer, number three, had proved a little more elusive. He'd taken me as far as liking the smell, but not the taste.

'Have you drinking the stuff yet,' he adds.

I nod.

Silence.

'So now what?' Jas breaks the conversation drought.

Now what? I don't know. We're in London. The possibilities are endless. I give him the eye. 'Were you really going to shut yourself up in a hotel room and scarf down the minibar?'

'I might have ordered room service…'

I can't believe what I'm hearing. 'You're in London for the night and you'd stay in and order room service?'

'I said I'd watch a movie. If I watch a movie, then it counts as doing something.'

'Not in London it doesn't.'

'People live here, you know. Spend nights at home on the couch watching TV, go to bed at nine-thirty and then get up and head to work in the morning.'

'But not me. And not you. You're supposed to be on holiday, remember?'

Jas watches the luggage carousel go round for a moment before he turns back to me. 'Let's go. Cab it in?'

I remember something then. 'Oh. Where are you going to stay?'

'Where are you staying?'

'Some divey 18–35 semi-hostel thing. It came cheap with the tour. Believe me, you won't want to stay there.'

'And you do?'

I shrug. 'I don't mind. It's just a bed.'

It's right about now that Jas gets that evil plotting expression that I haven't seen for years. 'Oh, no,' I say. 'What're you up to?'

He sticks both hands out in front of me, fists closed. 'Pick one.'

I give him a dubious look. 'Why? Which one sells Zamiel my soul?'

'Funny. Pick one.'

I reach out and touch his left hand, our eyes locked. Jas winks at me. 'Exquisite choice, madam,' he says, using his best English accent—which is just plain bad.

'And what did I just choose so exquisitely?' I sound a little more than doubtful.

'You chose Brown's Hotel.'

'Are you going to stay there?'

'*We're* going to stay there.'

I take a step back. '*We're* going to stay there?' My voice rises a tad.

'My treat.' Jas nods.

'Is that right?' I shake my head, furious. People are staring at us now, realising we're arguing. I don't care. Who does he think he is? 'Look, if you're going to come on this trip with me, you're not going to play the rock star and pay for everything.'

'Ah, come on.' Jas steps forward, closer to me. 'I'm not trying to pay for everything. Only want to make it up to you. Just this once. Least I can do. I'm going to be butting in on your holiday, sponging off your room on the tour. I owe you.'

Yeah, right. This still smacks of rock star to me. But then I see his expression—it's convincing. I exhale. 'It's just that I want to do this how I'm supposed to do it. This trip was a present and I'm not going to have you making fun of it.'

'I'm not making fun of it, Charlie. All I want is to show you a good time. Thanks for letting me come. That such a bad thing?'

I take another look at him. Still convincing. 'Well, no. It's just that I want to do everything properly. If you're going to come with me on this thing, you come as you. Not as some flashy person who can buy his way in and out of anything and everything.'

'Have I acted like that so far?'

I pause.

'Have I?'

'No,' is my grudging reply. 'Not yet, anyway. But I'm just making sure you don't start.'

'Don't think I'm going to be able to start anything with you around. Sounds like you're going to keep me firmly anchored to earth.'

'I have to be sure, that's all.' At least everyone's stopped staring at us now.

'Didn't sound like you were too sure about the 18-35 hostel.'

I finally uncross my arms. 'I don't mean to sound ungrateful, really…it's fine. I understand you're just trying to be nice. We'll stay at the Brown place, whatever it's called.'

Jas's makes a noise, disgusted. 'The Brown place? You'd think the oldest five-star hotel in London would deserve maybe a *little* more respect.'

I point at him. 'Rock star?'

'Sorry.' He grins.

We spend the next five minutes arguing on a new topic—whether we should take the Tube or cab it into the city. I try to win him over on the less expensive option, but don't have the energy for victory. We make our way out to the cab rank and wait.

'So what was the other hand?' I ask while we're standing in line.

'The other end of the spectrum. The Sanderson. Modern. Very.'

'And Brown's isn't?'

'Nope. All wood panelling and buttered crumpets for the genteel.'

'Sounds pretty good. But I'm going to insist on buying dinner.' I point a finger at me.

'Done. I'm a rock star, remember? Can't buy my own dinner.'

I'm too tired to give anything but a withering look in return.

Chapter Eight

I crash and burn about three seconds after sitting down in the cab. As big and as comfy as those first class seats are, it's still hard to sleep on a plane. Especially when you're busy gas-bagging with your lost ex-flatmate. I try desperately not to do that nodding off thing. You know—the embarrassing nodding off, hearing a noise and jerking awake thing? Even worse, Jas notices, and starts poking me each time my head lolls forward, warning me that I really need to stay awake until at least early evening if we want the sleeping thing to pan out properly.

Somewhere between the fourth and fifth poke, however, he must give up, because the next thing I know we're parked in front of Brown's and I sit up to see our luggage already on the way inside.

'You can always sleep here.' Jas grins at me, leaning his hands on top of the cab and bending his head down between them to watch me. I sit up, suddenly very awake, and bring one hand to my face. 'It's OK,' he adds. 'You didn't dribble. This time.'

Inside, Jas tries to edge me over to one side of the counter while he discusses the rooms the hotel has available. When I hear them, the rates make me choke. I take him aside and we have another 'discussion' and 'agree' on a twin room rather than two singles. We check out the room itself—which I, mocking Jas's bad accent, declare 'luvverly'. There are more phone calls—to the travel agency, so they know to pick us up from here tomorrow rather than the hostel. And to Kath and Mark, so they know where I am—Kath makes me put Jas on the phone to prove that he's not really a Za-miel kind of guy all the time.

Business out of the way, we throw down a pick-me-up coffee or two, or three, and set out. I've decided a brisk walk through Mayfair and over to Hyde Park is the go, and Jas agrees. By the time we've crossed half of Hyde Park we're tired already. In the end we stroll the rest of the way over to Rotten Row and collapse on the grass for a minute or two to watch the horses trot by—if there are any.

Jas leans back on his elbows and starts plucking stray bits of grass out of the ground with his fingers. We both watch in silence as a couple walk past, arms intertwined.

'Get down to the juicy stuff, Charles. Tell me all about your love life,' he says when they're out of earshot.

'Ha! What love life?'

'Haven't been seeing anyone?' He turns his head to look at me.

'Seeing anyone? No, not really.' I sigh. 'I've done a few of the first date things. First in Byron, and then Kath and Mark set me up with absolutely anyone single they knew.'

'No good?'

I roll over onto my stomach. 'Don't let me fall asleep, OK?'

Jas nods. 'Not a pretty sight anyway…'

I ignore him. 'As I was saying—no, they weren't much chop. And it was so painful.'

'What? Painful?'

'Not in the physical sense of the word. I mean mentally painful. There's just so much effort involved, isn't there? First there's the finding out as much about them as you can from other people thing, the getting ready for the date thing, the thinking of things to say so the conversation doesn't dry out thing, and the kiss or not to kiss thing when the date's over…'

'Know what you mean.'

I snort. 'Sure you do. I'm sure dating is a *real* problem when you're world-famous. People wouldn't be interested in you at all. And you'd have to go to such boring, inexpensive places. Like Paris for lunch.'

Jas snorts back. 'Thought we'd been through all that? Worked out that maybe all those things you've heard about me aren't exactly true? That my life isn't *quite* as glamorous as it…'

'So it's harder for you, is it? Harder than it is for everyone else?' I cut Jas off at the pass.

He plucks a few more blades of grass out of the ground and brings them up to his face to inspect them more closely. 'Yeah. In some ways.' His eyes flick to me for only a second.

'Ha!'

'No. Reckon I'm being fair. I've been on both sides of the fame fence. This side's harder. That so difficult for you to believe?'

'Gee, I don't know. Maybe they should start making a new TV show—*When Stars Whinge*.'

'OK, OK. Get your point. I don't mean harder, exactly. Just different. It has its own added set of problems.'

'Like?'

Jas thinks about this a bit before answering. 'It's the media's fault, mainly. People get these ideas about you. Think they already know you from what they've read around the place when really they know nothing about you at all.'

'Mmmm?'

He eyes me. 'You believed it all, didn't you? Lived with me for almost a year, day in, day out, and you still believed it.'

'Like what?'

'Like what's-his-face having his tongue stuck down my throat.'

'Well, he did. I saw it with my own eyes.'

'You know what I mean. You believed there was something going on between us.'

'Hmmm.' Guilty as charged. I smile. 'I didn't believe all of it…'

'Sure. OK, then. How about the other pig thing? The real pig thing. That's a good example. The bestiality thing. Nice, huh? Pigs, apparently. I have a penchant for pigs. Great conversation starter on first dates, that one.'

I turn fully, surprised. 'Actually, I hadn't heard that one. Maybe you should check what people know first before you go blurting it all out. I can just see it on a dating agency form: "Jas, twenty-nine, six foot four, enjoys romantic walks on the beach, lazy Sundays in bed. And pigs. The bigger and pinker the better." Come on, Jas. You've got to leave some mystery for the second date.'

'Yeah.'

'At least it's not all your fault. It sounds like it's Zamiel who's letting you down on the dating front.' I laugh. 'Maybe you should just comfort yourself with the fact that at least he's getting some. Even if it is with a pig.'

'It'd be funny if it weren't almost true.' Jas pauses then, thinking. 'You know, it's strange—the sex thing with Zamiel. He's supposed to be quite androgynous. Wasn't meant to have sex at all. Not supposed to need to. If anything, I think he'd bud—you know? He'd grow another little Zamiel off his arm or something. That's my theory, anyway.'

'Great. Thanks for that.'

'Yeah. I was joking. About the budding thing.'

'Right. I just didn't know there was a whole psychological profile going on behind the scenes. Anyway, you were saying there's been no one?'

I think it takes him a second to realise I'm talking about dating again. 'Like you said, first date here, first date there, piggy in the middle. No, really, even if the first date's OK, I never get a second one. Always in the wrong state, or the wrong country or something.'

I yawn, not being able to help myself. 'You sound like me—dating's been thrown into the too-hard basket. I've decided I'm going with fate now. It's easier. I've become a big believer in fate lately. If it's meant to happen, it's meant to happen, and that's that.'

Jas rolls over onto his stomach now too, crossing his arms out in front of him. He puts his head on the side so he can see me.

'What?' I say eventually.

'You're different.'

I sit up a bit. 'What do you mean, different?'

'You've changed.'

'What? How?' What does he mean?

Jas frowns. 'Before you were always doing, doing, doing. Like you never took a breath. You never would have said that before. The thing about fate. You would've talked about making things happen.'

I'm surprised at his comment. 'Really?'

He nods.

Uneasy, I laugh. 'It must be old age that's changed me. I'm slowing down.' I glance around me. 'Hey, aren't there shops around here?' I say, changing the subject. 'Harvey Nichols? Harrods?'

'You should know. You used to live here.'

'Oh, come on. Only until I was five!' Jas is right, though. I was born in London and lived here with my mother and, for a few years, my father, who died when I was three. I haven't been back since I was a child, but before I left I wasn't exactly of Harvey Nichols/Harrods shopping type age.

'I don't think there's any shops around here…' Jas says, then starts whistling guiltily.

'Nice try, buddy.' I haul myself up and then give him my hand.

'Worth a shot.' He grins.

For the next hour or so I drag Jas around Knightsbridge, shopping. Then, energy levels almost non-existent, we head back to Mayfair with my booty. Sinking onto our respective beds, we both decide we're too tired to go out for dinner and order up some room service instead. I make Jas promise I can take him out for a slap-up dinner in Germany, telling him, if he's lucky, he might even get *two* sausages with his sauerkraut.

By six-thirty the food's all gone and we can barely keep our eyes open. Wearily, we both crawl into our beds. I turn my bedside light out first, while Jas takes in the delights of a little more local television. I'm just dozing off when he turns the TV and his own light out and I wake up a little. I stare at the opposite wall and realise I can hear him breathing. Awake now, I think about how strange it is that we've met up again like this. All because of a videotape falling onto my unsuspecting noggin.

I really didn't think I'd ever see Jas again, and now here he is, breathing beside me. And he's the same. Almost exactly the same. I mean, he obviously has more money, and he does seem a little more sure of himself—the way he walks and speaks to people—but other than that he's the same old Jas. The guy I used to share a flat with what feels like a million years ago. Still staring at the wall, I remember what he told me in the park. That *I've* changed. *I'm* different. Am I? Well, I guess I am. Facing death does that to you, I guess. Whether it's your own or somebody else's.

Things are different between the two of us, that's for sure. And I just wish I could feel like I used to. That I could tell Jas anything. I spotted him looking at me questioningly a couple of times today and it made me feel terrible to hold things back. Like when he asked me about uni. How slack did I seem there? It was a fair call on his part—you'd think someone could finish off one subject in two years. And I'm quite aware that I haven't told Jas much about what I've been doing since I saw him last and that he's probably noticed. But it's difficult. Complicated. And if we're going to be busy on the tour, and then he's going to go back to work, to his new life, what's the point of telling him everything I've been doing over the last few years? I don't want to go into it. Mum. Me. It's easier for both of us just to have a good time. Not to worry about the past. To start afresh and simply enjoy the short time we have together.

I hear Jas roll over to face me and my body stiffens involuntarily. I can feel his eyes on the back of my head and instantly I know what he's going to say.

'Charlie,' he says. 'We need to talk.'

I think about pretending I'm asleep, but then the words begin tumbling out. 'You know, we don't,' I say with a small shake of my head. 'Really. It's OK. It's just…all that…I'm over it. I don't feel that way any more. About you, I mean. It's all in the past.'

I wake up at four-thirty a.m. and try, unsuccessfully, to fall back asleep for the next half an hour. By five-fifteen, I can't lie still for a minute longer, and sit up a bit to look around me in the light that's available.

'You awake?' I hear Jas's voice in the semi-dark.

'Sorry, did I wake you up?'

'No, I've been lying here staring at the ceiling for an hour or so. Obviously went to sleep too early.' He turns his bed-side light on.

I swing my legs over the side of the bed, suddenly glad that I treated myself to some new Peter Alexander pyjamas for the trip. 'Want a cup of tea?' I ask Jas, not quite meeting his eyes in case he wants to bring up last night's topic of discussion. The one I'd chosen to pass on.

'*Ja*, that would be *sehr gut*.'

'What?' He sounds way too cheery for this time of the morning.

'Just practising my German. Don't get excited. That's as much as I know.'

'You sound like the Swedish chef from the Muppets.' I yawn as I go over to fill the kettle.

'Swedish, German. They're lucky they'll be getting any-thing out of me. Languages aren't exactly a gift of mine.'

'Oh, that reminds me,' I say, abandoning my tea-making. I go over to my bag and pull the little book out. 'Here we are.' I hold it up.

'What's that?'

'German phrasebook.' I throw it over to Jas before heading back to our tea.

Jas sits up. 'Money, travel, telling the time… What is it with these books?'

'What do you mean?'

He flops back down, still reading. 'Why don't they ever tell you anything you need to know?'

'Such as?'

'Like how much do you need to bribe the *maître d'* to get the best table in the restaurant? Where do you park your car if you want to come back and have it still sitting there?'

'I thought that was your chauffeur's problem?'

Jas puts the book down. 'If I've told you once, I've told you a thousand times…'

'…garbage night is Monday night.' I finish his sentence and then we both laugh.

I never used to remember to put out the bins on a Monday night, even though it was one of the jobs I'd picked to do around the apartment. Jas always ended up doing it for me, and when he came back from the task he'd make me recite the phrase ten times to show me up.

He puts the book up and starts reading again. 'Here's one that's universal. *Ich will mein Tanzenbeine schwingen.*'

I dump the two teabags in the bin. 'Now you just sound like you're choking. What's it mean?'

'I want to shake my dancing legs.'

Carrying the two cups of tea across the room, I laugh and spill some over the side of each cup. 'Sorry.'

'Jesus. No saucer! You do know where we are?'

'Don't get all hoity-toity with me, mister—room service doesn't start till six a.m. You can demand your saucer then.' I put both the cups down on the bedside table and sit down on my bed. 'Here, let me have a look.' I hold my hand out. Jas passes me the phrasebook. Five minutes or so later, I shake my head. 'I don't remember any of this.'

'You studied German?'

I nod. 'Sort of. Years 8 to 10. Study didn't really come into it, though. That's probably why they threw me out.'

'They threw you out of German?'

'The teacher *suggested* that maybe German wasn't the language for me and that it might be better if I studied French instead.'

'Nice. So you did French?'

I laugh. 'No. I packed it all in and did geography.'

'So we should at least be OK if we get lost?'

I look up at this. 'Don't count on it. I got a C.'

'I won't. Hey, you remembered!' Jas says, having taken a sip of his tea. 'Black and three-quarters.'

I raise an eyebrow. 'Of course I remembered. I was practically your tea slave.'

'Yeah. So, what *do* you remember from German? You going to be useful at all this trip? Apart from tea-making?'

I close the phrasebook. 'Probably not. The thing I remember best was these books we had. You know—like the readers they give you when you're learning to read in primary school?'

Jas nods, presumably remembering good old Dick, Jane, Spot and Fluff.

'There was something about a dog named Lumpi and someone's uncle, Onkel Ernst, I think his name was. I distinctly remember one book where the family kept confusing them, which seemed a bit stupid. He must've been one really ugly uncle, or a spectacularly large and hair-free dog.'

'Sounds a bit surreal. Who wrote that little number? Freud?'

'It may as well have been. It wasn't very helpful in deal-ing with everyday life. I mean, how many kids confuse their dog with their uncle? And if they did they'd be far more likely to get a good smack on the head for it, rather than a long and detailed family conversation.'

'So that's it? All you remember?'

'Well, that and "99 Luftballons", of course.'

'Course.' Jas nods.

'Hang on, what's this?' About to put the phrasebook away, I spot something sticking out of it. A piece of paper. I unfold it and skim it for a moment or two. 'It's from Mark. Here.' I turn it around so Jas can read the heading. 'Dirty crap to say in German! He says "Thought this might come in handy. Don't tell Kath…"'

'If he's saying "don't tell Kath" it must be good. Give us one.'

I hum as I look down the page. 'How about this: *Ich habe einen Anschiß von den Bullen bekommen.*'

'Yeah?'

I glance up. 'Those cops really raked me over the coals.'

Jas laughs. 'Hopefully I won't need that one. Any oth-ers?'

'Um…hmmm, some of these are pretty dirty. No won-der he didn't show them to Kath. You should see her now she's a mother. Mark and I don't even get to say damn any more.'

'Dirty, you say? Great!'

'You don't have to get *quite* so excited.'

'Ah, come on. I know all the rude words. I'm just… searching for new and interesting combinations now.'

'OK, OK, um…*Ohne Gummi kannst du dir einen Tripper holen.* You can get the clap if you don't wear a rubber.'

Jas laughs again. 'That's not dirty—that's a fact, baby.'

'Baby? That's a new one in your repertoire. I'll need to pick myself up a rock star phrasebook next. Here we go. I've got another one. You'll like this: *Der Höhepunkt der Fete war der Gruppenfick danach.* The highlight of the party was the gang-bang afterwards. That one should come in useful for Zamiel, at least.'

'Oh.'

Jas sounds like he's forgotten something. 'What?'

'Nothing. Nothing. Give us one more. One of the really dirty ones.'

'One more and that's it, pervie boy.' I point a finger at him. 'Here, you go: *Wo ist Tom? Er holt sich in der Garage einen runter.* Where's Tom? He's jacking off in the garage.'

He laughs again. 'That's more like it. Might even have to learn that one off by heart.'

I fold the piece of paper up then. 'What's the time?'

'Just on six.'

We look at each other. 'Breakfast!'

We've got two hours to fill before the tour bus will arrive to pick us up and, perusing the menu, we decide that the only reasonable thing to do is to eat as much as we can to pass the time. It takes us a good fifteen minutes to decide on exactly what we'll have, and in the end we both choose the full English breakfast with lots of side orders, including one of black pudding. We probably won't eat it, but we're curious enough to push it around on our plates for a while so we can say we've had a cultural food experience.

The two-hour plan doesn't exactly pull itself off, however, because twenty minutes after the knock on the door and the delivery of the breakfast tray, breakfast is gone. I forget my sad vegetarianism and Jas and I both wolf down our food as if we've never eaten before. When we're done, only the black pudding, a bacon rind and a toast crust or two remain.

'I'm so full.' I lie back on my bed with a groan. 'Something tells me I'm going to outgrow all my pants on this tour, even if it is only five days long.'

Jas flops onto his bed as well. 'Good. Outgrow them. You're too skinny.'

'Ha!' I say to the ceiling. 'Too skinny. That's a good one. Who said that thing about you can never be too skinny? You can never be too rich or too thin—that's it.'

'Probably someone with a large overdraft and a raging case of bulimia. You *are* too skinny. You've lost heaps of weight.'

'I didn't try. And just remember I don't work at a café any more. I haven't got hummingbird cake and white chocolate macadamia blondies staring me in the face all day. In Byron it's lentil burgers and wheatgrass shots or nothing. Take your pick.'

'Nothing, thanks. With extra sauce. But what about now? Living with Kath and Mark? Responsible adults and all that. Don't they cook?'

This really makes me laugh. 'Let's say they *try*. I do most of the cooking when I'm around. And if I'm not, I think they live on Lean Cuisine.'

'Nothing wrong with frozen dinners.'

I turn my head to look at Jas. 'I didn't say there *was* anything wrong with frozen dinners. I'm quite partial to the Lean Cuisine vegetable cannelloni myself. Larger serve, of course.'

'Course.'

'OK.' I push myself up with my elbows. 'Shower. You mind if I go first?'

'Go for it.'

I have my shower and douse myself with citrus shower gel in the hope that it'll unfuzz my head. The three cups of coffee helped, but I'm not quite up to speed yet. When I re-emerge—dressed, hair partially dried, slap on and ready to go—Jas is fast asleep.

'Hey.' I pat him on the arm and he jumps. 'Want a shower now? I'm all set, so I'm going out for a quick walk around. We've still got another forty-five minutes or so.'

He nods and makes his way into the bathroom, closing the door behind him. 'Oi! Did an orange explode in here?' his muffled voice says.

'See you soon.' I don't give him the reply he's after.

Half an hour later, I'm back. Jas is watching TV. 'Mission accomplished,' I say through my full mouth, offering him a white paper bag.

'Mission?'

'Pear drops.'

Jas pokes his nose into the bag. 'Lollies?'

'They're not lollies. They're sweeties,' I correct him with a proper English accent. 'Pear drops. Real pear drops. Not like the fake ones we get at home.'

He chooses a yellow one and sticks it into his mouth. Then, just as fast, he reaches over, grabs a tissue and spits it out. 'Charlie, that's revolting. Tastes like nail polish remover.'

I roll my eyes. 'Philistine. They're an acquired taste. I bet Zamiel wouldn't spit it out.'

I get a look. 'Anything tastes good after drinking chicken's blood. Put them away before they kill somebody.' Jas checks his watch then. 'We've got to get downstairs.'

He's right, I think, checking the time.

'Shit.'

I turn around and look at Jas. He's rolled over and is now

inspecting his tiny mobile phone. It starts to beep incessantly again. Just like yesterday. 'More messages?' I ask.

'It's nothing.' He slams it down on the bedside table as he gets up.

I go over. 'My—seventy-eight messages today.'

Jas snatches the phone up then. I watch as he turns it off and sticks it on his belt next to something else. A pager. It's turned off as well.

'Calm down. Aren't you going to get your messages again?'

He makes a noise. 'No point. Know who they're from. Zed. My manager. Zed the dickhead.'

I make a face. OK. I'll have to remember that. We don't much care for Zed. I'm starting to think he's getting a teensy bit upset about some phone messages from his manager, even if there are seventy-eight of them. Zed must want something. Badly. I go over to finish up packing my bag. 'Why is he calling you when you're on holiday? And don't you want to know what he wants? It might be important.'

'I know what he wants. Just wish he'd piss off, really.' Jas runs his hands through his hair.

This makes me pause. Fine. Whatever. This must be the moody rock star stuff I haven't had a chance to see yet, I think. I decide to ignore it and busy myself scooping up the last few items of mine that are sitting around the room— my book, a packet of tissues. 'Ready?' I ask Jas when I've zipped up my suitcase.

Jas nods. 'Sorry. It's just that it really gets my back up. You don't know how he is. He's the most annoying person on earth.'

I give him a quick smile. 'OK.' I start to head for the door, suitcase in tow. 'Enough said. Let's go.'

'What're you doing?' Jas is still standing beside his bed.

'Um, going downstairs.'

'You can't take your own bag. Not at Brown's.'

I drop the suitcase like a hot potato.

Jas picks up the phone and calls Reception. After a word or two he puts the phone down again. 'Now we can go. Come on, *philistine*.'

Chapter Nine

Downstairs, Jas takes a seat on one of the leather couches. 'Don't we have to settle the bill?' I hover beside him.

He waves a hand. 'All done. While you were out.'

'Jas…' I start.

'What? Not this again. I told you it was my treat.'

I sigh. 'But not dinner and the phone calls and break-fast and…'

He shrugs. 'Doesn't matter. It's just money. Don't worry about it.' He picks up a copy of GQ and starts reading.

I stand there for another second or two. 'OK. Well, um, thanks.' I pick up a magazine as well, and go to sit on the couch opposite him. Just money. I shake my head slightly behind my open magazine. I wonder if Jas realises any more how much normal people have to think about 'just money' on a daily basis. About 'just money' to pay the electricity and the phone, 'just money' to buy groceries and fix the car with. It's the rock star thing again.

Jas puts down his magazine now and gets up from the

couch. He starts pacing around the lobby and I watch him with one eye, the other fixed on my reading material, as he makes his way around the room. He seems agitated. But, like I thought last night, there it is again—he looks so much more sure of himself, so much more self-confident than he used to. There's just something about him now. Almost like an aura. He glances over at me and I quickly return to my magazine. Half a page into the article I'm reading, I bring my hand up to my mouth as I yawn. God, I'm tired.

I think I spent about half of last night willing myself to go to sleep, but really replaying the day over and over in my mind. The video landing on my head. Meeting up with Jas. Getting to London. OK, so I'm lying. Most of the tiny amount of energy I had left last night was used up trying not to remember Jas's and my last night in the apartment. I just couldn't stop thinking about it.

And it's funny that after all this time I still feel completely stupid about That Night. As if it only happened yesterday. As if I should have known Jas was gay. But, really, how was I supposed to know? After all, he was sleeping with women. *Lots of them.* Slowly, I look up from my magazine to watch Jas again, but he turns my way and I lift the magazine up a little higher, out of his view. I shouldn't feel stupid about it. I know that. I mean, it's not as if I could have come out and asked him about his sex life up front. How do you ask that kind of thing? Hey, Jas, mate. Are you gay, or bi, or what? You can hardly ask a prospective flatmate and, well, after that it's a bit late, isn't it? You're kind of supposed to *know* which way someone leans if you're living with them.

The thought had, of course, crossed my mind in the past couple of years that maybe Jas was bisexual. That would explain everything. The guys I kept seeing with him on TV— because, despite what Jas said, it wasn't just piglet-face the media had paired him up with—*and* the girls of the Magnolia Lodge kitchen brigade. And being bi was a fashionable rock star kind of thing to do. To be. It was strange, though, that the media had never picked up on it. Like I said, it was fashionable—it would've been a *better* story. Orgies with supermodels, that kind of thing. Right up Zamiel's alley, really.

God, who knows? And what does it matter, anyway? Either way, it's got nothing to do with me. Still, when did this all get so complicated? I remember my mother having The Talk with me when I was in primary school. It went something along the lines of 'When a man and a woman love each other...' Of course, Mum being Mum, they never got married—they just had babies and lived happily ever after together 'if that was what everyone wanted'. But it wasn't as complicated as all this. This is the Snakes and Ladders of sexuality, and something tells me I've been left behind on square one.

My eyes flick up at Jas one more time. He's inspecting the few paintings hanging on the wall and I yawn and think of my lack of sleep again. Maybe I would have got a bit more if he hadn't wanted to 'talk'. I still can't believe he had the guts to bring up our past like that. But Jas must have known I'd kept getting flashes of That Night all day. He must have known I was thinking about it to bring it up like that. After all, I knew instantly what he meant when he said the words 'we need to talk'. He could have meant anything. And me, of course, I just said the first thing that came to mind—the least embarrassing thing. The thing that would get me out of trouble, out of the whole situation the fastest. That's why I blurted those words out—'I don't feel that way any more'. It was the first thing that came into my mind. But the truth is, I think, watching Jas pace the room…the truth is I don't know how I feel about Jas at all.

'Charlotte Notting and Jasper Ash?' A guy walks towards my couch holding a clipboard. He's a welcome distraction from my thoughts. I stand up.

'Charlie,' I say, shaking the loud Mambo board-shorts and jumper-bedecked guy's hand.

'Jas.' Jas comes over to do the same.

'Great. I'm Shane. Your tour guide. Right?'

Jas and I both glance at each other and then back at Shane, surprised at his get up and 'out there' accent. 'You're Australian,' I say, stating the obvious.

'Gold Coast, yeah,' he says, holding both thumbs up. 'Those your bags?'

The two of us nod dumbly as the doorman, overhearing, comes to take them outside for us.

Shane whistles at this and turns three hundred and sixty degrees, inspecting the hotel. 'Not exactly roughing it, are you, eh? Come on, then, you're the last two.' He heads outside to the waiting bus, gesturing for us to follow.

We wait until our bags have been stowed underneath, then climb on board and take two seats near the middle as the bus pulls out. 'Right,' Shane says, up at the front, microphone in hand. 'That's everyone, so we're off—like a bucket of dead jellyfish.'

There's a chuckle from the passengers at this.

'Like that one, do ya?' Shane says. 'Well, there's plenty more where that one came from, believe you me.'

I turn to Jas then. 'I can't believe I've come halfway across the world to see a bit of culture and Shane "bucket of dead jellyfish" man from the Gold Coast is supposed to be pointing it out to me.'

Jas's eyes widen at this. 'Culture? Who said anything

about culture? It's Oktoberfest. It's all about the beer. Which means he's probably an expert in his field.'

I hadn't thought about it like that, but have to admit Jas is probably right.

When I tune back in, Shane's still talking. 'Today's a bit of a killer, travelwise. We're going to be taking the ferry to Calais from Dover, ripping through France and getting to good old Munich at about one a.m. I'll fill you in on the details as we scarper.'

'Great,' Jas says, rubbing his hands together as he turns to me. 'Always wanted to rip through France.'

'Hey, me too.' I laugh. 'Lifelong dream.'

Shane pipes up again then. 'But what we're going to do now is get to know each other a bit better. Warm fuzzies and all that. I'm going to get everyone to come up to the microphone in turn and say their names and a bit about themselves. I'll start, eh?'

'Beer and surfing,' I say to Jas. 'I bet you five bucks.'

Jas looks at me as if I'm crazy. 'Sure. Because I was going to bet on him collecting antique silver teaspoons and entering his pedigree Persian cat, Herr Fluffy, in cat shows.'

I poke my tongue out before turning my attention back to the front of the bus.

'Like I said, my name's Shane, and I'm from the Gold Coast, Australia—the best place in the world. Yeah. I like beer—' there's a cheer from the tour group when he says this '—and surfing and playing the guitar. And chicks, of course.'

Damn, missed one, I think, hoping Jas wasn't listening too hard.

'Missed two,' Jas leans over and says.

Ignore it, ignore it, Charlie, I tell myself, but can't help it. 'One.'

'Missed the chicks as well. That's two.'

I roll my eyes at him. 'I thought that went without saying.'

Jas starts to say something, but Shane begins talking again up at the front of the bus. 'OK, I know where most of youse are from. Here's to the good old Beer-drinking Society…'

There's an ear-splitting cheer at this. Everyone on the bus besides us seems to be from the Beer-drinking Society.

'But there're also a few of you who are virgins. First-timers. A few new faces around the bus. Guess we've all got to start somewhere, don't we?'

They cheer again.

'Right. We'll get started then, from the back. Sweetheart, you're up.' Shane points to a girl sitting on the back seat.

Sweetheart? I snort.

Jas and I listen as each person goes up to the front of the bus to take their turn at the microphone. There's an Irish couple, and a girl and her friend from London, but besides them everyone who gets up to speak seems to be from the Beer-drinking Society of some university in Sydney. I wonder how such a large bunch of students managed to cough up enough money for a trip like this. When I was studying full-time I was lucky if I had enough money to pay for luxuries like textbooks, let alone a trip to Europe.

I look at Jas and he mirrors my surprised expression. And in that one moment that passes between us I'm instantly glad I didn't have to come on this trip on my own. I can't see myself getting in with the Beer-drinking Society, and the only other choices would have been gooseberrying with the Irish couple or tagging along with the girls from London, who are probably fine on their own. The third option would have been making friends with Shane which, right now, doesn't look like much of a possibility. We'd probably go off like a frog in a sock, to put it in his terms.

Eventually it's my turn. I monkey my way up front, holding onto the tops of the seats one by one as I go.

'OK, Posh Spice,' Shane says, passing me the microphone.

I give him a weary sigh as I take it. Obviously this is going to be my new name, thrust upon me because of the hotel I spent the night in, even though I chose it by picking Jas's left hand rather than his right one. And honestly—Posh Spice? I couldn't even be mistaken for the girl by a drunk in a dark alley. I am neither dressed in Gucci—instead, I'm wearing the next best thing: a daggy ensemble of my oldest jeans, a black stretch shirt, padded black vest and Birkenstocks—nor immaculately made up, with only a bit of a half-hearted attempt with some tinted moisturiser and a cap to hide my not very well blow-dried hair. But, no. I am now Posh Spice.

Oh, well, better than Nana Mouskouri, I guess.

'Hi,' I say. 'I'm Charlie. That's short for Charlotte, but I hate Charlotte. I'm from Australia—Byron Bay, actually, which the few of you who aren't from Australia may have heard of. I was given this trip as a present, even though I don't like beer…' There's a whole lot of noise from people at this. Jeers, mainly. I wave my free hand. 'But I'm willing to learn, so I'm counting on all of you to ease me into drinking it. My friend Jas, who you'll meet in a minute, couldn't get me to drink the stuff, not even the wussy one you're supposed to stick a piece of lemon in, so think of it as a challenge.' I give the microphone back to Shane.

'Love ya work, babe,' he says, with a wink.

I give him a little smile back. Something tells me that five days of Shane is going to be more than enough culture for me.

On my way back up the bus, I meet Jas coming down. 'Great. Thanks for the intro. Jas the wussy beer-coaching loser,' he says.

'No worries.' I give him a smack on the butt and send him on his way.

I sit down in my seat and listen as Jas takes the microphone. 'OK. Well, I'm Jasper Ash—Jas, really...'

'Oh, my God!' A girl screams at the top of her lungs. Everyone turns to the back of the bus, where she's sitting, to see what's going on. It's one of the London girls. 'Oh, my God!' She stands up then, and points right at Jas. 'It's Zamiel. Zamiel! Oh, my God! Oh, my God!'

Everyone stops gawking at her and stares at Jas instead. There's complete silence for a minute or two. Except, of course, from the girl up at the back, who's hyperventilating now. Most people on the bus are moving their eyes from the girl, to Jas, to each other, and back to the girl again, but not me—all my attention is focused on Jas, waiting to see what he's going to do. As I watch him this weird thing happens—this kind of glazed look comes over his face.

'What?' he says, eyeing the screamer.

She doesn't answer him, but turns to the people near her on the bus instead. 'It's Zamiel,' she says. 'You know—from Spawn. You're Zamiel.' She finally looks back at him.

Jas's eyes flick over to me for a second and I wonder if I should do something. But what? Strip to create a diversion?

A murmur starts up around the bus that gets louder and louder as time ticks past.

I keep watching Jas. He doesn't seem to be coping with being spotted particularly well, which surprises me. Doesn't he have to deal with this kind of thing all the time? I shoot him a 'what do you want me to do?' look, and this seems to bring him back to earth. Finally there's some action. He does a very bad double take when the girl moves her attention to him once more. Ouch. Not quite believable, in my opinion.

'Zamiel? Spawn? What're you talking about?' he says.

The girl pauses, flustered. 'You're not Zamiel?' she asks.

'Course not.'

'But you look just like him. And you're Australian.'

Jas shakes his head. 'No, I'm not. I'm not Australian. I'm from, er, New Zealand.'

I watch as Shane, privy to our details, gives him the eye.

'Oh,' the girl says.

Jas pauses for a moment. 'People have said that before, though. About the Zamiel thing. Guess I do look a bit like him. I met him once. Part of a lookalike competition. His real name's…' Jas glances out the bus window for a second '…Fox. Justin Fox.'

Justin Fox? Where'd that come from? Still watching Jas, I notice him take another quick glance out of the bus window. Right where he'd looked before. Just as the bus pulls away from a red light I manage to turn in my seat and check what he's looking at. It's a pub. The Fox and Hounds.

'Justin Fox? Oh. I didn't know that was his real name.' And with that the girl sits back down slowly beside her friend, who is obviously not as big a Zamiel fan as she only seems confused by the whole 'you're Zamiel' deal.

'Yeah. Better not tell anyone, though. Think it's a bit of a secret. Not even sure I was supposed to know,' Jas blurts out, then goes to pass the microphone back to Shane. But Shane says something to him and Jas takes the microphone back again. 'Right. Sorry. As I was saying, I'm Jas and…I'm from New Zealand where I…er…farm sheep. A lot of sheep. On a…er…sheep station. It's very green where I live and…that's about it.'

'Tell us about your woolly girlfriends!' an Australian pipes up from the back.

Jas runs a hand through his hair. 'Funny. I don't sleep with the sheep. Well, only with Barbara, but she's special.'

There's a moment's silence before everyone laughs, realising he really *is* joking. Jas gives the microphone back to Shane, fast, then makes his way back to his seat looking a bit the worse for wear.

I can't stop laughing. When he sits back down, I pull him closer to me by his jacket. 'A sheep farmer on a sheep station…?'

'Shhh,' he says.

But it's too late. I'm on a roll now. 'It's very green? Have you even *been* to New Zealand?'

'Nope. Had to dredge it up from what I've seen on the tourism ads on TV.'

I start laughing again. 'And Justin Fox? Or should that be Justin Fox and Hounds? At least you didn't come out with something like Justin Time. Now, that would've been good. And Barbara? I'd love to meet Barbara!'

Jas gives me a look and I know enough to shut up. We settle back to listen as the microphone is handed from person to person.

Chapter Ten

The drive to Dover takes over two hours, and it's gone eleven before we're able to get off the bus and stretch our legs around the ferry. It's a good feeling, finally being able to move again. It's as if I've been cooped up for weeks. First on the plane, now this. And there's more to come. Plenty more. I've got no idea how I'm going to last till we arrive in Munich in the early hours of the morning.

'Don't get seasick, do you?' Jas asks as we climb the stairs up to the top deck.

'No. Why? Do you?'

He shakes his head. 'Just checking. Seen enough vomit for three lifetimes.'

'There's a bit of vomit on the road, is there?'

Jas nods. 'The boys of Spawn aren't exactly into clean living.'

We lean on a railing and watch the White Cliffs of Dover as the ferry pulls out of the dock. 'It's beautiful,' I say to Jas, trying to change the subject away from vomit. 'I didn't know Dover was so close to London.'

'Where'd you think it was?'

I laugh. 'I *told* you I got a C.'

'Um, hi,' someone says then, and both Jas and I turn around to see who it is. 'I'm Sharon.'

'Right. From the bus,' Jas says, not needing to.

Sharon. Likes pubs, *Big Brother*, *Survivor*, her cat, Blackie and hates working as an admin assistant. I remember from her turn at the microphone. Not to mention the fact that her 'it's Zamiel'—'you're Zamiel' harpy-like screeches are still ringing in my ears.

'Sorry about that before. I just got a bit carried away. I'm a big Spawn fan.'

'Yeah. Me too,' Jas says.

I try not to laugh at that one. 'Me three,' I pipe up. 'Though I hear their manager's a bit of a dickhead.'

Sharon and Jas both glance at me. But Sharon's attention returns to Jas quick-smart.

'I must've looked like a right idiot.' She laughs.

'Course not,' Jas says.

'I went to their concert. The last one in London. It was great.' She turns slightly with this, as if to angle me out of the conversation altogether. I spot her friend then—Tara, I think her name is—over near the cafeteria, watching us.

'Was it?' Jas takes a step to the side, holding onto the railing now. He obviously wants out of this conversation, and fast.

'You said you'd met him? That you'd met Zamiel?'

Jas nods.

'That must've been fantastic. He's so...' She takes another step round, really forcing me out.

'Sexy?' I say, and Sharon looks over at me. 'Oh, I know,'

I continue, hamming it up. 'I mean, when you see him, don't you just want to run your hands all over that leather?'

She nods at me. 'Yes!'

'And his long hair! I'd give anything to run my hands through that…' I keep going.

'Oh, I *love* his hair,' she says animatedly.

'And those boots. Wouldn't you just love to take them off and, well, sniff them?'

This makes her pause. She gives me a strange look, but doesn't know what to make of my comment, so goes to Jas instead. 'Well, um, anyway—I just wanted to say I'm sorry about the fuss. I'll see you around.'

'Sure,' Jas says.

We both watch Sharon walk off in the direction of the cafeteria.

Jas waits till she's well out of earshot and is talking to Tara. 'What the…?'

'A girl's allowed to have a few fantasies, isn't she?' I laugh, and we both turn back to the view again.

When there's nothing left to see but water, we go inside and get a cup of coffee. I slide into the window seat of one of the tables and pull out the paper bag from my backpack. 'Another pear drop?' I say, offering Jas the packet.

'Not in this lifetime.'

Sharon walks past our table and gives Jas a small wave.

'She's going to find out it's you soon enough,' I say when she's gone.

'The Justin Fox thing should put her off for a bit. Hopefully.'

I suck away. 'She'll figure it out. She's not Einstein, but she'll figure it out. One sexual favour in Shane's direction to see what kind of sheep you farm and you're a goner,' I say. 'Don't think he won't oblige. He'll be relatively cheap too, I'd say. A hand job would probably do it.'

'Charlie, that's disgusting.'

'What? Shane, the hand job, or the pear drop?'

'All three.'

I shrug. I've been known to be disgusting from time to time. This shouldn't come as such a big shock to Jas. 'You'd better eat something. Remember we're not stopping for lunch till after two.'

'All right, all right! I'll eat something, Mother,' Jas says, and gets up to see what they've got.

As I watch him go, I spot Sharon at a nearby table. She eyes Jas all the way to the counter, or as far as her vision will let her without actively turning around and being obvious about it. She sees me observing her after a while and goes back to her coffee. Still sucking away on my pear drop, I shake my head. I'd bet my life on the fact that on his way back to the table it'll be all hands on deck to check out his butt. I turn my attention to Jas and—not that *I'm* checking out his butt—notice that his mobile and pager are fastened onto his belt, ready to be reached for at a moment's notice. I wonder absentmindedly why he's still wearing them when they've been switched off the entire trip. Force of habit, I guess.

All too soon we're back on the bus and heading for Reims—during which time I realise a coffee, a Coke and half a bottle of water was probably a mistake for both caffeine and toilet-trip related reasons. For the first hour or so I fidget in my seat, intermittently jumping up to make trips to the bathroom. I wonder again how I'm going to make it to Munich. Or even *if* I'm going to make it to Munich—the way I'm going, everyone will probably get sick of me and drop me by the roadside somewhere in France.

As we head east, Shane tells us a bit about the Champagne region. 'It's got a bit of everything, this place,' he says, reading from a sheet of paper. 'Rolling plains, lakes, water meadows, dense forest, hills…'

'What's a water meadow?' someone pipes up.

'Dunno, mate,' he says. 'It just says water meadow here, right on the sheet, so that's all I know. I'll find out for you, if you like, when we get to Reims.' He returns to his sheet of paper for a moment, then looks back up again. 'Oh, yeah. I almost missed the most important bit. You'll be pleased to hear that the Champagne region is, of course, famous for its *booze*…'

There's a mighty cheer from the Beer-drinking Society as Shane says the magic word.

'And there's a cathedral too, if you like that kind of thing.' He crumples up the sheet of paper and pushes it into the driver's seat pocket.

'Not me,' I say to Jas.

'But now we get to the fun bit,' Shane continues, reaching over into his own seat pocket and pulling out another piece of paper and what seems to be a tape. He sticks the tape into the bus's tape deck. 'We're going to learn a true-blue German beer-drinking song.'

There's a cheer. I'm starting to wonder if there's a sign up somewhere I'm just not seeing that says *Cheer Now*.

'Each tour I teach a different song, so even if you've been on this trip before, like Damien, the right honourable president of the Beer-drinking Society, who happens to be on his fourth bender—' he points out a guy near the front of the bus '—you won't know this one.'

Jas and I look at each other. People have done this trip four times?

'The one we're going to learn's called "There's no Beer

in Hawaii". Mind you, that's not really true. There's plenty of beer in Hawaii. I happen to know because I drank most of it once, when I was there for ten days, but we'll just have to pretend there isn't, eh? OK, here we go. We'll listen to it once in full, then we'll start to learn the words, right?' He glances up. 'Right?'

'Right!' we all say back this time.

Shane goes around the bus, handing us each a photo-copied sheet of the words in both German and English. We spend the next half-hour or so singing along to the tape.

The lyrics are, um, interesting. And, I notice when we finish up, probably engrained on my long-term memory. Before I can try to delete them, Shane's up at the front of the bus again.

'OK, now that's out of the way, there're only two more things you have to learn in German to get by on this trip and they never change. What are they, Damien?' Shane points to the president of the amber fluid drinkers.

'*Zwei Bier, bitte!*' Damien yells out rather too loudly. Rather as if Shane is a drill sergeant and he's on parade.

'*Und?*' Shane says.

'*Wo ist die Toilette, bitte?*'

'That's right, my friend. For those of you that didn't catch that, Damien just said the two most important phrases in the German language. He said, *"Zwei Bier, bitte"*—which means "Two beers, please"—and *"Wo ist die Toilette, bitte?"* which means "Where's the toilet, please?" That's all you need to know, kids.'

We spend the next ten minutes repeating these two phrases over and over.

Just as I'm getting a headache, Shane gets us to stop. 'Now, you'd better remember those two German lovelies, because if you don't and someone hears you say one of them in English—' he picks up a large tin that looks like a Fosters beer can '—you'll have to pay a few euros into the kitty. We spend what we've collected out on the town during our last night in Munich, so you can be sure it all goes to a good cause. Your livers.'

There's another cheer.

'So, what do we say?' Shane says.

Everyone pipes up in unison, *'Zwei Bier, bitte! Und, wo ist die Toilette, bitte?'*

I think I want to cry. But as I can't seem to squeeze a tear out, I send up a silent prayer instead. Please, God, let it be over soon.

Jas taps me on the arm. 'Are you OK?'

'Just tell me one thing. Were we like that as students?' I know what his answer is going to be—a solid no.

Jas grins from ear to ear. 'Hell, yes!'

Chapter Eleven

Over the next few hours I start to feel a tiny bit sorry for ocker Shane. On paper, his job sounds cruisey—guide a busload of people through a five-day booze-fest—but in reality it's something akin to babysitting.

He seems exhausted already, only half a day into the tour, and I have to suppress a giggle when he pops in a video for us all to watch—*Ten Things I Hate About You* dubbed in German with English subtitles—and sinks down into his seat with a sigh in exactly the same way Kath's mother friends do seconds after they push *The Lion King*, *The Wiggles*, *Pocahontas* or whatever's the go this week into the VCR to satiate their two-year-olds. After a cup of tea and a chocolate biscuit they're usually a bit more ready to face the rest of the day. Shane settles for a muesli bar.

Poor guy, I think. He's not going to get his cup of tea. So, to give him a break, I watch the video quietly, like a good little tourist, while Jas reads.

It isn't long, however, before Shane's on his feet again.

'OK, guys and beer wenches.' He stands up at the front of the bus as it slows to a stop. 'We've got an hour here in Reims, and I reckon you should make the most of it as we won't be stopping again till eight. So, off you go…'

'Off like what?' Damien pipes up.

'Off like a fifteen-year-old at a nudie bar, pres,' Shane answers quickly, and everyone laughs. 'Oh, and remember to go to the toilet *before* you get back on the bus. You don't want it to get backed up like it did on the last tour, believe me.'

Jas and I get up and file out of the bus like everyone else. When we're outside, I hand my bag over to him as we start off along the street. I want to pull my jacket on as it's surprisingly chilly and I don't want to catch a cold. I take a deep breath in, which makes me cough, and my hands immediately go up to feel my throat. Maybe I'm already catching a cold, I think, poking and prodding my glands. No. It's just the cold air. I continue with pulling my jacket on. I'm just being silly.

'You OK?' Jas asks.

I nod. 'Fine. It's just cold.'

It isn't until I've got my jacket on, taken my backpack from Jas and fiddled around putting it on my back again that I pay attention to what's around me. But when I do, I stop, my throat forgotten. 'Wow. Look at that.' I point out the structure at the end of the street to Jas.

'It's been there the whole time. Believe me.'

'Is that so? I take it that's the cathedral?'

'I'd say so. Yeah.'

'It's gorgeous.' I stand in silence for a moment, staring at its white frothiness. 'All that detail—it's just like a wedding cake.' I keep standing and staring. After a minute or so I pull back in surprise as I realise that my sculptor's eye kicked in for a while there. One minute I was standing and admiring the place, the next minute I was looking specifically at things like light and shade, curves and lines. And I really am surprised.

A few years ago I couldn't do the washing-up without seeing things through my sculptor's eye. I've heard other artists say it too. I once read a piece a photographer had written about how he saw the entire world, every day, through a viewfinder he couldn't shut off. I was never that bad, but I have to admit that since I stopped sculpting, almost two years ago, I've noticed a difference—the way I see things has been changing back to normal. Especially over the last year, my eyes have begun to see things, like the cathedral in front of me, for what they simply are.

I walk up to the cathedral, drawn to it, completely forgetting about Jas, who trails along behind me in silence. I don't walk up to the door and enter, however, but move off to the left-hand side.

'Hey,' Jas says. 'Don't you want to go in?'

I look up above me at the façade. There's a row of angels and I stare at the folds of their skirts, mesmerised. They're amazing. I reach out and touch the stone in front of me—cold and smooth. I run one hand over it, then the other, before my eyes move back up to the angels again. 'Come here.' I turn around and beckon to Jas, who's waiting a few steps behind me.

He comes on over.

'Give me your hand,' I say, still with one of mine on the stone. He gives me his right hand unquestioningly and I take it and run it over the surface beside mine. Then I stop, my hand still over the top of his. 'Now look up.' He turns his gaze to the angels above and I watch as I see the realisation dawn on his face that someone, some time, somewhere, made the angels come out of the same stone. He moves his gaze back down to me.

'Pretty amazing, isn't it?' I smile as I slowly let my hand drop.

Jas runs his over the wall one more time before letting it fall to his side.

'Want to go inside?' I nod my head towards the door.

'Sure.'

When we exit the cathedral fifteen minutes later, we both squint as the bright sunlight hits our eyes. A child walks past us with an ice-cream and we stop, letting him cross in front of us.

'That reminds me,' Jas says.

'Of what?' I glance up at him.

'I'm hungry. Starving.'

'That's what happens when you knock back people's perfectly good pear drops. Come on, we'll have a walk around and see if we can find something to eat. Where did Shane tell us to go again?'

Of course neither of us has listened to a word Shane's said.

'Follow that guy.' Jas points out a man crossing the street when we've decided we're officially lost. 'He looks hungry.'

And, funnily enough, the guy must be, because a few streets later we're where we were supposed to be about half an hour ago.

We walk around for a while, taking a look at all the food on offer, before Jas stops. 'What about here?' he says, pointing up to one café's sign. '*Café le Paris.* We're only setting foot on French soil for about an hour. Better go somewhere that actually sounds French.'

'What, *le* McDonald's isn't French enough for you?' We'd passed one a while back that I'd pointed out to him before

I'd remembered how much he used to hate the place. Obviously he still does, by the expression on his face.

Jas pulls out two nearby chairs from a table and we take a seat. We peruse the menu and decide to share a pizza, of all things, then pick out two strange little bottom-heavy orange drinks that have French writing all over them—our one concession to actually being in France. When we've ordered, we sit back in our chairs and take in the view—the fountain with people milling around, some sitting on its stone base, stretching their legs out and enjoying a moment or two of sunshine, the cream-coloured buildings surrounding the square, sandwiched together like Monte Carlo biscuits.

Yep, I could sit here for quite a while, I think. But it's quiet at the café and the food comes reasonably quickly.

'Great,' Jas says, suddenly looking all too like a starving dog.

As a big whiff of pizza smell hits me, I realise I'm starting to get pretty hungry as well, even after my big breakfast. I eat two of the large slices of pizza and pick at a third one as I watch Jas. I'd forgotten how much he used to eat. I guess you have to when you're that tall. There's just more of you to feed, isn't there? He finishes his half of the pizza in no time.

'Eat the rest of mine,' I urge him. 'I'm not going to. Just do it slower this time, or people will start asking about the last time I fed you.'

'Too long ago,' he says, and starts in on the rest of the pizza.

I sit back and take in the view, sipping on my orange drink while Jas polishes off the pizza. It's lovely here. It's a shame we have to pass through all these places so quickly and miss out on exploring them properly.

When he's finished, Jas leans back in his chair as well, with a contented sigh. We sit in companionable silence for a while, taking in the atmosphere. I catch a glimpse of the cathedral in the distance and Jas cranes his neck to see what I'm looking at, before leaning back once more with a 'hmpf'.

'What?'

'Ah, nothing.'

'No, what is it?' I can tell that he's thinking something. Something about me.

Jas shrugs. 'You just surprised me back there before.'

'Surprised you how?' I put my drink down on the table.

He shrugs again. 'You used to be a bit more blasé about what your mother did for a living. That's all.'

Did I? I look at Jas for a second, then back at the cathedral. I don't know what to say to this.

'We've got to go. Three o'clock, Shane said. Yeah?'

'Mmmm,' I say, checking the time.

We get up and start to stroll back in what we think is the direction of the bus, but manage to get a bit lost again.

'You're supposed to be good at this directional stuff.' I point a finger at Jas a few streets later.

'Why? Because I'm male? I get lost better than anyone else I know.'

'Now, there's a claim to fame.' I stop now, trying to get my bearings. 'Oh.'

'What?'

'Um, hang on a second, I just have to, um, go somewhere,' I say, and run a few steps down the street and straight into a shop that says 'Chocolatier' in large letters above its doorway.

It takes a few moments for Jas to realise what's happening and catch up with me. But not before I've spied some choice-looking nougat. 'You know you'll get hungry later,' I tell him as I buy a few bars.

He gives a short laugh as I stuff the bars in my backpack. 'Nice to know you're always thinking about me.'

The lady in the chocolate shop gives us directions back to the cathedral, from where we think we might just be able to kick our poor directional skills into action and find the bus again.

A few minutes later we round a corner and the bus comes into sight. We head up the street towards it.

'Charlie, look out!' Jas grabs my arm.

'What?' I glance down to see I've just missed the pile.

I move my gaze back up, a big smile on my face. An evil smile, which grows even more depraved as I recall more and more about the floor three rule at Magnolia Lodge. One of the residents on our floor—Mrs Harrow, an invalid—owned a Chihuahua. A not-very-well-house-trained Chihuahua, who sometimes escaped out of her flat and left messes in the hall. Small messes, but messes all the same. Mrs Harrow's home help didn't think anything outside of Mrs Harrow's apartment was her problem, so the floor residents came up with a solution. Whoever saw it first cleaned it up. Once, Jas and I had alighted from the lift at the same time to find a neatly deposited pile right in our line of vision. We'd spent the next half an hour chasing each other around the Lodge, arguing about who'd seen it first.

Now, I slowly bring my finger up to point at Jas. 'You saw it first!' I start walking backwards towards the bus.

He grins back.

I walk a bit faster.

His grin gets wider. 'No, you saw it first and pretended not to see it.' He points back.

I turn around and start running. 'Prove it!' I laugh. And I don't care who's watching, I just keep running. All the way to the bus, where I stop and lean against it, exhausted.

'I *hated* finding it first,' I say to Jas, still laughing when he catches up.

'I think we all did.' He leans on the bus as well. 'But hang on…' Jas pauses, turning his head.

'What?'

'Can't seem to remember what we were just talking about. Ah, that's it—the fact that *you* saw it first.'

'Don't start.' I use my last stores of energy to push myself off the bus and poke him in the chest. 'I'm too weak.'

Jas watches me puffing away. 'You really need to go to the gym more often.'

The gym. As if. I used to love going to the gym, but haven't been for over a year. I just sigh in reply and make my way up the stairs of the bus. Jas follows and Shane, standing up the top of the steps, winks at us as we pass.

When Shane's done the head-count, and it seems no one's gone AWOL in Reims, we set off. He picks up the microphone. 'Anyone got to pay up? Any money due in the kitty?'

Everyone's attention turns to the last couple of rows, where there's something going on. Eventually one guy stands up.

'There's always one,' Shane says. 'We'll forgive you this time, because we're in France, but as soon as we hit Germany that's it, fellas. No excuses, right?'

There's silence.

'Right?'

'Right,' we say in unison, starting to get the hang of this now.

'That's *ja*, to you. In a few hours, anyway,' he says. 'And don't you forget it. Oh, and I found out what a water meadow is. It's a bit of grassland next to a river that farmers flood artificially. But only at certain times of the year.'

'What times of the year?' someone pipes up from the back.

Shane gives the guy a dirty look and then laughs. 'Now you're just starting to piss me off. Right, another vid then, shall we?' He pops one in, then turns the microphone off and sits back down.

This time it's a Mel Gibson movie. I watch about the first ten minutes before I fall asleep, my head on Jas's shoulder. Three-quarters of the way through the movie I wake up and watch ten minutes or so of Mel running around like a headless chicken before I fall asleep again. And when I wake up the next time there's a Meg Ryan movie on. I realise that we're alternating—chick flick, boy flick.

We stop in Karlsruhe before long, as planned, and Jas and I eat something nasty and fried in a *Biergarten*. When we're done, we stretch our legs a bit, and soon enough it's time to get back on the dreaded bus.

'I don't want to go,' I whine at Jas as we walk back to our seats. 'The bus sucks.'

'You're just going to go back to sleep. What's the difference? Here, give me your bag.' He takes it when I pass it to him and opens the zip, moving one hand around inside. 'Now…' He passes me something that I can't quite see in the dark. 'Quit whining. Eat some nougat.'

This doesn't sound like such a bad idea, so I do. And he's right, of course. Not about quitting whining—nothing could make me do that—but about the sleeping. Because half an hour later I'm asleep again. It only takes me that long because the Beer-drinking Society has started up a rousing rendition of Slim Dusty's 'I Love to Have a Beer with Duncan' and they just happen to know all five verses off by heart.

When I wake up next, it's with a jump. I open my eyes, confused, taking a second or two to remember where I am and what's going on. When I do, I turn my head to gaze up at Jas. He's wide awake. Reading. One hand holding his book awkwardly and the other…around me. I wait, expecting my body to stiffen like it did in bed last night, but it doesn't. Surprised, my eyes lift to meet Jas's and he smiles, looking down at me.

'It's OK.' He smooths his free hand down my cheek, just like I guided his hand down the stone wall of the cathedral today. 'There's been no dribbling to worry about. No dribbling at all.'

I smile and, still dreamily half asleep, settle back down to sleep some more.

Chapter Twelve

Of course with all that sleep I wake up again in what can only be called the middle of the night. I tiptoe around the room, unpacking the clothes I need for the day, having the quietest shower possible, scratching my pen as non-scratchingly as I can over the few postcards I write and sneaking down to the lobby to call Kath and tell her how things are going. When I get back upstairs, Jas is still fast asleep.

Lucky bastard.

I pull out one of the chairs from the small table beside the TV and sit down to check out the breakfast menu. It's not very exciting, and every so often I find my eyes wandering over to Jas's face. Eventually I put the menu down and just watch him. It's funny that even though he's on holiday he hasn't been able to wind down. To me, it seems as if he always has one eye fixed over his shoulder. Though with crazies like Sharon on the loose I'm hardly surprised.

Jas rolls over and my eyes jump quickly to his face, checking to see if he's awake. He's not. Double bastard, I think to myself as I spot his eyelashes. I'd forgotten what gorgeous long, doubly thick eyelashes he has. Completely wasted on him, of course. I had to drag him over to the bathroom mirror to show him he even *had* eyelashes the day I pointed them out at the apartment. He wasn't suitably impressed with the comparison between his and my stumpy ones. 'Swap you,' I think he said.

Typical Jas.

I suppress a laugh, but then stop as I remember something. Last night. I saw those eyelashes last night. Up close. I glance at Jas's face again, smooshed against his pillow, and my chest feels tight. Too close. Way, way too close. I turn around now to face in the opposite direction.

God, I'm such a fool.

This, all of this, should be enough. I should be happy just that we're on this trip together. Happy that Jas and I are friends again. I look down at the table and pick up my postcards. I turn each one over slowly in my hands. I should be happy that I *have* a friend again, in fact.

I'd lost most of my friends—all of them—really, over the last few years, as I shuttled back and forth from Byron to Sydney. Julie from high school, Katerina from uni, Sally from waitressing at the café. I turned down their offers of help when I was at my lowest. My most selfish. When I couldn't face anyone but Kath and Mark. And I know I've got to make it up to them all somehow—even if they don't want to be friends again. The postcards I'm writing are a start. An olive branch now that I'm finally getting my life back together.

But Jas is here now and I have the opportunity to fix things with him. I was stupid not calling him back. I just didn't want to have to deal with the embarrassment of That Night. And because I couldn't deal with things like an adult, I lost what was once the best friendship I'd ever had.

Stupid. Stupid. Stupid.

And I know the answer to that question now, the question I was pondering yesterday morning. I really *don't* feel that way about Jas any more. I just want our old friendship back. I want things to return to the way they were before I wrecked them. We used to have the best time together. I'm not going to be juvenile enough to endanger that again.

'Hey,' Jas says, startling me. 'You're up.'

I swivel in my chair. 'Yep,' I say, a bit too brightly. 'First stop today—new body clock.'

'You get used to it.' Jas yawns. 'I can sleep any time, anywhere now. Buses, planes, couches, stretched across four guitar cases with an amp as a pillow…'

I roll my eyes. 'Lucky you.'

'Comes in handy.'

'Want me to order some breakfast?' I ask, holding up the menu.

Jas jumps out of bed. 'Yeah, you pick. I'll just have a quick shower. We've got to be downstairs soon.'

I order us up some toast, fruit salad and coffee. Enough to keep us going until we hit the land of sausages and sauerkraut.

When Jas and I are finished eating, we head downstairs to meet up with the group.

Shane's doing a head-count in the lobby. Well, OK, a wig-count. Because this morning all of the Beer-drinking Society members are wearing wigs. All kinds of wigs—big black afro wigs, red Pippi Longstocking plaits, rainbow curls. I think about asking someone what the wigs are for, but my brain gives up on the task of forming the appropriate sentences. It's too early and I haven't had my second cup of coffee yet.

'That seems to be it,' he says, after a few more people turn up. He claps his hands together. 'Right, people, this is it. As you can see, it's wig day for the Beer-drinking Society once again, which means you can stop crossing the days off your calendar. The first day of the big "O" has arrived. Today we're going to be taking a brisk walk over to watch the opening parade, and then, following that, you'll get to see the Mayor tap the first barrel of beer. If you get pulled away from the group, don't worry—just follow the crowd and you'll be right. I'll be outside the main gate at both five p.m. and ten-thirty p.m., if you want someone to walk back with you to the hotel. Or feel free to come back yourself at any time. I'd advise on the ten-thirty slot, though, because that, ladies and gentlemen, is when the beer stops.'

There's a moan from someone up at the back of the group then. Probably President Damien, serial Oktoberfest visitor and, it's looking like, resident nutcase. The rest of the Beer-drinking Society moan in unison after him. It's as if they can't believe the beer actually stops.

'Yes, yes, I know it's an inconvenience, but they have to give the waitresses a rest some time, so they'll still be alive and kicking next year,' Shane continues. 'OK—a tip or two for you. There are fourteen different beer halls, but unless you're in and seated inside one of them by three p.m., you will not get a seat. I repeat that. You will not get a seat after three p.m. And what happens if you don't have a seat, Damien?' He glances around the crowd for the regular. It *is* him up at the back. As I'd thought.

'No beer.'

'What's that you say, Damien?'

'No beer! *Kein Bier.*'

What is this, some kind of cult?

'Too right, my friend,' Shane continues. 'That is unless you're in the Hofbräu tent. Which leads me to my next tip.

Stay out of the Hofbräu tent. Avoid it at all costs unless you're full-blooded Australian or Irish. If you are not Australian or Irish, you will not be able to handle the Hofbräu tent. Ladies of any nationality, if you do dare to go in there, please don't do it alone—take note that the Italians *will* go for your arse. *Herren und Damen*, you have been officially warned.' Finished with his speech, Shane heads towards the hotel's front door. 'And we're off…' he starts.

Everyone quietens down, waiting to hear what he's going to say this time.

'…like a maggot in a dead dog.'

There's a cheer from the Beer drinking Society.

I really need that second cup of coffee. I look up at Jas and shake my head. 'I'll give you one guess where they're going to head straight to when everything opens up.'

'Er…' Jas scratches his head deliberately. 'Could it be…the Hofbräu tent?'

'You guessed it.'

Outside, Shane moves into action, turning around on the footpath and walking backwards for a few steps. 'Come on, people, let's move it. We don't want to be late.' He steps up the pace a bit.

We keep walking street by street, considerably faster as we go along, and everyone warms up. It's freezing out, and I can see my breath huff and puff in front of me as my legs whisk along trying to keep up with Jas's pace—unfortunately these are also stumpy, like my eyelashes. After a while, Sharon and her sidekick Tara pass Jas and I by. As they go, Sharon gives Jas a meaningful look. One of those 'I'm trying to flirt with you' long, unbroken gazes.

'Somebody likes you,' I sing-song under my breath to Jas. 'I think you've got yourself a groupie.'

'Great. Just what I need—another groupie.'

I look up at him, surprised. 'So you really have groupies? Like, lots of them?'

Jas stops me until everyone passes and we're at the back of the group. 'Don't want anyone to hear,' he says, before he continues. 'Groupies, yeah. Plenty of them. There's even a couple of semi-normal ones too. The ones who don't think I'm God almighty and claim they like the music. Must be deaf.'

'And do they really hang around outside your hotel room and things like that?'

Jas nods.

'Wow.' I whistle. 'So, what do they want?'

Jas's face seems a bit blank. 'Beats me.' But then he smiles and runs his hands down over his chest, past his hips to his legs. 'My body?' He grins. 'Who wouldn't?'

I hit his arm. 'You dag. Nice to see how modest you still are!'

Jas laughs. 'Yeah, just call me "Jenny from the Block."'

I groan. 'But, really?' I get serious again. After all, I want to know all this stuff. It's not every day you get to quiz a rock star, is it? 'What *do* they want?'

Jas shrugs. 'Usually they want to have it off with Zamiel. Me, I try not to think about it. Understanding groupies isn't a good place to be at.'

'So, *have* you ever slept with any of them?' is my next question.

Jas looks at me as if I'm an idiot. 'This is what I mean. Why would you say that? Am I really that different?'

I raise an eyebrow. 'Answer the question.'

'Jesus. No. Course not. You should see them. They dress like him. Zamiel, I mean. Not my scene.'

'And the other guys in the band?'

'That's different. Let's just say we have a security guard who knows their types.'

My eyes widen and my pace slows. 'You mean he picks them out of the audience, or something?'

'Pretty much. They like an all-you-can-eat smorgasbord after each show.'

'Hey, you two!' Shane calls out to us from up at the front of the group. 'Step on it!'

'Sorry!' I yell back, and Jas and I run a bit to catch up.

Over the next few streets the crowd starts to get thicker and thicker, but Shane pushes on. We slow down, having to negotiate our way through.

'That must be really strange—having people outside your hotel all the time, just waiting to see you,' I say to Jas. 'I can't imagine it.'

But Jas shakes his head at this. 'They're not waiting to see me.'

'Well, waiting to see Zamiel. Same thing.'

He shakes his head again, harder this time. 'That's what no one understands. Not the same thing at all. Always reminds me of when I was a kid and someone—my dad, I think—told me there was an actor inside Big Bird on *Sesame Street*. That it was just a costume. But the guy, the actor—you never saw him. Had no idea what he looked like for real. That's me. I'm no one. Nothing.'

'Jas!'

'What?'

'Don't say that!'

'Say what?'

I catch his arm. 'That you're no one. That you're nothing. That's a terrible thing to say.'

'Why? It's true.'

I shake his elbow. 'It's only true on the you-know-who front.' I have to be more careful now we're surrounded by people. 'But if all that ended tomorrow, so what? You're still you. And that's better than being you-know-who any day. To me, anyway.'

Shane stops now and, slowly, the group stops with him.

Jas sighs. 'I should take you on the road. Write me some mantras. At least get you to meet Zed.'

'Zed the dickhead?'

'That's the one.'

'Maybe you should fire Zed if he doesn't tell you things like that often enough.'

Jas laughs then. 'Maybe.'

There's a flash of neon yellow then, as someone falls in beside us. Damien. Complete with yellow wired plaits sticking out at right angles, no less.

'Hey! You guys been before?' he asks me. 'To Oktoberfest?'

'No,' I tell him.

'Didn't think so. Bloody hell. You have *really* been missing out.'

I frown. What do we have? 'Oktoberfest Virgins' written on our foreheads? I turn and check him out. The poor guy looks as if he's about to wet himself he's so excited. 'We're here now.'

'It's the best. I come back every year.'

Jas and I look at each other. So we keep hearing. I can tell he's thinking the same thing I am. I turn back to Damien, interested. 'How do you guys afford it? Being students and all?'

He sticks his thumbs up Shane-style, 'Fundraising.'

'Fundraising?'

'Yeah. You know—raffle tickets and beer-tastings, that kind of thing. And we run the uni toga party every year. The stuff we pick up after that pays for a couple of our tours as it is.'

'What sort of things do they leave?' I ask.

'Mobiles. Laptops. Three-hundred-count Egyptian cotton sheet sets they've pinched from their parents to wear as togas. They never claim any of it.'

Jas is staring at the guy goggle-eyed now. 'No one comes back for their lost laptop?'

'We put on such a good show, the next day they probably don't even remember they took it with them. Well, better go catch up with my drinking buddies. See you later.'

Jas and I watch Damien skip away like a frisky impala. I'm still watching when there's a nudge to my elbow.

'Somebody likes you,' Jas sing-songs my own words back at me.

'Ugh. Just my luck.'

We start to hear it then. A marching band. It seems this is where we're going to watch the parade from. I catch sight of Damien's wig pushing its way to the front of the crowd to get a better view. That poor boy. For a second or two I worry about how he fares in the real world and what he's going to do when he finishes uni. But I stop myself smartly. Who am I kidding? He'll probably be an Oktoberfest tour guide.

I can hear the parade coming closer and closer now, but unfortunately can't see a thing. I look up at Jas the giraffe, who has a great view. At five-foot-five, I'm left jumping around like a three-year-old, trying to see above the crowd.

'I'd offer you a spot on my shoulders. Might put my back out, though.'

'Gee, thanks. I can just see myself up there, waving around in the breeze with all the kiddies on their dads' shoulders. Maybe I should check with Damien. I'm sure he's got a spare keg around somewhere I could stand on.'

'Wouldn't surprise me. I'll just have to tell you what's

going on. There's a few different bands coming, and then, up the middle, there's some horses with kind of…er…wagons or something. With waitresses on top?'

I nod. 'Mark told me about that. It's the brewery floats. I had a go at him for it.'

'Why?' Jas asks.

'Well, when I was a waitress I never got a day off to swan around on a float in a parade.'

'How many beers could you carry at once?'

'About two.'

'Yeah? I think they've got about six in each hand.'

'OK.' I scrunch my nose up. 'Point taken.' I take my backpack off for a minute and search around for the photocopied information sheets that came with my tour itinerary. When I find them, I have a quick read through. 'After this, we have to make a run for it to the Schottenhamel tent to see the Mayor tap the first barrel of beer. Everything should get going after that.'

Jas nods. 'In a big way, I'm guessing. This is huge.'

'Is it ever.' I can see the marching bands passing by now, and the mood of the crowd around us has lifted both visibly and audibly. Everyone waves at the people on the floats and in the decorated carriages. What really gets my attention, however, is the crowd. They're having what looks like the time of their lives. A number of them are even wearing what seems to be national dress, with the guys in leather trousers and braces and tiny, quirky little hats. The women have long skirts and jackets, or cotton dresses with white low-cut tops underneath. Dirndl, I think they're called.

All the German good cheer going on around me makes me think of the parades I've been to back home. Somehow I can't see Australians doing this—the national dress thing. A flag here or there, yes. A spot of face-painting, of course.

But national dress? The closest we have to national dress is thongs, shorts, a white towelling hat, matching zinc on the nose and the obligatory esky.

We watch the entire parade, and then get pushed along in the crowd with everyone else until we're in what must be the Schottenhamel tent. Jas keeps a firm hold on me— I think in case I get trampled underfoot. We're right up at the back when we finally stop moving. And when I say back, I mean *back*.

'How many people do you think are in here?' I glance up at him.

He takes a look around him: 'I'd say ten thousand at least.'

'No way? Really?' But I believe him. After a few years of moving around from stadium to stadium he probably knows how many people a place can hold the second his eyes sweep over it.

The atmosphere gets rowdier by the minute. Eventually I see what all the fuss is about. There's a guy up at the front, on the stage. Holding something that's shaped like a golden tap. He's surrounded by the media and there's a bit of stuffing around before he seems to get on with what he's supposed to be doing. Then, all of a sudden—I'm inspecting the guy next to me's funny-looking leather braces at the time—there's this *bang*, *bang* which makes me jump. When I see him again, the guy is shoving the golden tap into the barrel and, this accomplished, he turns around and yells something in German. Everyone cheers heartily.

'Should I go up and get us a cold one?' Jas laughs.

'Be my guest, Superman.'

I'm still clutching my photocopied pages. Jas taps them with one finger. 'So now what?'

People are starting to push past us, making their way out of the tent. 'Apparently we're free. Let's get out of here before we get crushed to death.'

Chapter Thirteen

Outside, we both stop for a moment and take a few deep breaths, filling our lungs. It's sunnier now, and much warmer than before. I take off my jacket and tie it around my waist as I check out what's happening around me. It's the usual sideshow sort of stuff, with the only truly different thing being the fact that the place is dotted with these huge beer tents. People are spilling in and out of the tents as if there won't be any beer left in half an hour, even though it's only just gone midday.

I'm starting to think that when these people drink beer they're serious about drinking beer.

'Hey, you two.' Shane surprises us, approaching from behind and laying an arm on each of our shoulders. 'Jas and Charlie, right? Weird names.'

'Um, thanks,' I say, and both of us turn around.

'Won't stay a second. Beer to taste, people to see. I just wanted to find out...' He looks at Jas for a moment, as if sizing him up. 'It is you, isn't it, mate? You *are* that Zamiel guy. You're not from New Zealand, anyway. You've got an Australian passport. I checked after the sheep farming thing. Sounded a bit dodgy, that.'

There it is again, that glazed look. The same as I'd seen on the bus. Jas's eyes start to dart around. 'Er…'

'Thirsty?' I ask Jas, giving him a moment. He shakes his head. 'Shane?'

'Nope.'

'Well, I am. I'm just going to buy a bottle of water.' I point out the nearby drinks stand, where a small queue is forming. 'Mind this for me?' I drop my backpack down on the wooden bench beside us.

'No worries.' Jas sinks down to take a seat next to it. Shane sits down as well.

I go over and line up, trying to work out how many Australian dollars there are to a euro—and I'm quickly learning that whatever you're converting to it's never enough. When I'm next in line, I turn around to check what's going on. Jas and Shane are deep in conversation. I watch with one eye, the other eye keeping track of how the queue is going. Jas is talking, talking, talking. He reaches for something. His wallet. Shane waves his hands, no. Jas puts it away again. Now Shane's talking, talking, talking. Jas laughs. Shane laughs. They shake hands. And that's it. Shane walks off, giving me a wave as he passes.

I nod and wave back.

'So, what was all that about?' I ask when I get back to Jas.

He laughs some more. 'Was actually quite funny. Didn't think that anyone would recognise me—not travelling like this…as me, I mean. Doesn't happen often—only with the diehard fans. But Shane's got my details.'

I nod, taking a sip of water then offering it to Jas.

He waves a hand. 'No, thanks. It's just that you forget sometimes. What people can find out about you. Some of them have even tracked my parents down. Turned up at their house.'

'I bet that went down well.' I'm sure Jas's parents aren't exactly *supportive* of his career. They never thought he should have studied music in the first place.

Jas sighs. 'Yeah. It was hardly tea and scones on the front verandah. Anyway, Shane knows it's me, and I didn't want it to get out, so I thought I'd offer him some...' He pauses. 'I hate saying this, but offer him some money. You know— shut him up. If he told anyone the media would be interested. They love trying to catch me out of character. It'd wreck the trip if they found out. For everyone.'

I never thought about it like that—that the media would like nothing more than to catch Zamiel without his make-up on. Kind of in the same way they love doing it to Cameron Diaz—though I have to admit those kind of pics make me feel a whole lot better while I queue at the supermarket. 'So he didn't take it? What's so funny about that? I wouldn't if I was him. You're on holiday after all, and he *is* the tour guide. He owes you at least a bit of privacy.'

'Wasn't that that was funny. It was the whole ocker Australian thing. He confessed he's doing the same thing as me—living a double life, that is. He's really a student. Guess what he's studying?'

'Um, Modern Dance?' I try to pick the most unlikely thing.

'Close. Fine Arts.'

I laugh. 'I hope he's doing better than me. So the whole surfer bit's a pile of rubbish?'

'He said the tour company wanted an ocker Australian for this tour—you know, to do the whole Australian "beer is life" thing. Apparently they're the only guides who come back from this trip alive when the Beer-drinking Society's on board. They don't respect anyone else. We shook on it. I keep his secret, he keeps mine.'

'Sounds like a fair trade.'

'Yeah.'

We look at each other.

'So…' Jas starts.

'So, now I'm hydrated we're going on that.' I point over and upwards.

'The Ferris wheel?' Jas isn't impressed.

'What? You're not a Ferris wheel kind of guy?'

'Ah…'

'Think of it as being about planning and strategy. It's a good vantage point. We'll be able to see everything from up there and plan our day.' It's always far more convincing to the male of the species if you put it in guy-speak.

Jas nods. 'Course. If it's all about planning and strategy, the Ferris wheel it has to be. I'm sure Sun-tzu wrote all about Ferris wheels in *The Art of War.*'

We have our three turns around on the Ferris wheel, and by the time we're done there's a plan in place. A few rides, then a beer tent and some food.

Putting the plan into action, we spend the next hour or so going on a number of the vomit-inducing upside-down rides. More than a few, in fact, because I make the mistake of buying a book of tickets. It seems to be cheaper than buying separate ones, and it is. But then we find out they're all for the same ride. We go on that particular vomit-inducing upside-down ride five times between us.

Tickets used up, we're standing in the street once more—now, strangely, a wobbly-looking street. 'Lunch?' I turn to Jas, my voice croaky from compulsory ride screaming.

'Lunch?' he repeats.

'Yes, lunch.'

'Don't you feel sick?'

I shake my head. I might be seeing double, but I don't feel sick.

'Lucky you.' Jas grimaces.

We head for the Wirtsbudenstrasse and walk down the street doing a quick inspection of all the beer tents as we go so we can decide which will be our first. The Augustiner seems fairly laid back, the Hofbräu is raucous already and it's not even two p.m. The Schottenhammel tent, where we started off this morning, is just plain too big. If we lost one another in there it's likely we'd never meet up again in this lifetime or the next. At the end of the street we stop and shrug at each other.

'I don't know,' I say. 'They're all different, but the same.'

'What if…?'

'Don't look now.' I grab Jas's arm and angle him in the opposite direction.

'What? What is it?'

'Sharon. The groupie. At eleven o'clock.'

Jas takes a quick glance over his shoulder even though I've told him not to. 'Where?'

'She's headed straight for us,' I continue. 'Closing, closing…' I grab his hand and start running then. 'Go, go, go, go, go,' I say, as if we're on some kind of Navy SEAL Oktoberfest-type mission. I run us into the closest tent—the Löwenbräu. We pause for just a second as the huge lion above the entrance roars something at us. Löwenbräu, I think. Jas and I stare at each other incredulously.

'Never heard any of the lions do that when I went on safari last year,' he says.

Inside, still holding Jas's hand, I take a few steps to the left so that Sharon, if she's following us, won't be able to find us. That said, I don't really know why Sharon would be following us. Or why we're running away from her. Frankly, I don't even know if she saw us. There's just something about that girl I don't like.

Finally I drop Jas's hand and we both take a moment to view the scene around us.

'Holy…'

'…shit?' Jas, ever the gentleman, finishes the sentence off for me.

'Something like that,' I agree.

This tent—it's like nothing I've ever seen before. Table after long table full of people drinking gigantic mugs of beer, singing and laughing and talking at the tops of their voices. One whole side of the tent seems to be taken up with different kinds of food for sale. The place smells like old beer, frying meat and something sour. Sauerkraut?

I tug on Jas's sleeve, unable to speak, as a woman pushes past us. Eventually I get it together. 'What the hell?' I point to what the woman's carrying in her hand. It looks like something edible. Something edible on a stick.

Both of us watch, silently, as she keeps walking.

'Is that…?' Jas starts.

Unfortunately it is, I think. It's a fish, or an eel, or something. It looks cooked—oh, I really hope it's cooked—and it's impaled. She keeps right on walking, the stick bobbing up and down.

I shake my head at Jas. 'Now, that's just disgusting. What's wrong with a plain old dagwood dog dipped in tomato sauce? Why do they have to make a whole living beast portable?'

'It's not like dagwood dogs are vegetarian. They're made of meat,' he says.

'You think so? What kind? Dog?'

'They're meat *flavoured…*'

'I think that's where it ends.'

'Yeah, probably. Come on. Place is filling up. Better find us a seat.'

I look around for a couple of spare places and spot Damien and co over on the far right. The left side of the tent is suddenly very appealing.

We spend the next few minutes walking up and down the aisles trying to find somewhere we can fit both our butts in together. Finally, we find a likely spot. 'Thanks,' I say to the guy who moves up a bit for us. He replies in German, and I smile and shrug. 'Sorry!'

A waitress passes by and Jas and I watch in awe as she lugs ten huge mugs of beer, not a drip spilling over the sides.

'Paul would love her,' Jas says with a laugh.

'Paul who?'

'Paul the drummer from Spawn. Blonde and busty. And, most importantly, she can carry ten litres of beer at once.'

I snort. 'Paul sounds like a really nice guy. Really into girls' *personalities.*'

'Yeah. That's Paul.' Jas waves a hand and orders us two beers. 'Right. Must be time for some of that tasty pork knuckle that Shane was telling us about last night.'

'Pass.'

'Chips and mayonnaise?'

'You're reading my stomach. Want me to get them?' I go to stand up, but Jas puts a hand on my shoulder.

'It's a war zone out there. I'll go.'

'OK. Thanks. Oh, and I'd love a lemonade if they've got one.'

'See what I can do,' he says, and gets up to head off in the direction of the food.

'Hey, someone's—' I whip my head around as I hear the thump of someone sitting down in Jas's seat. It's Shane.

'Are you spying on us?' I smile.

'Small world, kiddo. Small world.' Then, 'Oh, sorry. For a moment there I forgot you knew.'

I laugh.

'I am spying, actually. But not on you.' He nods off to the right. 'On them.'

I glance over at the bewigged group that I'd spotted before. Damien's in there with them and he's having the time of his life.

'Got to keep an eye on what's going on. I have to account for lost bodies at the end of the trip, and those ones can get rowdy if you don't watch them closely. They've had a broken leg in their group before. Some cracked ribs too. Just means trips to the hospital and paperwork for me, so prevention's the key.'

I nod. The injuries really don't surprise me. 'So, what's with the wigs?'

'Beats me. Started before my time, anyway. First day's wig day, second day's flag day, third day's pyjama day. That's all I need to know. Can't complain, really. Makes them easier to spot.'

I nod again. Well, did I really expect it to make sense? 'Did you want something to eat? Jas's just gone off for some food.'

'No way. I got food poisoning here once. I live on muesli bars now. Here's a tip: avoid the sausages.'

'Thanks, but I'd already figured that one out myself. They don't look exactly, um, appetising.'

'They're not. Especially the third time they come up.'

'Ugh.' I make a face.

'Sorry. Forgot again. What I really wanted was to ask you something.'

'About Jas?' My eyes move in his direction.

'Sort of. I wanted to ask if you two are, you know…' he crosses two fingers, '…together?'

I pause, not knowing what to say. 'We, er, came together, if that's what you mean.'

'Way-hey!' Shane says, then jerks his head back as if he's surprised. 'Christ. Sorry. Can't help myself, can I? I get a bit like that on these tours. It's like working at Disneyland, you know? You tend to stay in character after you get in the suit.'

'I'm sure Jas would understand. Um, why do you want to know? About Jas and me, I mean?'

Shane waves his hands. 'I just need to know what's going on. What I'm in for. Anyway, better be off,' he says, getting up.

'Um, sure,' I reply. 'See you around.'

Well, that was weird, I think as I watch Shane leave. I thought for a moment there that… No. It's too silly. He was probably just trying to work us out. After years of Beer-drinking Society fun he's no doubt mastered the act of predicting disaster before it happens. Like he said, he needs to know what's going on. I shrug slightly and then turn to check on Jas one more time as my stomach grumbles.

People are hungry, it seems, because over at the food side of town Jas hasn't moved that far up the line. These lot are obviously a famished as well as a beer-thirsty nation. After a few minutes I must seem lonely, because the guy beside me taps me on the shoulder and starts entertaining me with his very colourful life story.

In German.

He's flinging his arms around, spilling beer here and there. Every so often I nod at him to keep him happy.

When Jas arrives back our beers have turned up and the German guy is still going off at me.

'What's he talking about?' Jas whispers as he puts our tray on the table.

'Beats me, but I can assure you he hasn't said a word about Lumpi the dog or Onkel Ernst yet.'

The guy taps me on the shoulder again, and I turn back to him to see what he wants.

Which is right when he plants a big fat, wet, sloppy kiss on my cheek.

Jas and I both sit there with our mouths open.

The guy grins and holds up his beer at us. *'Prost!'*

I laugh then. A laugh that comes right up from the bottom of my stomach. 'This is insane,' I say to the guys on either side of me, then hold my beer up too. *'Prost!'*

Chapter Fourteen

'You're a saint,' I sigh as I polish off the last of my chips and mayonnaise and wipe my fingers on my paper napkin.

'I know. Hey, what did Shane want before? Saw you having a chat.'

I pause. 'Nothing, really.' I scrunch up my face, returning to my earlier thoughts. 'Actually, I'm not sure…'

'What do you mean?'

'I think,' I say with a saucy smile, and start to run my hands down over my chest, 'he may have wanted my body. Who wouldn't?'

Jas laughs. 'You're crazy.' But then he stops laughing. 'What do you mean?' he says again.

'It was kind of weird. He was asking about us. But kind of strangely. Like he wanted to ask me on a date or something.'

'On a date?' Jas's face reads disbelief.

I snort. 'Some people have lowered themselves that far, you know.'

'Charlie, I didn't…'

'Sure you didn't. Anyway, I probably read it all wrong. I usually do.'

Jas obviously doesn't get my That Night reference. 'What did you tell him?' He leans forward.

I repeat my exact words, as it doesn't look as if he's going to settle for anything else. 'Forget about it,' I say when I'm done. 'It was nothing.' I hold up my beer, changing the topic. 'Quite creamy, isn't it?'

'You can tell what it tastes like from three tiny sips, can you?'

'Six sips. Big ones. And at least I'm *trying*.' I glare as I uncap my lemonade.

Jas watches as I pour quite a bit into my beer before he realises what's going on. He grabs the bottle from me when he does, splashing some on the table. 'What the hell do you think you're doing?'

'Making a shandy,' I say innocently, loving every moment of his horror. I knew he'd react like this.

'On *top* of the table? Where everyone can see?'

'It is legal.'

'You sure? I reckon you're lucky you haven't already been scalped or knee-capped or something. Taken out the back to the beer abusers' room. What's the matter with you?'

'Why can't I make…?' I start, but Jas claps his hand over my mouth and only removes it when it looks as if I'm about to bite him.

'Do you realise what a sad human being you are? Drinking a shandy. At Oktoberfest. You don't deserve to be here.'

'That's what I tried to tell Mark. I mean, what did I ever do to him?'

'Funny.'

I stand firm. I want my damn shandy and I want it now.

'Do I look like I care what people think? I can't help it if I don't like beer.'

'No. You don't look like you care. That's what worries me. And you *can* help it. I'm supposed to be coaching you. Yeah? If you'd put anchovies on your cereal I would have stopped you. This is the same. My life's calling and all that.'

I sigh dramatically.

'OK,' Jas reminds me. 'We went through this with the olives. And the anchovies. "They're too salty," you said, spitting them out. "They're too fishy," you said, spitting them out. What's going to be so different about beer? You already like the smell—that's a good start.'

I pick up the beer and sniff it. 'I guess…'

Jas watches me for a minute or two as I alternately sniff the beer then turn up my nose as I taste it. 'Jesus. I've never seen anyone so miserable about drinking bloody beer. Now, take another sip.'

I take another sip.

'Wasn't so bad, was it?'

I put it back down on the table. 'It's OK, I guess. I mean, I'd drink it if I was dying of thirst in the desert or something.'

'Now there's a compliment to the Löwenbräu people.'

'I'm sure they'll cope. Most people here are drinking enough for two as it is. Anyway, what do *you* think of it?' I ask then. 'Being such a beer connoisseur.'

'I think it's pretty good. It is creamy, like you said. Not bad at all. Sure it'd go nicely with fish on a stick.'

We sit then—Jas finishing off his beer, me sipping mine. When Jas is done and I decide I'm finished, it's made pretty plain to us that it's time to move on—people are circling us like vultures, waiting for our seats.

Out in the street again, we take in a few lungfuls of non-beery air and start patrolling the grounds. We walk up and down the streets people-watching, not talking to each other much and not really feeling the need to. Companionable silence. I always liked that about my relationship with Jas. The fact that we didn't have to talk to fill the gaps. We point things out to each other here and there as we walk—kids making a mess of themselves with fairy floss, another fish on a stick, *ugh*, a kid who's won a stuffed gorilla almost as big as she is.

We're laughing at the gorilla when I stop dead in my tracks. 'Look.' I point at a stall on my right.

It's Zamiel. Zamiel on a balloon. A balloon, of all things! Because, of course, that's what you'd put on a German kids' balloon, isn't it? Or any kids' balloon for that matter. A fallen angel wearing make-up and a cow and a half's worth of leather. Still, I guess it's not any worse than some of the things the Brothers Grimm came up with. 'And over there.' I point out another stall that's giving away Zamiel figurines as prizes. I glance up at Jas before I start walking again. 'That's weird. To see them here, at Oktoberfest. You're really famous, aren't you? It's really weird. To me—I don't know—you don't seem all that different, I suppose.'

'I'm not all that different. And it's not weird, it's sick,' he says. There's no missing the venom in his voice. And I've never seen his face look like this before.

'Sick?' I say quietly, my pace slowing.

'It's…' Jas starts to say something, then seems to change his mind. 'I mean *I'm* sick of it, that's all. I'm supposed to be on holiday, remember?'

'Sure…whatever.' I eye him, unconvinced.

'What?' He runs his hands through his hair.

'You know, if you don't like your job, maybe you should get out of it and do something else.'

Jas snorts. 'Easy for you to say.'

Really? 'And why is that?' I can tell, just tell by the expression on his face, that he thinks I've been fluffing around with my life. Living in Byron Bay in a gingerbread cottage. Reading a little. Pottering around the garden. Filling my days with shopping and sunning myself on the beach. Cooking gourmet meals. Staying with the relatives when I get a bit lonesome. 'You're a shit, Jas.'

'What? I didn't say anything!'

'You didn't have to.' I give him a dirty look. 'You know, I don't care what you think about my life; we're talking about yours. If you hate your job this much you're just wasting your life away if you don't chuck it in.' I'm about to tell him more, but then turn instead, with a huff. I start walking off, faster and faster, not turning back to see if Jas is following.

The crowd's starting to get thicker now that it's past four p.m. As I half run up the street there's a noise behind me— a loud *whoop* from one of the rides. I turn to look at what's going on and realise that I've lost sight of Jas. Even though I know he can't be too far away, this gives me a real start. I begin scanning the heads in the crowd more carefully, and I'm getting worried when all of a sudden I see him again.

The crowd, like a school of fish, parts just for a second. And there he is, staring right back at me.

Shitty as I am, I smile involuntarily as soon as I spot him. One of those stupid, goofy, unwilling smiles that you can't stop. As it spreads across my face I recognise the fact that I'm really happy to be here, at Oktoberfest. That I'm genuinely glad Mark chose this stupid excuse for excessive beer-drinking and the attached flights that gave me the opportunity to catch up with Jas again. It's a strange feeling, that smile. Something that I think I might not have felt for quite some time.

Jas walks up to me, grinning as well. But when he reaches me his expression fades to a frown. 'Don't ever do that again!'

'OK,' I say. I didn't enjoy the experience that much myself. I pull him off to one side, out of the flow of revellers. 'I'm not trying to be bossy, it's just that I want to see you happy. If you hate being Zamiel, you can't throw your whole life away doing it. You've got to find what makes you happy and run with it—it doesn't matter what anybody else wants. God, if I've learnt anything in the last few years, it's that.'

Jas sighs. 'I know. I know. Keep telling myself that, but it's difficult…'

I nod. 'Of course it's difficult. It's loads of money and a job people would kill for. But it's not worth your health. Or your sanity.' I smile then. 'I'll shut up now, and stop lecturing, shall I?' I reach out and touch his arm. 'Friends?'

Jas puts a hand over mine. 'Friends.'

I check my watch then, and see that it's almost four-thirty. 'Did you want to meet Shane at five and go back to the hotel? Or do you want to stay on?'

'Let's go. I'm buggered.'

'OK. How about one more thing, and then we'll go back, have dinner and get an early night?'

'Sounds great.'

'What about that?' I point and Jas follows my finger over. 'Shit. No.'

'What?' I look up in surprise.

'Er…' His eyes are glued to the object in the distance.

I look back over. It's not exactly something to worry about. I was pointing out one of those throwing games. I turn back to Jas. 'You've had a bad experience with these things?'

'I'm not great at throwing things, OK? I might have even gone to, er, remedial throwing lessons at school.'

'What?' I'm practically on the floor laughing now. 'You're joking, right?'

'No.'

Oh, dear. I stop laughing now, because Jas is definitely not joking.

'Hate those things. It's like some kind of testosterone test. You always look like a loser unless you win the big teddy bear. Or gorilla, as the case may be.'

I stare up at him. Where is all this coming from?

'Not that I have a testosterone problem,' he adds loudly, making a few people near us look over.

I keep staring. I don't think anyone would think for a second that Jas has a testosterone problem. Six-foot-four, reasonably muscular, with a full head of hair and rock star stubble, clad in vintage jeans, a black Marcs T-shirt and a well-worn brown suede jacket. He doesn't exactly look *feminine*.

I pat him on the arm. 'Of course you don't.'

'I don't!'

'I know!'

'All right then…' He sulks.

I lead Jas over to the stand and give the guy behind the counter the correct amount of money. In return, he gives us three balls each, which we have to shoot through a tiny basketball-like net right at the back of the booth. 'You go first,' I say to Jas.

'Probably not a good…'

'Go *on*,' I urge. 'Make an idiot of yourself. It's what it's all about.'

He throws the first ball, which hits the wall and bounces off. The wrong wall entirely, I might add. So does the next ball, but on the opposite wall.

'Oh,' I say.

'Never seen me throw anything before, have you?' he asks, putting the third ball down.

'Well, no…' I admit. 'Not now that I think about it.' I smile at the image that comes into my mind. 'Good thing it's the girls who have to throw their undies on stage at *you*!'

'Bitch,' he mutters, but then laughs.

It's then that I spot Shane in the distance, watching us.

'Blame it on being tall. Poor hand–eye co-ordination,' Jas adds.

I turn my attention away from Shane and roll my eyes at his excuse. 'If that was true I should be a professional basketball player, given my height.' I put my three balls down on the counter beside his last one. 'Here, let me show you.' I bend down to drag over a wooden step meant for the kiddies and place it behind Jas before I step up onto it, making us almost the same height. I reach down and pick up the four balls, place one in Jas's palm and lift his hand.

'Don't throw it so hard this time,' I say. 'Let it arc and just drop in. No effort.'

'Sure, no effort…' he scoffs.

I sigh. 'Just try it, OK?' Out of the corner of my eye I see that Shane is still watching us, but I decide not to tell Jas—especially after his testosterone comments. Now, together, we swing out. When my arm bends over, I simply let go of the ball. We hold our breath as we watch it arc up…

…and drop to the floor.

'It's OK,' I say. 'We've got three more to go.'

'Stop breathing on my neck! You're putting me off!'

'So that's the problem.' I laugh. 'OK. Here we go again.' Our arms come up and we throw the ball, which arcs and this time drops straight into the ring, not even touching the net below it.

The next two balls do the same thing.

'See? Let this be a lesson to you—you should listen to me more often,' I say when we're done, and turn Jas around by the shoulders to give him a hug. But then, when he goes to pull away, by some feat of awkwardness I'm still holding him. I pull back then. Quickly. Awkwardly…

And fall off the step.

'Jesus. You OK?'

'Sorry—sorry,' I mumble, not looking at Jas. My ankle hurts and I reach down to rub it.

'Sorry for what? For falling off the step? Hey, your ankle…'

The guy behind the stand says something in German. 'I'm all right,' I say.

The teenage boy who's been throwing balls beside us turns around then. 'He says he's not going to give you a gorilla because you were standing on the children's step.'

I look up now. 'Charming!' I say, trying to sound as if I don't care, but actually feeling rather as if I'm going to bawl.

'Stuff him.' Jas crouches down. 'I'll beat him up for you later. Is your ankle OK?'

'It's fine. I just jolted it.' My eyes flick around, looking at various patches of grass. I eventually convince him I'm OK—my face, I'm sure, a lovely strawberry-red.

But when I do glance up again I see something rather strange—Shane's still watching us. And when I meet *his* eyes he doesn't look away.

Chapter Fifteen

Late, we hurry to meet Shane, who thankfully manages to distract us as he swaps tales of Hofbräu tent madness with the few wiggy Beer-drinking Society people who are waiting to walk back to the hotel. By the time we get back to our room I'm completely exhausted. Really exhausted after the day I've had. I worry for a second that I'm getting sick again, but then decide I'm being ridiculous. I'm just tired. I flop down on my bed.

'Going to have a quick shower,' Jas says, heading in to the bathroom.

There's a knock on the door.

'It's OK.' I get up. 'I'll get it. You have your shower.'

I go over and open the door to find that it's room service—the guy's holding a silver bucket filled with ice and a bottle of champagne.

'There must be a mistake,' I say. 'We didn't order any champagne.'

'Room 213?'

I nod.

'Yes.' He nods, checking a piece of paper that he's holding in his hand. He nods again, then comes in and puts the bucket on the table.

'But we didn't order any champagne,' I repeat.

He shrugs and shows me the piece of paper. He's right—it does say 'Room 213'. I look up at him again and shrug too. He goes then, closing the door behind him. I watch him leave, thinking he must be all of seventeen or eighteen and realise that if his bit of paper says 'Room 213' he's going to take whatever he's got to room 213 and leave it there. It's up to me to sort it out from here. I don't think he's exactly viewing this as a career job.

'Who was it?' Jas yells from the bathroom over the noise of the shower.

'Room service with a bottle of champagne,' I yell back. 'You didn't order any, did you?'

'Nope.'

'I didn't think so. It's a mistake. I'm going to go downstairs and check it out, OK?'

'Yeah.'

I grab my wallet and head downstairs to the front desk.

'Hi,' I say to the girl who's manning the desk when I get there. I don't think I've seen the same girl twice the whole time we've been here. They must be making them out in the back.

She eyes me warily, knowing that I want something but not having heard what it is yet.

'We've just been sent a bottle of champagne. Room 213. It must be a mistake, though, because we didn't order any.'

She clickety-clacks on the computer for a few moments.

'No. It's right. A gift.' She's American.

'A gift?' I look at her. 'From who?'

'I can't say.'

'Why ever not?'

She eyes me.

I lean on the counter then. 'Please?'

Nothing. But then I remember—she's American. Tipping time. I pull out fifteen euros. That should do it. I hope. I slip it to her over the counter.

She gives me a quick smile then. 'It's from Shane. Your tour guide.'

Shane? I try for one more bit of information. 'Do you know where he is?'

'I think I saw him in the bar a while ago.'

'Thanks.' Amazing what fifteen euros will buy you these days, isn't it?

I make my way across the lobby and over to the bar. I haven't been in there yet, and as I walk in I remember why. I glanced inside yesterday night as we walked past, but was hardly drawn in by the decor. Not that I'm that picky when it comes to bar decor, but it really is pretty dingy. The kind of place that hasn't been modernised since it was fitted out with green and black carpet and a green vinyl bar in the sixties. God only knows how many cigarettes have been stubbed out on the carpet and how many spilt beers are helping to keep the green colour fresh.

I spot Shane at the end of the bar, chatting to the barman, and start towards him. 'Hey,' I say when I get there. I hoist myself up onto the bar stool next to him.

'Hey, yourself,' he says. 'Want a drink?'

'Um, OK. Scotch and dry, thanks.'

'You heard the lady, my good man,' Shane says to the barman.

I decide it's best to get straight down to business. 'You sent us a bottle of champagne?'

Shane nods, taking a sip of his beer.

'Whatever for?'

He moves his eyes over to meet mine. 'I thought you needed a helping hand.'

I don't understand. 'A what?'

'You know. A little social lubricant.'

'What for?'

He turns on his stool to face me properly. 'What for? For you and Jas. You know, romance and everything.' He says 'romance' as if it's a dirty word.

'Oh,' I say as the barman gives me my drink. I go to pay him, but Shane waves him away, motioning for him to put it on his tab. I take a big gulp of that drink. 'I wasn't lying before, you know. Jas and I...we're not—not together,' I stutter. I wonder if I should convince him by explaining Jas is gay, but I can't really, can I? That should be the kind of thing he tells people himself, not me.

'Right,' Shane says then. 'I just thought you were being cagey about it because of the Zamiel thing...'

'We used to live together. For a year or so. That's all. But we haven't seen each other for a while. We're just friends. Really.'

'Oh, so there was never...?' He trails off again.

I pause just a second too long.

'Aha.' He points now, smiling. 'I knew there was something. But it's all over?'

I snort. 'Oh, yes. It's definitely over.' I take a sip of my drink. 'You could say it wilted and died.'

'Right...' Shane gives me strange look.

'We met up again by accident. He wasn't even booked on this trip until two days ago.'

'I see.'

Something catches my eye then, behind us. It's Sharon,

hovering in the background. 'What's she want?' I lean over nearer to Shane.

He lowers his voice accordingly, now he's in non-ocker mode. 'She's been wondering where Jas is. She doesn't know, though—about the Zamiel connection, that is. Just thinks he's a bit of all right at the moment. I've been trying to keep her off the scent.'

'Thanks.'

'I, um, wanted to ask. Seeing as you're in Byron Bay and all, and I live on the Gold Coast, maybe we could get together some time when we're both back home?'

I pull back, surprised. So I *was* right earlier today. I wasn't imagining things. I laugh, remembering my first impression of Shane—how I thought I'd rather kiss a dead possum. But now I think I rather like Shane and his Aussie act.

'You don't have to laugh about it,' he says.

'No, sorry about that.' I wave a hand. 'I was just remembering when I first met you. I couldn't have ever seen us going on a date. But I'd love to. Really.'

'Great.'

I grab a pen off the barman and write my home phone number and e-mail address on a coaster. 'There you go.' I hand the piece of cardboard over to him.

'Yeah. Yeah—thanks for that, mate.' Shane slaps me on the back as he takes the coaster from me and I cough. But then I turn and see Sharon and a few other people from the bus standing a bit closer than before. They could probably hear us if they tried hard enough.

I stand up and push my bar stool in. 'Um, thanks for the drink,' I whisper. 'And the champagne, of course.'

'No problemo.' He winks as the Beer-drinking Society start to envelop him, chatting away.

I feel his eyes follow me all the way across the room.

★ ★ ★

When I come in the door, Jas turns the TV off.

I go over, lift the champagne out of the bucket and stare at it thoughtfully.

'So…?' Jas says.

'Hmmm? Oh, sorry. The champagne—it was a mistake. We can keep it, though. Want to open it up?'

'You sure? That's a pretty big mistake for room service. My guess is it's probably from somebody.'

'Beats me,' I lie.

'OK. Fine. I'll just get changed.' He's wearing one of the hotel bathrobes.

I put the bottle back in the bucket and go to lie down on my bed. 'I've had it.'

'Yeah?'

I turn my head. 'Remember, I got up hours earlier than you did.'

Jas grabs some jeans and a T-shirt and heads for the bathroom. 'Just be a minute.'

But when he emerges again I'm already dozing off. 'You still want the champagne?' he asks.

'Mmmm. Just going to have a little nap,' I say, pulling up the covers.

I sleep straight through the night.

My going to bed at six p.m. means, once again, that I'm up way too early. Bright-eyed and bushy-tailed. When I've run through the few things I have to do, I sit on the end of Jas's bed and start jumping. Softly at first. Then a bit harder. Then harder again.

He rolls over and groans. 'If you don't get off my bed right now, I'll have to kill you.'

I bounce a tad harder.

'Isn't there anything on TV?'

'The news and cartoons. But I don't even understand the cartoons. They talk too fast.'

'What's there not to understand about a cartoon?'

I stop bouncing then, and get up. But I'm back in less than ten seconds. I wave the room service menu in Jas's face. 'What do you want for breakfast?'

'Too early for breakfast.' Roll. Another groan.

'No, it's not. It's already been on for an hour.'

'That means it's only seven o'clock. Damn. I'm awake now.' Jas pushes himself up and yawns. 'You're a pain in the butt, Charlotte.'

'Don't call me that, *Jasper*.' I point at him with the menu.

'What're we doing today?'

'You know something?' I go over and sit on my own bed again. I have a quick bounce. 'Your bed's definitely softer.'

'Great. We'll swap tonight. Don't care. How can you have this much energy in the morning? You on something, or what?'

I stop bouncing. 'I thought I was getting sick the last couple of days. But I'm not—when I woke up this morning I felt great. So now I'm chirpy, all right? I'm high on life.'

'You been watching the Christian channel? Fine. I'm happy for you. Happy that you're not sick. Now, what are we doing today?'

'I thought we should probably have a quick whip around the festival one more time—you know, take some pictures, buy some souvenirs. Then we can skip this afternoon and tomorrow and have a scout around Munich instead. Some real culture. How about that?'

'Sounds great. One condition.'

'What's that?'

'You stay up late tonight. No bed experiments tomorrow morning.'

I wave a hand. 'No problem there. We're going out tonight with the group, remember? The night out on the town? I think we're going to some funky karaoke place.'

'Funky karaoke?'

'Mmmm.'

'Aren't they mutually exclusive words?'

'Just because you don't need the backing tape and the little white ball…'

Jas grins. 'I guess I am kinda good.'

I throw a pillow at him.

On purpose, we sneakily leave the hotel half an hour after the rest of the group's already gone. We take our time wandering towards the Oktoberfest grounds, ditching room service and stopping for breakfast and a coffee on the way. When we get there, we decide that, along with the photos and souvenirs, we'll brave the Hofbräu tent, despite Shane's warnings—though as Australian citizens we should technically be OK. I buy a beer stein for Mark, a calendar for Kath and a couple of T-shirts for the twins. Unfortunately they don't have the 'My auntie went to Oktoberfest and all we got were these stupid matching T-shirts because we're twins' variety. That done, we head on over to see some hardcore Oktoberfest-style partying.

People are spilling in and out of the Hofbräu tent at a seriously high rate as we make our way through the entrance. It's much busier inside than the other tents seem at this hour. The smell, however, is the same—sweat, beer, sausages.

The first thing I notice is that the Hofbräu tent is an every beer-drinker to himself kind of event. It's not like the other tents, where you have to be seated to get a beer. Here you can drink wherever you want. It's complete chaos, but when I think about it a bit harder I realise it's probably the only way. A riot squad would have a hard time getting this crowd to sit down and form some kind of order. It'd be like asking people nicely to be seated and quiet while they're fighting for air in a soccer stadium crush. The second thing I notice is that everyone's suddenly speaking English. Most of them with an Australian or New Zealand accent. I look up at Jas.

'OK?' he says.

I nod. So far. But then I see the expression on Jas's face and look back down again. He's staring at something in the distance in utter disbelief. I follow his gaze through the crowd and see it immediately.

It's Damien. President Damien.

President Damien who is now absolutely starkers, standing in the middle of a ring of red, white and blue people. The members of the Beer-drinking Society. Mainly red, white and blue because they're covered in Australian flags. Flags draped around their shoulders. Fake tattoo flags on their arms. Painted flag faces. I remember Shane's words then—today is 'flag day'. Damien himself is downing stein after stein of beer, not even stopping for a breath.

'Aussie, Aussie, Aussie, oi, oi, oi!' the ring start yelling in unison.

He downs another stein.

I'm wondering how many litres of beer a stomach can physically hold before lunchtime when Shane appears as if from nowhere. He tackles Damien, grabs his flag off the ground, wraps it around him and drags the guy off in one swift movement. Quite balletic, really. Everyone watches them go. Shane is heading for the men's, Damien's head under one arm, flag trailing. As they pass by, Jas yells at Shane, 'Need a hand, mate?'

Shane shakes his head. 'No, thanks. All in the job description.' Damien struggles then, and Shane tightens his grasp. 'Come on, fella. If you struggle it'll just make it harder for both of us.' They keep going.

I keep right on standing in the same spot, watching Damien, naked as the day he was born now that the flag's fallen off again. Expression: disbelief.

'Don't look.' Jas reaches over to cover my eyes with one hand. 'A sight like that could put you off your beer for ever.'

When he lets his hand fall, I glance up. 'You'd think he'd know better than to do that in autumn,' I say.

Jas cranes his head and guesses what I'm hinting at. 'Shrinkage. Never a good look for a little Aussie battler, is it?'

'No, not really. Especially when it seems he wasn't exactly gifted to start with.'

The show over, we both look around us. Beside us, in front of us, behind us, people are sinking litres of beer at an alarming pace.

'You want to stay?' Jas asks.

I shake my head. 'No, but I've got to go to the bathroom first. It's all too much excitement for me.'

Jas nods. 'I'll wait here.'

I start off in the direction of the ladies', figuring out fairly fast that where Oktoberfest is concerned being vertically challenged is a pain. All I can see is the people directly around me. Finally I reach the hallway that leads to the bathrooms and sigh a sigh of relief. Still, even the hallway is crowded, and I have to pick my way through the people lining each of the walls to get to the bathroom.

'Hey.' I whip around halfway down the hall as I feel a distinct pinch on my behind. 'Ow! Hey!' There's another one. And another. I turn, first to my right, then to my left. 'Ow! Stop that! Ow!' The guys on either side of me lean in closer. 'Ow!' I slap one. *Cut that out!'* Slap. Slap.

The Italians. I remember Shane's words.

'Don't touch me,' I warn one of the guys on my left as I see his arm dart forward. 'I mean it! Ow! I said I *mean* it!' Staring me right in the eye, he pinches a nasty little pinch that I just know will bruise. The others jeer and wave at his amazing sexual prowess. I go to turn again so I can leg it out of here, the way I came, but before I can…someone picks me up from behind.

'Right. That's it!' I yell, and the Italians cheer and wave madly. I can't see who the guy is, but I reach back and slap him on the neck. Then, with all my might, I kick him in his right shin with my heel.

'Hey!' he says with perfect Australian English.

'Jas?'

'Yes, Jas. Stop kicking me!'

'Sorry,' I say, bouncing up and down as Jas whisks me awkwardly through the Hofbräu crowd. As we run past, the crowd claps and wolf whistles. It isn't until we're outside the tent that he puts me back down again.

I wait for the ground to settle beneath my feet, my body feeling as if it's just been through a washing machine. On the long cycle. After a while, my mouth starts moving up and down, but I'm unable to say anything so I give myself a minute and try again. 'What are you…?' I start laughing when my voice comes back to me. I can't complete my sentence. I laugh harder and harder until I stop breathing, croak like a frog, and slowly collapse down to take a seat beside the tent.

Jas watches me as I crumple. 'What's so funny?'

Now I really laugh. I only manage to stop long enough to say the word 'bodyguard'.

'What?'

I don't answer. Can't answer. I'm crying now, gulping for air, big, fat tears running down my face. 'Just like Kevin

Costner in *The Bodyguard*. That scene in the nightclub.' I wipe my face with one hand. It's a struggle to get the few words out and I'm not sure if Jas understands. I'm talking about the scene from the movie *The Bodyguard*. Where Kevin Costner, playing the bodyguard, picks up Whitney Houston, playing a world-famous singer, when she gets into a spot of trouble with her fans in a nightclub. He ends up carrying her to safety and being the hero of the day. 'Where's my limo, hey?' I say, and crack up all over again. I try to get up, fail, and sit back down. 'It's a good thing I don't have a sister, that's all I can say.'

Jas shakes his head. 'You should be grateful!' he tells me, but then starts laughing himself.

I hoot at this, and finally manage to crawl up into a standing position again. 'The day I can't stop some Italian who's shorter than me pinching my butt, I'll tell you about it,' I say.

'Fine.'

'Fine!' I repeat back at him. I laugh again and link an arm around Jas's. 'Come on, you big dag. I'll go later.'

'Come on where?'

Good point, I think. I tug on Jas's elbow then, and grin. 'Let's do something completely stupid.'

'I thought we just did, according to you.'

I roll my eyes. 'Sour puss.'

'Something stupid it is, then. Like what?'

'I don't know! Come *on*. Let's live a little. *Do* something for once.'

'OK. OK! You pick.'

I stop tugging for a second and glance around me. 'Um…' Still looking, I find my 'something' then, and my eyes widen accordingly. 'All right! Wait here.' I drop Jas's arm and run over to the nearby stall.

I come back with two big gingerbread hearts on some ribbon. 'Bend down,' I order, and Jas bends down. I put one of them—the one with the blue ribbon—around his neck. He pulls it out with one hand so he can inspect it as he stands upright again.

'Yeah. Blue ribbon. That's masculine. No one'll beat me up for having an iced gingerbread heart around my neck now. What does it say?' He squints as he tries to read the writing upside down *and* in German.

'It says "Kiss me".'

Jas makes a face. 'Now I really will get beaten up. Probably twice over. All the men because I look like a dickhead, and then all the homophobes'll line up for a second go.'

I don't say anything, but busy myself adjusting my own gingerbread heart.

'Thanks. Nice to know you care,' he adds.

'What? Oh, no one's going to beat you up,' I say, with a wave of one hand. 'Right. Next stupid thing. Let's go.'

'That wasn't it?' Jas protests meekly, but I've already grabbed his arm again and am pushing through the crowds. 'This is so corny.' He shakes his head. 'You'll be making me go into the House of Horrors next.'

'Where?' I whip around. 'Where's the House of Horrors?' I love those things. But then I spot something even better. 'Ooohhh. No, I'm not. I'm not going to make you go into the House of Horrors, but I *am* going to make you go in there.'

I pay for us to go into the sideshow and we're both ushered into a little amphitheatre and seated. Even though it's dim inside, it doesn't take Jas long to work out just what kind of sideshow I've dragged him into. It's a circus. But not any kind of circus. There certainly aren't any lions or elephants here. The main ring is more like a tiny stage, and everything on it—a soccer field, a country village—is made on a miniature scale. And I've read and heard about these things, but I never thought they were real…

It's a flea circus.

An actual, real, live flea circus.

Speaking of fleas, I notice then that we're only sitting a metre or so away from the ring itself. I start to frown then. I've heard something else as well—don't fleas jump? Like, really, really long distances? Kilometres in flea lengths, even? Or am I just being stupid—maybe the fleas aren't even real? You know—like at flea markets? I look over at Jas.

'Freakshow,' he whispers.

'That's quite a comment, coming from you, Mr Z,' I reply.

Jas and I wait for the other few seats to fill up and they do—far more quickly than you'd expect. The ringmaster—fleamaster?—a woman, comes over after a bit and talks to us to fill in the time.

'So, how does this all work?' I ask her. A good generic, I'm-not-an-idiot sort of question.

'It is a family secret,' she says, waggling her finger at me.

I check it for fleas. Nothing. The fleamaster, thank God, is clean.

'You must be pretty busy,' I continue. 'Don't fleas live only a couple days, or weeks, or something?'

The fleamaster shakes her head at that. 'This is one of the biggest misconceptions about fleas.'

I try not to laugh when she says that. People have misconceptions about fleas? I thought it was simple. They live on animals, they bite, they suck blood. Where do the misconceptions fit in? I start to wonder if there are things about fleas I just haven't heard about. Maybe there are fleas who've gone on to have long and illustrious careers singing opera? In banking? Diplomacy?

She continues. 'It takes six months or so before they are ready to be trained, then around three months to train them. For three months after that they perform in the circus.'

'Then what? You put them out to pasture on the back of a nice hairy dog as part of their retirement plan?' I joke.

She turns and stares me down. 'No. Then they die.'

Right. OK.

With the amphitheatre full now, the fleamaster leaves to begin the show.

And what a show it is. By the end I am a flea-believer, because I see it all. Fleas playing soccer. Fleas riding a train. Fleas pulling in a chariot race. They must be the happiest little fleas on earth, those fleas.

'Well,' I say when Jas and I are back outside again. 'I, for one, will never flea-bomb the house again. Think of the work they could be doing for me! Cleaning, ironing, doing the dishes. I've been mad, killing them off all these years.'

Jas laughs. 'Could've saved a packet giving up our cars and being pulled around in little chariots.'

'We've been fools,' I groan. 'Fools.'

We turn at exactly the same time.

'Let's get out of here,' we say in unison.

And I couldn't agree with either of us more.

Chapter Sixteen

In the same way Jas had run me out of the Hofbräu tent, we run again now. Wildly, arms flailing, not caring who sees. We keep right on running—out of the festival grounds, past one street, and another, and another—until we're completely breathless. It's only when we can run no further that we stop and lean up against a brick wall. I giggle, and a middle-aged lady wearing fur gives me a look.

'Well, hello,' Jas says, smiling at her sassily. She huffs and walks off.

We collapse into laughter once more.

'Man, I've had it,' Jas groans.

I'm still breathing so hard I can't reply. Instead, I slide down the wall and sit on the footpath. When I recover a little, I open up my backpack that's been resting in front of me and search around. There it is. I pull out the guidebook.

'Any ideas on what you want to do?'

'I made a few notes. What about you? Anything you really want to see?' I open up the inside front cover, where

I've jotted down the sights that I thought I'd be interested in. I start to read them. 'Oh,' I say, before Jas has a chance to answer my question.

'What?'

'I've just remembered. There *is* something I want to do.'

'What's that?'

'There's a piece of Mum's sculpture in an art gallery here. I thought I'd go take a look.' I leaf through the pages to find the location map for the gallery. 'Here.' I pass the book to Jas.

'Brilliant! That's not far from here.'

We grab a sandwich and a hot chocolate each before we start for the art gallery. It's only a few streets away from the warm coffee shop we've just eaten in, but as we walk over I'm grateful I took a second hot chocolate with me on the way. It's freezing out, and I warm my hands around the cup as we go, jacket done up and scarf wrapped around my neck.

'Well, this is it,' I say to Jas as I throw my cup into a bin at the bottom of the gallery steps.

'Yep,' he replies as we start the short climb.

It's as we reach the top that I realise this doesn't feel right. I turn and look down the steps, then back up at the gallery, then at Jas. 'Um…' I say.

'What is it?' He stops.

'I feel really awful, but would you mind if I went in and saw it alone?'

Jas shakes his head. 'Course not. I understand.'

'Really?'

'Yes, really.'

Despite Jas's words, I still pause.

'I mean it. Here—give me the guidebook and I'll have a read. There's some seats inside the entry there.'

I look. 'Are you sure?'

'Go!'

'OK, but only if you pick out something for us to do to-morrow. Something special. Your choice.'

'Done deal.' Jas shakes my hand.

We enter the building together and I leave Jas sitting on the wooden seats. When he's settled, I keep going. Right up to the man at the information desk inside the next set of doors.

'Hi,' I say.

He grunts, not moving his eyes from the counter. 'The Rubens is down the first hall on your right, turn left, third painting on the left of the doorway.'

My eyes widen. 'That's, um, great, but I don't want to see the Rubens.'

He looks up now.

'I want to see the Notting.'

'The Notting?'

'Yes.' I nod. 'It's a sandstone sculpture.'

'Oh, the…' The guy makes a sweeping gesture over his stomach.

I nod again.

He gets up now, and asks me to follow him. We walk down several rooms, past more paintings than I can count. I don't look at any of them. I'm focused now—focused on getting there. As we keep walking I realise my breathing is getting more and more shallow. That my hands and fore-head are clammy and hot. I take a deep breath as we turn a corner…

And then I exhale.

Because suddenly there it is. The guy leaves me with a murmur and I stand and stare from way across the room at the spotlit piece. It's a woman. A pregnant woman—sitting on the floor, her legs outstretched and one hand behind her, holding her up. Her other hand rests on her smooth, round belly. I walk over slowly, slowly, step by step, closer and closer, until I'm standing right in front of her, only the small white wooden ridge the piece is mounted on separating us.

My hands itch to reach out and stroke the ball of her stomach in front of me, but as I stretch my arm out I become aware that I'm in an art gallery and I can't. I shouldn't. The itching, however, doesn't stop, and I decide soon enough that I don't care if they throw me out. I reach forward a second time and run a hand over and around the mound. It's so smooth. I extend my other hand and run it over at the same time. I keep my hands on the piece until I feel I'm done. Then I step back a pace or two and sit down on the floor.

And I must sit there for ages, because when someone's hand is placed on my shoulder from behind I startle as if I've just been woken up.

'Sorry. You OK?' Jas asks, sitting down beside me.

I nod.

'Want me to go? You want some more time?'

'Stay.'

Jas's eyes move to the sculpture and I hear him exhale. Just as I did before. 'It's really beautiful, Charlie.'

I nod again. But then, with Jas's interruption, everything I've been feeling since the moment I first walked into this room weighs down upon me and the words spill out, falling over each other as I speak too quickly. 'Why didn't she *tell* me anything?'

As I tear my eyes from the woman and stare at the floor I fully expect that I'll have to explain my words to Jas.

But I don't. Jas gets what I mean immediately. 'She probably thought she had all the time in the world, Charlie.'

Well, she didn't, I think, the ridges gathering on my forehead. It takes me a few minutes of silence to shake some of the anger away so I can speak again. 'It's just so unfair.'

'It is unfair,' Jas agrees.

I can't stay angry for long, and now I sigh. 'It's just that I've spent the last few years floundering and she never prepared me for that. She never showed me things could be hard. Everything was so…easy for her.'

Jas turns away from the sculpture. 'You know that's not true.'

'Isn't it?' I snort.

'No. You know how hard she worked to get the recognition she did. You know better than anybody how tough the tough times really were.'

I think back to before the house in Byron Bay, to some of the tiny one-bedroom apartments we lived in. Then there was the dilapidated old wooden house we shared with another family—Mum having to work on her art at the community centre, relying on grants to get by. I know Jas is right, but somehow, through my teenager's eyes, the past is blurred and stained. 'But why didn't she show *me* how to do that?' I hit the floor with one hand. 'And why wasn't she one of those proper mothers?'

'Proper mothers?' When I meet Jas's eyes he doesn't look impressed.

'We never…you know—clicked like that. Like mother and daughter. I used to see other girls my age with their mothers. Shopping, their arms around each other. Going to the movies. Having cake and coffee. We weren't like that. We argued. Constantly. About anything! We always got on each other's nerves and…'

Jas laughs.

'What?'

'Charlie, take it from me. Your mother loved you like nothing I've ever seen. And you felt the same way about her. You still do. Don't you know what the problem was?'

I stare at him in silence.

'You're made from exactly the same mould.'

'Me?' I say, shocked. 'And Mum? Us?'

He laughs again. 'Yes, you and your mum. Your sculpture. Your mannerisms. You even look more and more like her each day.'

I glance down at myself, unconvinced. Do I? I frown. 'Then why don't I feel like that? Why don't I feel like I know how to do what she did? How to make everything work out in the end?' My voice sounds shrill and bounces off the too-white walls until there's silence again.

Jas looks at me hard. 'You know how.'

Our eyes lock; I go to shake my head. But at the last moment something holds me back from doing it—the thought that maybe, just maybe, he's right. Maybe underneath all my worry and fretting I *do* know how. Maybe I do know how to push myself through to the end of these last two years and close the door behind me. Maybe I do know how to move on with my life.

And maybe I even have the strength to do both. Starting now.

I stand up quickly, decisively, and go over to my mother's work. This time I stroke the piece's head. 'Right—um. OK, then. I think…I think I'm going to do this,' I say, running my hand over her hair. 'I think I can…no, I *know* I can do it.'

Jas stands up as well. 'Do what?' he asks as he comes over.

I bite my lip for a second before I turn my head to meet his gaze. 'I've got half a piece at home. Part of a pair Mum was working on before she died. *Sisters*, it's called. I want to finish it. For Annie and Daisy. And me. And Mum. I've sort of been thinking about it for a while now.'

'But…' Jas starts.

'I know.' I nod. 'I know it's not what I do. But maybe…maybe it could be. I'm not saying it'll be easy. It'd take time, I know. So, um, what do you think?'

His mouth hangs open.

'I can, you know. Really I can.' I try with all my heart to convince him, realising I've already more than convinced myself.

Finally Jas's mouth closes. But he doesn't say anything. Instead he takes a step over, so he's standing right in front of me. He cups my face in his hands and bends down to kiss me on the forehead before he gives me a hug. 'I know you can, too,' he says. 'I've known all along. I'm just surprised it took you so long to work it out.'

And then, standing there in the middle of the art gallery, he lets me cry all over that old suede jacket.

Jas and I walk back to the hotel in silence. I think I'm in shock. I simply can't believe that after all the years I've spent trying not to be compared to my mother, making sure that my work was so abstract and at the opposite end of the spectrum to hers, I'm now going to turn around and start where she started. Right at the beginning.

I just wish she was here to see it all.

I know it's the right thing to do. I've learnt a lot over the last few years, but the main thing I've been shown is that I don't need to care what other people think any more. From now on if I want to do something, I'm damn well going to do it and not let anyone or anything stand in my way.

'You OK?' Jas must see the workings of my brain written all over my blotchy, tear-stained face.

'Yep. Great.'

He swipes his card and opens the door to our room, letting me in first.

'Thanks.'

'You're welcome. Now, take a seat.'

I pause. 'Take a seat?'

'On the bed. Got something for you.'

I look up in surprise. 'For me?' I say, sitting down.

Jas hands me a plastic bag. One of the bags from his souvenir shopping this morning. 'Here you go—knock yourself out.'

'How'd you know I'd need cheering up?' I take the bag from him.

'I know everything, remember?'

'Sorry, I forgot for a second there…' I empty out the bag's tissue-paper-wrapped contents. After only a few rips, I recognise what's inside. I laugh as I hold it up. 'Oh, it's too cute!' I stand up, holding it out in front of me.

It's a dirndl. One of the Bavarian dresses. Complete with the little white shirt that goes underneath. 'Jas!' I scold, but he just laughs. Then, 'Thanks,' I say. 'I love it.'

Jas sits down on his bed. 'Know what the guy at the shop said?'

'What?' I'm holding the dress up to myself now, in front of the full-length mirror that's on the back of the bathroom door.

'You'll love this. That I should tell you to wear the shirt low. So everyone can have a good look at the wood in front of the cottage.'

'"The wood in front of the cottage…"' I repeat the phrase slowly, then whip around as realisation hits. 'Charming!'

'Don't think the wood's supposed to be spilling out of the top, like some of the waitresses seem to think is the go this year, but a bit wouldn't hurt, I guess.'

I glance down for a second. 'I don't think the landslide effect's going to be much of a problem for me.'

'Ah, come on. You must be a 10C. That's not so bad.'

Oh, my God. I *am* a 10C. I cross my arms over my chest. Jas laughs. 'Sorry.'

I eye him. 'Pretty good guess. Are you sure you haven't been partaking of the Spawn smorgasbord?'

'Funny. Go on—try it on.'

I hesitate, but then head for the bathroom, emerging dirndled a few minutes later. I do a twirl in the doorway. 'So, what do you think?'

Jas gives me a once-over, taking in the Heidi look. 'Definitely. Party must-have. Frock of the season.'

'But what about you?' I say then. 'You should've got yourself some of those dinky leather pants.'

This makes Jas laugh. 'Leather pants? You've got to be joking. I've got enough leather pants to last me a lifetime. Two lifetimes, in fact.'

'Mmmm, but you're living for two, remember?'

There's silence for a moment, which makes me look up from inspecting the embroidered hem of my dress.

Jas's eyes are focused on his mobile phone on the bedside table. It's still switched off.

'Jas?' I say.

'Huh? Yeah. Right. Living for two.' He laughs. But it doesn't sound quite right.

I shouldn't have made him think about work again, I chastise myself. I do another twirl. 'Hey, how about the wood in front of the cottage?' I only realise what I'm actually asking as the words come out of my mouth. I stop twirling to watch

Jas's eyes travel up my dirndl and finally come to rest on my chest.

Finally, he grins. 'Man, I love it when you dress up for me.'

Chapter Seventeen

After a good two-hour pre-karaoke night kip, I've lost my 'I've been having a good bawl' headache and feel I might just be able to take on the singing world. Lying face up on my bed, I turn my head to look at Jas, to see if he's awake and ready for our Big Night Out.

Yay. A Big Night Out. I love a good Big Night Out. And I haven't had one for...well, not since I was living with Jas, to tell the truth. I've had heaps of drunken dinners. Plenty of soused soirées. But no Big Night Out.

He's still asleep. I roll over and check the clock—six-thirty-seven p.m. Just enough time to have a shower, wash my hair, get all dolled up, have a snack, a drink or two, and meet Shane and co downstairs at eight, as organised.

But first a bladder-relief trip is in order. I slide out of bed and make for the bathroom. And I'm doing what a girl has to do when I spot Jas's mobile and his pager sitting on the bench. He must've brought them in here when he had a shower before. I pick up the mobile and fiddle around with it. I've never had one myself. I've never found the need. I turn it over carefully—it really is excruciatingly tiny—and then go to put it back down on the bench.

That's when I hear it. A *beep*! I realise I've pressed something. And that's when the phone starts ringing.

Still sitting on the toilet, I quickly grab a towel from the rack beside me and wrap the mobile in it to muffle the sound. I don't know which button to use to turn the thing off. I'm sure I could probably guess, but that would mean actually having to look, which means unmuffling, and I don't want Jas to wake up.

The damn thing rings and rings and rings. Finally, after what seems like an eternity, it stops. I breathe a sigh of relief and gingerly open up the towel, trying to work out how I can switch the thing off, when the ringing starts up again.

Oh, God. Now what? Maybe I should answer it? Maybe it's important? Still trying to muffle the ring, I stick my head inside the towel. 'Hello?' I say as quietly as I can.

'Listen, you little shit, I've been trying to call you for days. Where the fuck are you? If you don't—'

I take the phone and my head out of the towel then, and search for a button. Any button. There's a green one and a red one that look likely. Red's bad, right? Red's for ejector seat buttons and stopping lifts and starting fire alarms and things like that. I push the red one. I push it hard and for a long, long time. And suddenly the voice stops yelling. I think the phone even turns itself off, because there's nothing on the screen any more.

I decide not to pick up the pager.

I spend a good five minutes washing my hands, debating what I should do about this. About the phone call. Should I tell Jas someone called? I mean, I shouldn't have messed with the phone. But that guy on the other end of the line…Zed, I guess it was. Zed the dickhead. He was a nice piece of work, wasn't he? Not even a cheery hello. Just a 'Listen, you little shit.' I'm taking it that's why Jas has had his mobile and pager turned off all the time to start with. To avoid Zed. And if that's the case Jas won't want to know he called anyway. Right. So that's it. I won't tell him. If I hadn't turned the phone on by accident there'd just be another message in his message bank, and that's hardly likely to be missed, is it? The guilt I'll just have to live with…

I go back and crawl into bed then, thinking I might just have an extra fifteen minutes' rest after all the bathroom excitement. I get right under the covers, because, as everyone knows, nothing can get you under the covers—not even Zed. But just as I'm covering my head there's a knock on the door. Jas, still asleep, thank God, stirs.

'It's OK,' I tell him, throwing my blanket off. 'I'll get it.'

As I cross the room I remember my clothes—I'm still wearing the dirndl. Why I didn't notice before, I have no idea. I contemplate going to get one of the fluffy white bathrobes in the bathroom, but then decide I can't be bothered. So what if I'm wearing a dirndl? Hey, I've got the Oktoberfest bug, so sue me, I think, and I go and open the door in my full regalia.

Sharon's standing outside.

'Um, Shane just wanted to check that you guys are coming tonight,' she says and, being taller than me, peers in a very non-nonchalant fashion into Jas's and my room.

'Did he?' I try not to smile. I'd say she still hasn't worked the Zamiel/Jas thing out fully, and I wonder for a second what Shane's been telling her. All kinds of things, I expect. Either way, by the expectant lovesick gaze on the girl's face, I'm doubting whether it's *Shane* who really wants to know if we're going out or not tonight.

She nods, still peering. 'So, are you?'

'Well, yes.'

'Both of you?'

'Yes, both of us.'

'OK, great.' She stops peering now, satisfied that Jas will be making an appearance tonight. Then she gives my outfit the once-over. 'Are you going to wear that?'

'Maybe.' I don't give her any further explanation, leaving her to wonder if I prance around in a dirndl on a regular basis.

'Oh.' She seems a little unsure of what to make of this. 'OK. See you later, then.'

I close the door with a smile on my face. Something gives me the feeling we'll be seeing a lot of Sharon later on tonight. Or Jas will be, anyway. And, if she has her way, probably more than he wants.

I let Jas sleep on while I hog the bathroom. I do the whole wash the hair, shave the legs, dry the hair, primpy-preeny Big Night Out deal. I only check to see if the mobile's really turned off or not every five minutes or so. When I'm done, I don one of the bathrobes and go out into the room to sit at the table and paint my nails. I pick up the few souvenir postcards I bought that morning and flick through them absentmindedly. As I stick them back in their paper bag I spot the dirndl, where I've left it behind on my bed. Trust Jas to buy me something completely idiotic I never would have bought myself but just love anyway.

I watch him as he sleeps. It's really been great having him here, I think, as I eenie, meanie, miney, mo between the bottles of nail polish on the table. I don't think I'd be having half as good a time if I'd had to tag along with the likes of Sharon and Tara in the Hofbräu tent. I let a chuckle escape, thinking that Sharon probably couldn't have picked me up and saved me in such poor heroic fashion as Jas did today, either. And I can tell Kath and Mark are pleased I've got someone watching out for me too. They seemed to be worrying a fraction less when I called them before my kip. Yep. Jas being here has made all the difference.

I look down and concentrate on painting the fingernails on my right hand the sparkly blood-red I've chosen. It really has been great, spending this time with Jas. And I think I've almost accomplished what I decided I wanted—for us to get our old friendship back. The one we used to have. Well, *almost*. Things are still a bit strained at times, like after that embarrassing hug the other day where I held on too long, but we can't expect everything to get straight back to how it was right away, can we? We'll get there, though. Of course we will.

It's stupid, that thing people say about how men and women simply can't be friends. Rubbish. Of course they can! It's a ridiculous generalisation. And I guess the only way to disprove their silly theory is to show them all by example that they're wrong. For Jas and I to have the best, closest, platonic friendship ever.

I'm halfway through my little finger when I feel it…someone watching me.

But I have to wait to check. It takes two more strokes to finish the nail I'm painting. Finally I sneak a glance up at Jas, polish brush poised.

He's looking at me. Staring at me. And I know that for me to have felt it he's probably been doing it for quite a while.

As soon as he sees me seeing him, he closes his eyes again with a quick smile. And I tear my eyes away. I sit there, brush still poised in the same place, winded.

What a load—I put the brush back in the bottle—of shit.

Because right then, when our eyes met, all I wanted to do was get up, go over and get into bed with Jas. It was almost magnetic, the feeling I just got from his eyes. I sit like this, staring down at the tabletop, for the longest time.

What is wrong with me?

The man is gay.

I think.

Oh, I don't know. Either way, we've been through this. He isn't interested. Not in the way I want him to be interested, anyway.

I want to give myself a good smack on each cheek for being so stupid. Give myself a slap, hoping I'll wake up to myself. I have to realise a few things and I have to realise them fast. I mean, who do I think I'm fooling with all my 'best friend' bullshit?

Well, myself—for a while, maybe. But not very well.

I groan then, remembering Shane. Obviously Shane was able to see through me from the start. Why else would he ask so many questions about whether Jas and I were together? I look over at the champagne bottle, sitting on one of the bedside tables, still unopened. And, hell, if Shane was able to see through me, who else had? Probably everyone. My gaze flicks over to Jas. Please, no…he can't have.

I close my eyes, really, really hoping Jas hasn't noticed anything. How embarrassing would that be? For my own sanity I have to wake up to myself. Smell the coffee in both cups—as you might have noted, I never quite see the point of just one. Because I am torturing myself, always hoping that I'm going to get what I want from Jas when I know that it isn't going to happen. At least before, when we lived together and nothing happened between us, I had some hope. Hope that he might feel the same way. Now I know that isn't how he feels and *still* I keep right on trying. Why can't my brain deal with that? Get over it? He only wants to be friends.

Good friends. Best friends.

Blah. I feel like spitting at that phrase—*best friends*. It's so…sickening.

I remember back to when we lived together. Before I realised how I felt about Jas. When we used to do touchy-feely things all the time. A hug here. A kiss on the cheek there. But that's all it was—a moment in time. Of course it wasn't for me. Where I was concerned it meant a little bit more than it should have. But for Jas that's all it was. A moment. A gesture. Nothing more.

And there's the catch—'nothing more' simply isn't enough for me. I've been fooling myself, thinking I could settle for anything less than the whole relationship deal. Being friends was never going to cut it for me and I should have realised that sooner on this trip.

Though, really…get a grip, Charlie. As if being best buddies could have even worked for us in the real world anyway. It would have been practically impossible. I'd never see him. I mean, every week he's in a different city. It would have just been too hard. We would have fallen out of contact again within days. Because now that Jas is Zamiel he has a whole different life.

One that I'll never be involved in.

One that I'll never be *invited* to be involved in, more importantly. What it comes down to now is we're from different worlds. He's on the beautiful people team and I'm on the non-beautiful people team. And it's not that I'm being down on myself or anything, it's really just the cold, hard truth. We don't have anything in common any more—I am of the non-beautiful and Jas has his beautiful people world to go back to after this trip. Even if he does have to wear a whole lot of make-up and crack a whip to get through the door.

So that's it. Realism. It just wouldn't work out. Like the Capulets and the Montagues, our two sets are fated never to mix socially.

I catch a glimpse of my reflection in the mirror then, pulling faces, and wonder how the hell I got onto Shakespeare. Beats me. I start to wonder if I'm inadvertently sniffing nail polish fumes. Maybe I just imagined all of this, including Jas staring at me? I glance up at him hopefully. He's asleep, or pretending to be. Hoping he really is, I turn my attention back to the table and put every ounce of concentration into painting those last five nails and trying not to think about that bed and what's in it that I want so badly.

Well, maybe I think about it once. Or twice.

But not after I drink the miniature bottle of vodka and the miniature bottle of gin mixed with some tonic out of the mini-bar. After I've done that, I decide to forget about the whole thing. I'd just embarrass myself if I said anything and, after all, we've only got approximately seventy-two hours left to spend in each other's company before he flies to wherever he's got to go. I'm sure I can resist him for that long. Whatever Sharon might think, no one can be *that* irresistible.

God, maybe Mark should have booked me on a drugfest tour of Amsterdam instead of this Oktoberfest caper? Right about now I could do with some of just about every illegal substance that city has to offer. Then again—I inspect the nail polish bottle—sticking my nose too close to 'Bombshell Red' seems to be doing the trick all on its own.

When Jas gets up I order a club sandwich and a bowl of wedges from room service—food therapy—and we share this before we head downstairs.

We don't mention what happened before.

Downstairs, most of the people on the tour are already hanging around the lobby and Shane waves us over. 'Hey, I didn't know if you guys were coming. So, how's it all going?' he asks. 'Enjoying the festivities? Drinking the beer, love?' He gives me another slap on the back that makes me cough.

'Yep, it's great,' I say. 'Jas even bought me a dirndl today.'

'Kinky.' He laughs. 'Champagne must've done the trick.'

I go to say something, but he's turned around by the time I get my act together and is already talking to someone else in the group.

Jas hasn't heard us talking about the champagne. I still haven't told him about it, though I'm not quite sure why. He's busy looking about himself, as if for an escape route. 'Can't believe we're going to a karaoke bar. I might need a drink or two to get through this evening.'

'That shouldn't be much of a problem,' I tell him. 'I think drinks consumed is what tonight's all about.' I spot Sharon in the crowd then. She whispers something to her crony, Tara, beside her, and the girl looks over and points at Jas. Sharon grabs her hand, stopping her pointing, and says something before they both turn away. I sigh. 'Your admirer's back on the warpath again.' I turn Jas towards Sharon. 'She was at the door before, asking if we were coming. Apparently *Shane* wanted to know, but he's as surprised to see us as anyone.'

'Maybe I'll need a few more than two drinks. More like five. Six. Seven.'

'I'm sure Sharon would be more than happy to buy.'

Jas snorts in reply as Shane starts speaking to the group. Everyone quietens down in order to hear.

'OK, people, I think that's all of you now, so we're off—

like a rat up a drainpipe. We're going to be walking a few
streets down to Atomika, this funky little karaoke bar. I've
had a few words to my mates there, and they've agreed to
give us reduced drinks all night…'

A cheer from the group.

'On one condition. Everyone, and I mean *everyone*, has
to get up and have a croon.'

A boo from the group.

'Come on, it's not that bad. Just take advantage of those
reduced drinks and we'll probably be dragging you off the
stage. Now, let us be motionary.'

Jas looks at me worriedly. 'I can't sing.'

'This is no time to get stage-fright, Spawn-boy.'

He shakes his head. 'Shhh, not so loud. What I mean is,
if I sing she'll know who I am—that Sharon girl. She'll find
out.'

'So? Big deal. It's only a matter of time before she works
it out anyway.' I turn to go and follow the group, but Jas
catches me by the arm. I look up at him, wondering why
he's so worried.

'You don't understand. If she finds out, she'll tell people.
I know her type. The media'll be here in under an hour.'

'Do you really think the media would come?'

'They always come,' he groans.

I finally get it then. The Sharon and the media thing. I'd
been wondering about it since that day in Reims—Jas's fretting about the media taking a few photos, worrying that
Sharon would work it all out and alert them. It's bigger than
I thought. It's not that he doesn't want Sharon to find out
who he is and have to give her an autograph and have the
other people on the tour interested in him. It's more than
that. He thinks the media are going to turn up and he'll have
to give interview after interview. Photo after photo. Well,

fair enough. I'd hardly want a media entourage on my holiday. All Jas is after is a little privacy, and I don't blame him if that bathroom phone call from Zed's anything to go on.

I think about his problem for a moment before I come up with something. 'Um, how about if you faked it? Sang differently? No one's asking for a star performance from you tonight.'

'You think I could?' He seems relieved by my suggestion.

I check to see if he's being uppity, but he's not. 'Sing badly? Sure you can. If you don't think you're up to it, just follow my lead. I'm a pro at singing badly—even in the shower.'

He takes his hand off my arm then, and looks a bit less worried. 'Guess we'd better catch up with Shane.' I follow his lead and we walk quickly out through the door and up to the group, who are waiting at the lights.

The group walks briskly the rest of the way to the little bar. It's cold. Winter's coming. And to add to this I think people are still more than a little hungover from the day's festivities. This combination leaves us all reasonably quiet, and when Shane tries to start up a rousing chorus of 'everyone's favourite beer song' he doesn't get very far. As one, we walk even more briskly the rest of the way and the relief is visible throughout the group when we finally get to our destination a few streets later.

Inside, I have to admit to myself that the place really *is* pretty funky for a karaoke bar. It's very retro, with pink and red lighting, which makes it feel warm and cosy. There's a fifties-looking vinyl bar, and the place is dotted with little white vinyl bucket chairs and tables all facing…

…the stage.

You can feel everyone's eyes stare at it in trepidation as they enter the room. And then, when they've all seen it and worked out what it is, there is an instant lemming-like descent on the bar.

'Scotch?' Jas asks.

'Yep. Scotch and dry, I think. A double.'

'Right.'

I find a table and take a seat. Soon enough, Jas comes back. With four drinks. 'Thought we might need them. Dutch courage and all that.' He puts them down on the table.

'Thanks.' I take a sip out of one of my drinks. 'But what are you talking about—Dutch courage? You do this all the time. And usually in front of hundreds of thousands of people who are *paying* to see you.'

'Usually they're not intent on "discovering my true identity".' He says this in a deep voice, as if he's reading from an action-packed comic book.

He's definitely losing it, I think, taking a close look at him as I keep sipping—I really *do* need the Dutch courage. 'Don't worry about it. I'll find a song we can do together and I'll drown you out a bit. You'll be fine.'

Jas downs his beer in almost one go.

'If you're still able to stand upright in half an hour, that is.'

After everyone's had a couple of drinks, and a few stragglers have arrived at the club, Shane gets the ball rolling with 'California Girls' by the Beach Boys. He includes lots of lovely up-and-down suggestive hourglass-shaped hand movements for all the girls in the audience to enjoy. Poor guy, I think as I watch him trying his damnedest. I hope he's making a lot of money out of this job and that he doesn't end up having a psychiatric episode later on, when the flashbacks start. What do they call it? Post-traumatic Oktoberfest stress disorder, I think.

A few of the girls strut their stuff next, in groups of twos and threes. It's the usual showing-of-age time warp choices, such as 'Fernando' by Abba and 'Careless Whisper' by George Michael. That kind of thing. The kind of thing I need to be way, way drunker than I am right now to get up and embarrass myself with.

Give me half an hour.

When Jas and I have downed our fourth drink each, I decide I'd better get moving before I end up under the table. 'I'm going to find us a song,' I tell him.

Jas nods 'I'll source us a couple more drinks.'

It takes me a good ten minutes or so to work through the list of songs available. When I've made my choice and stuck us in line, I go back to our table. 'Guess what I chose?' I say to Jas as I sit down.

'What?'

'"99 Luftballons" by Nena—they had it.'

'What? In German?'

'Of course.'

'But I can't sing in German. Can't read it. All I can do is the "99 Luftballons" bit.'

I give him a look. 'Duh. That's the whole idea. I'll do the verses and you just come in with whatever you can work out. That way you don't have to do too much singing.'

Jas's face perks up then. 'Duh, yourself. Might even work. When are we on?'

'Not for a while yet. I think there are still about three or four people in front of us.'

'Here you go.' Jas pushes my two drinks closer to me.

Hmmm. Should I, or...? Of course I should. If I'm going to be carrying us up there I'm going to need it.

Jas and I sit back and clap along as a few guys have a go

on stage singing a Beatles song. After this, it's Sharon who makes her way up.

'Got a bad feeling about this.' Jas turns to me. 'A really bad feeling.'

And he's right to have that really bad feeling, because in the next few seconds we learn that Sharon's chosen a Spawn song, of all things. She struggles through it badly, all the time looking straight at Jas, which makes everyone else turn around and look too.

To make matters worse, pictures of Zamiel start flashing up on the video screen halfway through the song. Zamiel walking down the endless corridors of some stadium. Zamiel in the wings. Zamiel running on stage. Zamiel doing his famous S&M banned-in-twenty-countries scene. Zamiel's fans trying to get on the stage. Zamiel's bodyguards kicking the shit out of the fans trying to get on the stage. That kind of thing. Good clean, honest fun.

'Jesus…' Jas groans under his breath and lowers his head a little.

If he could fit, I think he'd try to slink underneath the table right now.

I try very, very hard not to laugh as I watch the video. It's hysterical seeing Jas as Zamiel—the bad boy of the music world—when I know he's really pretty much like a kitten. No, that's not fair and, frankly, a bit emasculating. Maybe more like a gummy old lion who's lost its teeth and roar but can still pace around its cage majestically. Anyway, kitten or lion, it's something that I never would have thought he had in him—pulling off a character like Zamiel. And I'm having a great old time until the end of the clip…when Zamiel does the stare thing.

Now, the stare thing's something I've tried to avoid seeing in the media, because it tends to give me the shivers.

It's been a pretty hard task dodging it over the last year or so, though, because it's Zamiel's favourite move and is invariably included in every Spawn video clip, ad et cetera. And the stare is just a stare when it comes down to it—really, that's all it is, just a stare.

But, boy, is it an effective one.

Because Zamiel's stare, with Jas's dark, dark eyes, whitened face and lashings of kohl eyeliner, is mesmerising. Like one of those hypnotic swirls. As you watch, you seem to go deeper and deeper in, and try as you might there's no pulling away. Just as I'd felt before, in the hotel room.

I squirm in my seat and avert my eyes from the video screen.

Thankfully, the song is over soon enough, and a group of guys from the Beer-drinking Society get up and sing Men at Work's 'Down Under'— screaming out the bits about Vegemite sandwiches. The song is Jas's saving grace. It gets everyone bar the English Sharon and Tara and the Irish couple singing along and forgetting about Zamiel, his likeness to Jas and the fact that Sharon can't seem to leave him alone.

Even though it's not on the way to her table, Sharon manages to walk past us as she crosses the floor to her seat. 'Hope you liked it,' she says to Jas with a lick of her lips.

He turns to me when she's out of earshot. 'Ugh. Did you see that?'

'I could hardly miss it.'

'What's she talking about, anyway? How could I like it? She bloody murdered that song up there.'

I know what'll take his mind of Sharon. 'Guess what?'

'What?'

'We're on next.'

Jas sinks the rest of his beer in reply.

A minute or two later, I'm dragging him up front. He's not exactly being supportive about me having to sing on stage when I've never done it before. I'm scared out of my wits, even with three and a half drinks under my belt. While we wait for the music to start up all I want to do is sprint straight out the front door of the bar.

But I don't.

I glance up at Jas, beside me, hoping for some words of encouragement, maybe even a few tips. But Jas, with his years of performing experience, looks as if he wants to do a runner as well. He doesn't, however. Instead, he picks up one of the microphones and hands me another one.

Here goes.

'Er, hi. We're Jas and Charlie. Again,' he says, introducing us. 'This is going to be harder for me than for Charlie. I don't speak any German—except, of course, for *Zwei Bier, bitte!* and *Wo ist die Toilette, bitte?* So anyone who can speak a bit, try and sing along with us…' He trails off as the music starts.

I take a big breath and watch as the words come up on the video screen. They're moving quickly and, being in German, I have to concentrate on them with all my might just to read them out.

I struggle through the first lines, trying to make the un-familiar words fit the tune. It's a while before the two words I do know finally flit across the screen. And when Jas sees them—*99 Luftballons*—he belts them out as loud as he can.

Everyone laughs.

I keep right on struggling through the next verse, but, having done this, things then seem to get a bit easier. The words begin to fit in, I start to feel less nervous and take in the atmosphere.

Beside me, Jas joins in with whatever he can work out from the screen—usually just the *99 Luftballons* bits, which everyone is now belting out every time they come up. Jas looks relieved when they join in, and as more and more people come on board he starts to visibly relax on stage.

Big mistake.

Because as soon as he relaxes I think he forgets why he didn't want to sing in the first place. And when he lets himself go, it's hard for him not to look like Zamiel did before. Drunk as Jas is, he seems at ease now, unlike everyone else who's been on stage this evening. It's his movements that give him away, I notice when I've got a spare moment. Everyone else was gawky and self-conscious. But not Jas. He knows how to move on a stage to make people watch him. He knows how to hold the microphone properly, knows how to use it properly. He has a presence, while I...

I just have a bad voice, I realise as I squawk a high note out particularly badly. I try to concentrate on my singing then and not watch Jas too much. Though it's difficult. Because watching him is, I hate to admit it...incredibly sexy.

I put it down to my Jim Morrison rock star thing. I could never understand that—why I found Jim Morrison so attractive. The man was grubby and drugged out of his mind, with dirty hair and clothes that had seen better years, let alone better days. Not my type at all. But somehow you didn't see those things when he was on stage. Off stage—blah. But when he was on stage there was no denying that man was some very choice eye candy. And as long as you couldn't smell him you were OK— the dream could live on.

What is it about women and the rock star thing? What makes a relatively plain guy suddenly so attractive when he's singing and there's hundreds of women drooling before him? Another mystery that will never be answered, along with 'Where'd the last chocolate biscuit go?' and 'Who left a tissue in their pocket in the wash?'

I try desperately to ignore the fact that Jas is beside me. I keep singing and try to control those stupid, stupid hormones of mine. But it's difficult, because the fact is I'm pissed. *Sehr* pissed.

I look out at the audience for a second or two and see Sharon watching us just that little bit too closely. Standing near her, Shane follows my gaze to see that I'm keeping an eye on her. He goes up to her then. Distracts her for a bit.

What a man—what a tour guide, I think, hoping Jas has seen his efforts.

Finally we reach the end of the song and everyone claps. Jas and I clamber off the stage. 'That's it for me,' he says. 'Never again. Come on, I'll buy you another drink after all your hard work.'

I decide not to tell him about the relaxing on stage thing. After all, it's over and done with, and if I tell him now he's only going to worry he's given himself away.

We pass Sharon and Shane on our way to the bar. 'Hope you liked it,' Jas simpers, and I pull him away from her. He's drunker than I thought and seems to be looking for trouble now. When I turn back Sharon's still watching us, not quite knowing what to make of it all, especially the comment. Shane winks.

'How much have you had?' I ask Jas as we sit down at the bar.

'Not enough,' he answers. 'Hey, look.' He points to a row of about fifteen bottles on the bar. 'Schnapps. And lots of it. Let's do it.'

'Do what?' I eye him warily, trying for the life of me to forget all the things I'd thought of doing *to* Jas only minutes ago.

'Them all, baby!'

That's what I thought he meant. I feel drunk just looking at the bottles. 'Maybe one.' I feel his arm brush mine
and my hormones kick in again. Down, hormones, down.
'Maybe a couple…'

'Great!' Jas says, and calls the barman over. A minute or
so later I have five shot glasses placed in front of me.

Pineapple, cinnamon, peppermint, butterscotch and
tropical.

We try each schnapps shot at the same time, starting with
the pineapple and working our way through. We use as
many poncey winemaking terms as we can to describe
them.

'This one's very…fruity,' Jas says, after tasting the tropical schnapps—the last shot.

I laugh at that. Really laugh. Tropical. Fruity. Actually,
it's quite hard to stop. Which makes me recognise the fact
that I have now missed the turn-off for Really, Really Pissed
and have instead taken the Completely Smashed exit ramp.

The party steps up a notch then. A group of guys get up
and attempt the Beatles' 'Twist and Shout' which everyone
sings along to. Next is 'Love Shack' by the B52s and then
'YMCA' by the Village People.

I swivel around on my seat to watch them, and when I
glance back a few minutes later Jas has a whole new line-
up of shot glasses in front of him. He sees me looking.

'Thought we should move onto singles,' he says. 'Got a
lot of flavours to cover.'

I shake my head. 'Not me. You're going to have to do
this round by yourself, unless you want to be picking me
up off the floor in the next ten minutes or so.'

Jas opens his mouth to argue, but then shuts it again and
shrugs. He picks up one shot glass and downs it in one go.

Then the next one.

And the next one.

And the next one.

One more and he's done.

'What are you trying to do? Put yourself on the liver transplant waiting list?'

'Nah, just makes her look better.' Jas points out Sharon, who happens to be staring at him. She waves. 'Man, she's thick,' Jas says, and immediately orders a couple of beers. 'Doesn't she know? Doesn't she get it?'

I begin to say there's a lot of things I'm not getting either this trip, when the barman places Jas's beers on the bar. 'That's enough, then,' I say in a motherly 'don't mess with me' tone, worrying about the number of drinks he's downed. He must be ninety per cent proof by now.

Group after group take the stage, and the evening starts to become a blur. The same songs appear over and over again but nobody seems to care—not now that they've got more than a few drinks under their belts. When there's a bit of a break, Jas taps me on the arm.

'What?' I lean in so I can hear him.

'Thanks for inviting me, Charlie,' he says. 'To Oktoberfest.'

'That's, um, OK.'

'I'm really, really happy,' he continues.

'I can see that.'

'Really, really, really happy.'

'That's great.' I pat him on the arm. 'Really, really, really great.'

He goes to stand up then. 'Where're you off to?' I say.

'Got to go…' he says, heading in the direction of the men's. He seems reasonably focused on getting there, and when Shane stops him halfway and starts talking to him I don't worry. He'll be fine. Shane will look after him. I turn back to the bar and order a glass of water.

I'm just sucking on a piece of ice from the bottom of the glass, thinking Jas is taking his time, when I hear it.

Hear him, that is. Jas.

I get up off the bar stool and turn around. He's up on the stage.

I walk down the few steps from the bar so I can see properly. Shane's still there. A few steps away. I make my way over to him.

'Where's Sharon?' My eyes search for her as I ask. She's not where she was before, at a table with a few of her friends.

'It's OK. I sent her off with a few of the Beer-drinking Society kids for some fags.'

I pause, thinking this over. 'Are you telling me you put him up to this?'

'But he *wanted* to sing.' Shane grins. 'Couldn't stop the man.'

Oh, no. At least Sharon's gone, I think, quickly checking the door before I turn back to watch Jas. He's as drunk as a skunk and I can only hope Sharon and co stay away for a few more minutes. Jas was so worried about it before—about being found out. The only reason he isn't now, and is cavorting around on stage as if he lives there, is because he's completely and utterly plastered.

'A command performance,' Shane says to me. 'I can't wait.'

The sad thing is, neither can I. I know I should go up there and wrench Jas from the stage, but I can't. I can't do anything but stand here and stare. My feet are glued to the floor and my eyes to Jas.

And then he starts.

I know the song as soon as I hear the first few bars. Violent Femmes, 'Add it Up.'

Jas begins right on cue, sounding way, way too good to be in some karaoke bar. Funky or not. Don't hurry back, Sharon. Don't hurry back...

He moves through the first verse expertly. It's halfway through the second verse, when he starts singing about why he can't get a screw, that I start to forget about Sharon.

Bugger Sharon.

And I forget about the little talk I had with myself in the room this evening too. The one about thinking I could resist this man if I wanted to.

Bugger the little talk.

Because. Jas. Looks. Fabulous.

He's really enjoying himself up there. And, just like before, he has that presence again. I watch, entranced. But then all of a sudden Jas starts to seem a bit taken aback. He's scanning the crowd, his eyes flitting from one face to the other. He looks back at the bar again—he's searching for me, I realise. A few more passes over the crowd and he spots me.

And that's when he moves into the third verse.

He gives it all he's got. Right at me. My knees go weak as the lyrics come flooding back to me. And then, right when I'm least expecting it, he does the stare. The Zamiel stare.

I am rooted to the spot, for want of a better word.

Shane leans over. 'So much for our date. My bets are on you getting some tonight...'

I unfreeze then. 'Hey, don't give me that crap. I know, remember? About the Fine Arts.' In my drunken state, I don't care who hears.

He nods. 'I know. It doesn't matter. I'd still bet on you getting some tonight.'

I start to argue. 'I told you, we're not…we don't…it's—' before I give up. And we both turn back to watch the rest of the performance.

When Jas finishes there's an almighty cheer. He makes his way off the stage—missing a few stairs here and there—and over to where Shane and I are standing. He flings one arm around my shoulders and I almost collapse under his weight as he leans on me for support.

'What happened to never again?' I ask him.

He laughs. 'Couldn't help myself.'

I give Shane a look. Sure.

Sharon arrives then, pushing her way in beside us and Shane. 'What's going on? Did I miss anything?'

Shane winks at us. 'Nothing, darling. Just some drunken old hack on stage.'

'I'd better sit you down,' I say to the wavering Jas, and, seeing there are no seats left at the tables down here, pull him off in the direction of the bar and decide I'll just have to pay the bartender *not* to serve him this time. When he's back on his stool, I order another few glasses of water.

'Here, drink this,' I say, pushing one over to him when they arrive.

He does as he's told, and has another one besides.

'Bit better?' I ask.

He nods. 'Needed that. But now I'm really going to have to do the FFP.'

'The what?'

'The first fatal piss. Of the evening. You watch. Be going every ten minutes after this.'

'I really didn't need to know that,' I say.

'You asked!'

I don't argue. I asked, true. I just didn't want to *know*. 'Go on—go.' I wave one hand at him.

He goes. This time, though, I watch him walk the whole way, not wanting any more accidental sing-alongs.

Which reminds me of what has just happened. The song. The stare thing. And it's then, watching him walk away, that I know I'm going to have to tell him what's going on. I can't just say 'bugger the little talk'—dismiss it like that. I'm going to have to lay down some rules. Because I really can't do this any more. It has to stop.

So that's it, I think. And right then and there, on the bar stool, I start to form my plan. I'm going to tell him. I'm going to tell him tonight, while I'm still drunk and have the guts to do it. I'm going to sit him down when we get back to the hotel and tell him I lied that night at Brown's— the night I told him I don't feel that way about him any more.

I only said that because I didn't know what else to say, and I think I was scared of endangering our friendship again. The truth is, I still have feelings for him. All kinds of feelings and most of them not very ladylike. In fact most of them could be attributed to the goddess Hussy, and she and I don't know how to stop them. Even knowing they're un-requited isn't enough to turn me off. Which means there's nothing left to do to make it stop but explain the way things are…

And then tell him that we shouldn't see each other any more.

It's the only solution. The only workable solution. I may have fooled myself for a good forty-eight hours or so back there, but when it comes down to it I can't just be friends. I've tried that this trip and it hasn't worked. Thus, it has to end.

I take a deep breath and swivel back around on my chair.

'You look serious,' Jas says, coming over to lean on the bar.

The bartender places a shot glass in front of me. When did he order that? 'What's this?' I ask.

'Cherry. You like cherry.'

'I don't know if I can…'

Jas moves in closer to me. So close I can feel his leg hot against mine. Oh, God. He puts the glass up to my lips and stares right into the back of my eyes. 'You can.'

I down the shot and ask the bartender for another two glasses of water.

As Jas and I drink them I sneak a look at him from time to time, wondering if I should just tell him now—get my little speech over and done with. But, no, I decide in the end, the hotel's better. We can talk there. Properly.

I drink two more glasses of water before my bladder tells me it's really time to hit the bathroom.

As I start to get up Sharon gets onto the stage and the first few bars of Bette Midler's 'The Rose' start up.

Everyone boos. And rightly so.

I knew I wouldn't have fitted in with those girls.

'Coming with you,' Jas says, as Sharon keeps singing, regardless of what the crowd thinks. 'Going to have to go again in a few minutes anyway. And who knows? Mightn't be able to hear her from back there.'

I stumble, and I mean *stumble*, my way across the floor in the direction of the ladies'. That one cherry schnapps has taken me way beyond completely smashed territory now. So far beyond it, in fact, that I'm starting to get the sinking feeling that I've had far, far too much to drink and that the stumbling is going to get much worse before it gets better.

I trip over one of the three steps that leads up to the corridor where the bathrooms are situated, and Jas grabs me by the waist to steady me. Then he moves in front and starts pulling me along with one hand, steering the way.

We walk down the corridor in silence. The ladies' is first, and Jas slows down to let me go in and then continues down the hall himself. Except that I forget to let go of his hand for some reason...

And me forgetting to let go of Jas's hand pulls him back.

He turns around, surprised, and moves back closer to me. It's then that I know I have to put my plan into action. I have to tell him. I have to tell him now. It can't wait any longer.

As he enters my personal space, I revise the plan quickly in my head:

1. Tell him I still have feelings for him (leaving out the part about them not being very ladylike).
2. Tell him I've tried, but I can't stop these feelings.
3. Tell him I know the feelings are unrequited.
4. Tell him that being friends isn't enough for me.
5. Tell him the only solution to the problem is to not see each other any more.

Right. That's it. Good one, Charlie. It's perfectly simple. A perfectly simple five-step plan. And, now that it's all straight in my mind I open my mouth and get ready to put the perfectly simple five-step plan into action.

But somehow things go a little bit astray.

Instead of moving into my carefully thought out speech, I push Jas up against the wall, grab his head to bring him down to my height and start kissing him.

He kisses me back. Really kisses me back.

And I don't think I've kissed like this since high school. Not with this kind of fervour.

As we keep going, people start to push past us in the not so wide hallway. But we don't care. We can't seem to keep our hands off each other.

It's disgraceful.

A pash-off. A drunken pash-off.

And it's good.

Fantastically, smashingly, lip-smackingly good.

Eventually, after what seems like hours, we break off. 'I have to go,' I say, nodding towards the ladies'. 'Desperately.' I start towards the door, but Jas grabs me before I get far and we're at it all over again. I break off once more. 'Really. I really, really have to go now.'

'Want me to come with you?' Jas says suggestively.

Yes! But, 'No!' is what comes out of my mouth. Unfortunately I'm not *that* drunk.

He starts down the hall towards the men's. 'Hurry.' He turns halfway down and points a finger at me in a distinctly rock star move. Which makes my knees tremble again. Shit, shit, shit. I'm pathetic. I'm a rock star junkie. I'll have posters all over my room next.

My bladder calls for my attention then, and I practically fall into the ladies'.

When I come out of the stall I wash my hands and take a good look at myself in the mirror. I'm a mess. My hair is everywhere but where it's supposed to be and I have mascara travelling all over my face—most of it taking a holiday underneath my eyes.

As I fix myself up a bit, I drunkenly recall Jas's last word to me—'hurry'. Remembering this, I look up at myself in the mirror again. What am I doing? I don't want to go through all this again—all the feelings I went through after That Night. I don't think I have the strength. *I thought he was gay*, a little voice inside me says. *Do you think I care what he is?* another little voice says back. *I just want some more of what we got in the corridor back there.* I take a deep breath and glance around me for the third little voice that should provide an answer. It isn't there.

But a condom machine is.

I eye it suspiciously, as if it's trying to tell me something. As if it's been put there for a sneaky purpose. Then I look back at the mirror. 'Fuck it,' I drawl. 'Maybe it's a sign.' Ever the optimist, I buy two condoms and stuff them in my pocket.

And as I leave the bathroom I wonder if Jas has brought any of those leather pants Zamiel likes to wear.

Chapter Eighteen

He's waiting for me in the hallway.

And it must be Jas's turn once more, because he grabs my arms and holds them up on the wall, and starts kissing me as soon as I'm within reaching distance.

My knees do the weak thing once more, though I can't really tell if it's the kissing or the alcohol.

God, I really hope he has those leather pants.

Something's telling me it might be the alcohol.

I break it off when I can't wait much longer. 'Let's go,' I say over Jas's groan. I grab his shirt. 'Let's go back to the hotel.'

Jas doesn't argue. In fact he makes just as fast a break out of that corridor and towards the main door of the bar as I do.

We bump into Sharon and Shane as we crash past the tables.

'Way-hey,' Shane yells, and gives us the thumbs-up.

I give him a glare in return. This is all his fault. Sort of. 'Can't stop,' I yell as we race out through the door and down the street. It's busy outside, with quite a bit of traffic and far more people than were on the streets before. The cold air hits me then, smack in the face, and I feel myself get drunker. But I don't care. It doesn't matter—nothing matters. Because as we wait for a set of lights to change so we can cross the road Jas pulls me towards him, so my back rests against his front. He reaches underneath my jacket, underneath my shirt and runs his hands over my bra. Then, to my surprise, underneath my bra.

But he's g— the first little voice starts up again.

Second little voice: *Shut up!*

The 'walk' sign comes on and we bolt off again. We run down the street, around the corner, around the next corner.

We don't have any trouble with directions tonight.

Finally we come to the hotel. We leg it through the lobby and stand, waiting for the lift. Waiting, waiting. Waiting too long. Waiting far too long.

I grab Jas's hand and he sees what I'm thinking. We head for the stairs.

We run up one flight, two flights…

And then we stop for a bit. My jacket comes off. His belt gets undone.

We're all over each other again, and my lips are starting to hurt, but who cares? Not me. We end up half-sitting, half-lying on the steps. And I'm quite happy where I am until I look up and see the security camera pointing right in our direction. Immediately, I imagine our little escapade being e-mailed to half the world's population.

'Oh, God, let's go,' I say, dragging Jas up. 'It's not much further.'

We run up the rest of the stairs, push the stairwell door open and keep running.

We're in the hallway now.

210, 211, 212…

213.

I fumble with the swipe card.

'Here,' Jas says. He takes it and swipes it expertly through the door.

And then we're inside.

The clothes seem to come off by themselves as we get further and further into the room. By the time we get to the bed I only have my jeans on, and even they're undone. I search inside the right pocket urgently—where I've put the condoms. Jas is doing the same kind of thing in one of the pockets of his jacket, which is now on the floor. At exactly the same time we produce two condoms each. Optimists.

I hold one up, dropping the other packet, and Jas flicks his two over his shoulder.

And then we get down to business.

It is the worst sex of my life.

The reasons it is the worst sex of my life, I realise, staring at the ceiling a few minutes later, are twofold:

1. It's over in about three and a half seconds
2. We're both too drunk to actually enjoy the three and a half seconds it lasts

I turn on my side to look at Jas. 'Well, that was, um…'

'Shit,' he says. 'It was shit. Sorry—I'm sorry. I'm just so drunk. Shouldn't have…'

'Don't worry about it,' I say, looking away, even though I know *I'm* going to.

How can I not?

And, hey, what happened to my perfectly simple plan? My speech? The one where I was going to tell Jas we shouldn't see each other any more? The one that fitted right in with my 'let's get Charlie's head sorted out' plans? That went down the drain fast, didn't it? Inside my non-sorted-out head, I groan long and loud. How humiliating. Though I guess I should thank my lucky stars that tonight I didn't get pushed away before we even started. That, if possible, had been even slightly *more* humiliating.

With this thought, I must have stopped torturing myself and fallen drunkenly asleep, because the next thing I know it's three-fifteen a.m. and I have to get up and make a run for the bathroom. Where I throw up.

For the first time, anyway.

Because I throw up again at three-fifty-seven, and again at four-thirty-two, and again at five-sixteen.

It's the fourth time that does it.

I didn't think it was humanly possible to feel worse than I felt a couple of hours ago, but I was wrong. I sit there and cling to the porcelain for dear life.

'That's it. I'm calling a doctor,' Jas says, getting up and holding his throbbing head—I'd woken him up during the second hurl. 'If you keep going like this you'll be dehydrated in no time. You're not keeping anything down. Not even water.'

'I'll be OK,' I say weakly, crawling back into bed, not looking at him. I don't want to think about last night. I don't want to think about anything. I just want to die.

'But it's not normal. You ever done this before?' He goes over to the table and pops a couple of paracetamol.

For a moment I'm worried he's talking about last night, wanting explanations, but then I realise we're still on the topic of my stomach contents. 'Have I ever thrown up this many times in a row? No. Why? Are you thinking of calling *The Guinness Book of World Records* people in?'

'Funny. What if it's a combination of things? Maybe it's something you ate as well.'

'Ate?' I open one eye.

'The smoked salmon sandwich. Remember? You said it was a bit old and tired.'

As soon as the words 'smoked salmon sandwich' come out of Jas's mouth I have to make the race to the bathroom again.

'Sorry,' he says from outside the bathroom door a few minutes later.

'I think it was just the schnapps that did it. But if you say those words again…' I moan with my head over the toilet.

'I won't. But I'm calling a doctor. Where's your insurance paperwork?'

'It's in my backpack.' I don't have the energy to argue—rare, for me. I must really be sick.

I spend a few minutes cleaning myself up in the bathroom while Jas is on the phone. I wash my face and brush my teeth. When I come back out I feel five per cent better for it. I slink back into bed one more time.

Jas puts the phone down as I'm pulling the covers up. 'Should have a doctor here within an hour.'

'Excellent.'

I feel a tad better when I hear this, and within a few minutes manage to fall asleep again. I wake up to a knock on the door. There's a cool washcloth on my forehead and a wastepaper basket lined with a plastic bag on the floor beside me—courtesy of Jas, I suppose.

I check the rest of the floor—he's picked up all the clothes. And the condoms. Oh, God.

At least I've done one thing right—I had the forethought to throw on my nightie on the way back from my first sick-run of the night.

Jas goes and gets the door.

I hear two voices talking in the small entry. As the doctor comes in Jas explains what's going on. He's young, the doctor, I notice quite quickly, but don't care when I see he's got a big brown professional-looking doctor's bag with him. A big brown professional-looking doctor's bag I just know is full of fantastic German drugs that are going to stop me being sick.

I lie still and let Jas do the talking. When it gets to the point where I know he's going to say the evil words, I try to block them out. It doesn't work. 'Smoked salmon sandwich,' I hear him say, and my stomach's off again. This time into the wastepaper basket.

'I told you not to say it.' I point at Jas when I'm finished.
'Sorry.'

The doctor comes over then. 'So, you have had a little too much *gemütlichkeit*, yes?'

'What's that?' I eye him suspiciously.

'It is a hard word to explain. It means something like a good time.'

'Too much of a good thing,' I say weakly, thinking of the schnapps. 'You could be on to something there.'

He asks me a few questions about when I started throwing up, what I ate, how much I drank, if I took any drugs of the illegal kind, et cetera. Then he asks the big question. The one I've been hoping Jas would disappear into thin air for. The one about am I on any prescription drugs and do I have any allergies?

'Um,' I say. 'I'm going to have to get something.' I start to get up, but Jas stops me.

'I'll get it.'

I lie down again. 'There's a folder. It should be tucked into the big pocket on the inside lid of my suitcase.'

Jas goes over and searches for it. He finds it without any trouble and brings it back to me, passing it over with a puzzled expression.

I hand it to the doctor. There's no point in going into detailed explanations. He's going to have to read it anyway.

'I see,' he says, looking up from the notes eventually. 'This is more complicated. I may have to make a few phone calls.'

I nod towards the phone. 'Help yourself.' He goes over, pulls a small notebook out of his bag, gets the numbers he needs and starts dialling.

Jas sits down on my bed. 'What's going on?'

'Oh, I just can't take a lot of drugs. Nothing to worry about.'

'Why not?'

I shrug. 'I just can't.'

'I don't understand.' Jas's brow creases.

The doctor's babbling away now, in German.

'There's been some...developments. It's boring. Nothing, really. Nothing to worry about.'

Jas doesn't look convinced, but I close my eyes anyway, too tired to think of anything else to say. I feel him get off the bed, and when I open my eyes again he's standing and staring out of the window.

The doctor puts down the phone. 'OK. I have spoken to a specialist and he says what I want to give you is fine. There should not be any problem.'

'What are you going to give me?' I say as he fumbles around in the now sinister-looking brown bag. I have a suspicious feeling that what he has in mind might just involve a needle. As he brings a few things out of the bag I realise it does.

A doozie of a needle, actually. A big, fat, German stonker of a needle.

He wants to put it in my butt, but I tell him my leg will be just fine, *danke schön*. There's been enough exposing of flesh in this room for one night. I grit my teeth and try to suppress my inner five-year-old as he jabs me.

But it's worth it—the needle. Because I start to feel better within minutes of the injection. I even feel as if I may be able to keep down the two paracetamol I'm allowed to take as well. I've lost that chokey 'it's just a matter of time before it's all coming up again' feeling now, and I realise I'm exhausted. All I want to do is sleep.

For days.

The doctor gets up off his chair after I've signed everything I have to sign and he's given me some phone numbers to ring if I need to. 'I guess you could say you have seen the best and the *wurst* of Oktoberfest.' He laughs as he makes his way to the door. 'It is a good joke, yes?'

'Mmmm.' I send him a poisonous glare across the room. It was schnapps, not *wurst*, you healthy-looking smart-arse, I think. Well, several helpings from the mini-bar, a couple of Scotch and drys and about 257 shots of schnapps.

As soon as he's gone, I crash and burn.

I wake up a few hours later, but only because Jas is tapping me on the shoulder.

'Charlie?'

'Mmmm?'

'I'm going to go out for a bit—take a walk around. Yeah?'

I look at him in awe. 'Don't you have a headache?'

He shakes his head.

Rock star bastard, I think. How can they abuse themselves so well and still get away with it every morning? Meanwhile my headache is still present, if fading a little. My stomach feels a whole lot better, however.

'You sleep. I'll keep my mobile on so you can call me when you wake up or if you need anything, all right?'

'Yep,' I say, my eyes closing on me again. 'Sleep.'

And I do.

Chapter Nineteen

I wake up again at around four. My headache's gone and I feel about five hundred per cent better than I did this morning. I've always had a fast recovery rate from things like this, but this feels fast even for me. There's a loud stomach rumble from beneath the bed covers. Hmmm. I think I may even feel up to eating.

I get up slowly, checking if all my body parts are still working. They are, surprisingly. My leg's a little sore from the injection, but it's nothing, really. I go over and grab a bottle of lemonade from the mini-bar, thinking of my mum as I twist off the lid. She always used to give me flat lemonade when I was sick, just like her own mother had given her, even though when I was well the liquid was on the 'No, Charlie' list because of its high sugar content.

I sit down at the table and sip from the bottle while I read the room service menu. I decide on fruit toast with no butter from the all-day breakfast menu and ring my order in.

While I'm waiting for my food I have a quick shower and put some fresh clothes on.

I'm halfway through my first piece of toast when the door rattles and Jas arrives.

'You're up,' he says. 'Should've called me.'

His mobile starts ringing as he says this, and he grabs it and presses a few buttons but doesn't answer the call.

'You're still not answering it?' I ask, looking up from my piece of fruit toast.

He shakes his head and puts the phone down near my plate on the table. There's a *beep-beep-beep* from it soon after.

'Just the message bank.'

I spot the words flash up on the miniature screen then. '114 calls missed. 113 messages.'

'Brought you some plain biscuits in case you were hungry,' Jas says, fishing around in his backpack and then placing them on the table.

'Thanks.'

'How're you feeling?' he asks. He doesn't sit down, but goes over to the window and stares out moodily as he did earlier this morning.

'Heaps better. Pretty much back to normal, surprisingly. I thought I was going to die. It certainly felt like it, anyway.'

Jas watches me carefully as I speak. 'Didn't look too hot for a while there.'

We both glance away then, Jas to the window and me to my toast, avoiding the real issue. The issue of the worst sex in the world. The worst sex in the world that was had by us.

Ugh.

I eat my second piece of toast and finish my lemonade while Jas takes a seat on his bed and flips through the TV channels. He taps his leg on the floor as he watches and I can tell he's agitated. On edge. Just like I'm feeling.

When I'm done with breakfast and have a bit of stodge in my stomach I feel even better than before. And with Jas looking as if he's about to get testy any moment now, I plan my escape. 'I might go down for a spa or something,' I say, going over to my suitcase to find my togs.

He switches the TV off then. 'Not so fast, sunshine.'

'Sorry?' I drop my suitcase lid and turn around.

'Tell me about this folder. The one you showed the doctor.'

I pause for a moment. 'Like I told you, it's nothing. I just can't take a lot of drugs. You know I'm the sensitive type…' I try to make a joke of it.

Jas doesn't crack a smile. 'But why? You never used to have any allergies or anything. Not that I knew of. It's something important, isn't it? Like your mum had. I could tell by the doctor's face. Something he had to speak to a specialist about too. What kind of specialist did he call?'

I decide to play dumb. 'I don't know who he called, do I? He was speaking German.'

'That right, is it? You have no idea who he might have called? No idea what kind of specialist he might have needed to talk to?'

I shrug.

'Stop *bullshitting*, Charlie.' Jas's voice rises. But then his expression changes. 'Just tell me you don't have the same thing your mum had. Please.'

'No, no. It's not that—believe me. And I'm not, um, bullshitting.' I cross my fingers behind my back.

'You are.'

I don't say anything.

'You *are*. You've been funny this whole trip about getting sick. Catching a cold or something. Poking your neck. I've seen you. Now, stop crossing your fingers behind your back and tell me what this is all about.'

I keep my mouth set in a firm line while I nonchalantly uncross my fingers behind my back. I may look cool, calm and collected, but my thoughts are all over the place. Soon enough, just like yesterday at the art gallery, my feelings rise up to choke me and my words overflow again. 'Well, what business is it of yours anyway? What if I did get sick? You're just going to go back to your little world and we won't see each other any more, so what does it matter?' I regret each word as soon as it comes out of my mouth. Why did I say that? It wasn't what I mean to say at all, and it's come out all wrong.

Jas gets up off the bed then, and starts pacing the room. 'What are you talking about—what business is it of mine? I thought we knew everything about each other. That used to be your big take on our friendship. Remember?'

'A few years ago it did.' I take a step over and stand behind one of the chairs. I hold onto its back as if it's going to protect me somehow. 'Things are different now.'

Jas stops pacing when I say this, and I can see I've made him angry—really angry. My mother used to be like that. She had this unlimited patience until you pushed her just that tiny bit too far over the edge and then she would just snap. He comes towards me and grabs my elbows. 'What's this about? Why are you keeping things from me?'

I push his hands off one at a time. 'That's pretty rich,' I say. '*I'm* keeping things from *you*? Keeping things from other people is your line of expertise, if I remember correctly.'

'What are you talking about? Why do I know close to

nothing about what's been going on in your life for the past two years? You've been evasive this whole trip.'

'Me? Evasive?' I laugh at this. 'How about you, with your mysterious phone calls and your five hundred mobile phone messages a day? Why don't you ever answer your calls, hey? What's going on there?'

'I told you. I'm on holiday.'

'Bullshit, you're on holiday,' I try, and as I say the words I watch closely for the expression on his face. I see what I'm looking for. I knew it. 'Aha! That was a pretty good guess, wasn't it? And it helped that I answered one of those calls. Your friend Zed. He's a charmer, isn't he? Why doesn't he know where you are? I mean, he's your manager. What are you doing? Are you on the run or something?'

'Me? On the run? More like you.'

'Oh, really, Mr "my life's so hard being in a made-up band". You're such a hypocrite. Remember how you used to go on and on about Milli Vanilli? What a waste of time and space they were? That it was shocking people like them got in the door of the music industry? Well, what a crock, *Zamiel*!'

'Jesus, you're infuriating.' Jas runs his hands through his hair.

There's a noise, then, at the door—as if someone's there. We both turn around and stare at it for a moment before Jas runs over and wrenches it open.

It's Sharon.

'I knew it!' she says. 'I knew all along that you're Zamiel.'

'If I were you,' Jas tells her, almost smoking at the ears, 'I would get the fuck out of here—*right now*!'

Sharon stands there, frozen, and a frightened expression comes over her face. Then, when she's got herself together a little, she turns and runs for it down the hallway. Jas sticks his head out through the door and watches her go before he's satisfied she's not coming back, then slams the door closed again.

He comes back over and stands in front of me. 'Where were we?'

'Let's see. If I remember correctly, you were accusing *me* of being on the run,' I say, crossing my arms.

'Look at you. You are in some ways, aren't you? I know your mum's death must have been hard, but what have you been doing with yourself for the past two years? Nothing, it seems! Sketching?' he spits. 'No exhibition. No degree. Nothing.'

'Nothing! That's nice. As if you'd know about what's been going on in my life. And what do you think *you've* been up to? Making the world a better place for us all to live in?'

'At least I'm doing something. At least I'm not living off my dead mother's money.'

We both pause then, shocked at what he's just said. And that's when I reach up and slap him right across the face.

Jas takes a step backwards.

We stand and stare at each other for what seems like for ever.

'I'm sorry,' he says finally. 'I shouldn't have said that.'

'You're damn right you shouldn't have.' I watch as the red mark spreads across his cheek.

'I just want to know what's going on,' he says miserably.

And it's this one small comment that washes all my anger away. He looks awful, and it's all my fault. Guilt settles in. Because he's right. I have been keeping things from him. Big things.

I turn the chair that I'm still holding onto around and take a seat.

Hunched over, I glance up at Jas after a while. He's holding his palm against his one red cheek and I feel terrible. I've hit him. Actually hit him. I don't think I've ever hit anyone like that before. 'I'm really sorry,' I say. 'I've never done that before. I can't believe I just did it, in fact.'

And as I look at him I know one thing for sure about us—we both owe each other more than a few explanations.

'Come on,' I motion to him. 'Sit down and I'll tell you about the folder.'

When he's sitting down, I take a few deep breaths, wondering how I'm going to say it. I hate the telling. At least I didn't have to tell my mother. Because how can you tell your own mother something like that? It's supposed to be the other way around, if you're unlucky enough to have to deal with it at all. But when it comes down to it there's only one way to do it, one way to say it—those three horrible words.

'I've had cancer,' I say (I always think there should be a cut to the first ad break of the midday movie each time these words exit my mouth).

'What?' Jas stands up. *'What?'*

I wait. Obviously he's heard what I've said. All reactions are different. From Kath I got, 'That's not funny, Charlie.' One of my friends simply burst into tears. It's strange, people's initial reaction to the phrase. Though no stranger than my own, I suppose, remembering how I ate the doctor's whole jar of jelly beans as she talked me through the news. I left the black ones lined up on her table in a neat row.

Jas keeps standing. 'You're joking.'

'Sit down,' I say. 'It's all over. For now, anyway.'

'What kind? When?'

'Hodgkin's,' I say. 'In my lymph glands.' I bring my hands up to my neck. 'I found out about a year and a half ago.'

'It's all over? You said it's all over. You're OK now?'

I nod. 'I'm in remission, anyway.'

His hands are skittering all over the table. Picking things up, putting things down. 'What's that mean? It's gone? Not coming back? What?'

'It means I'm fine for the time being.'

'It won't come back again, right?'

'It doesn't for lots of people. I'm planning on being one of them.'

'Jesus, Charlie. Why didn't you tell me? Why didn't you call?'

I roll my eyes. 'I was hardly going to call out of the blue and say "Guess what, I've got cancer. Want to be friends again now I'm sick?" was I? Why should it change anything? And what could you have done anyway? You're hardly ever in the country.'

'But I called. Kept calling…'

I sigh. 'I know. I just couldn't call back. I didn't want you of all people coming around with flowers, or something, and feeling sorry for me. It was bad enough feeling sorry for myself through it all without having to deal with everybody else's grief too. It wasn't just you—I let all my friends go. It was selfish, but I had to be like that. It was the only thing that worked for me at the time.'

'Jesus.' Jas is genuinely shocked. He's gone quite pale, which makes the red mark on his cheek seem even more distinct. 'First your mum and then… Man. All the time—all the things you've said this trip. You were talking about you. I thought you were talking about her.'

'What do you mean?'

'That's why you're different. It's not her. It's you. The thing you said about fate. And when you got angry at me for wasting my life. Being Zamiel. Throwing my life away. I thought you were thinking of her. But it was you.'

I nod and get up and fetch him some ice, wrapping it in one of the washcloths from the bathroom. While I'm moving around Jas sits in silence. I suppose he's digesting everything I've just laid on him, poor thing.

'Why didn't you tell me? When we met up on the plane?'

I shrug. 'What was the point? It's over. And you're just going to go back to…wherever. And I'm going to go home. It would have spoiled things. I wanted us to have a good time.'

'But it would have explained everything. Like you not having finished uni. What was I supposed to think about that?'

'I know. You must've thought I was a pretty sad specimen. Not having finished one subject in two years. That's a record, even for me.' Done wrapping the ice, I press it on to Jas's cheek and he brings one hand up to hold it in place, still not looking at me, still staring at the table.

I decide it's time to change the topic before he goes into a catatonic state. I know how this initial conversation goes if you don't break it off and give them time to think. Usually round and round in circles. 'Anyway, that's what I've been doing with my life,' I say quickly and, before Jas can ask anything else, pick up the mobile phone from the table. 'So, are you going to share too? When are you going to tell me what this is all about?'

'What?'

'You know what. All the messages. You're not on holiday, Jas, are you? What's the deal with this Zed guy?'

'OK…' Jas starts, but then a knock on the door interrupts him.

Being closer, I get up and go over to see who it is.

As soon as I do, I'm blinded by the flashes from what feels like a hundred cameras. Someone starts yelling and then other people join in. I hear my name and look up, and the cameras are off again. Someone else sticks their foot in the door as I shield my eyes, and at the same time the phone starts ringing.

Jas races over to me then. He kicks the foot out of the doorway before slamming it shut and bolting it. I run blindly over to the phone, which is still ringing, and pick it up. It's the front desk, babbling about how it's not their fault all these people are at the door. They keep on and on and eventually I have to hang up, because what they're saying isn't making any sense to me.

'What?' is all I can say as I rub my eyes.

He slams one hand against the wall as he walks back over from the door. 'I'm going to kill that little bitch,' he says.

'Who?'

'Karen, or Sharon, or whatever her stupid name is. She's gone straight out and blabbed to the media, the cow, just like I told you she would.' He looks around quickly, then comes over and grabs me by the shoulder. 'Right. Pull some clothes on and grab some stuff. Not everything. Just stuff for tonight.'

'Why?' I hold my shoulder.

'Sorry.' He rubs it. 'Didn't mean to be rough. Just do it. We've got to get out of here.'

I stand there for a moment, wanting to argue that people had to find out he was here some time, that the media will eventually get tired of waiting for the door to open. But when I see Jas's face he looks serious, so I start shoving things into my backpack and pulling some pants and a shirt on all at the same time. While I'm doing this Jas picks up his small diary from the bedside table and makes a couple of calls using his mobile.

I go and grab both our toiletry bags, and by the time he's done on the phone I'm ready.

'Who'd you call?' I ask as he races around grabbing a few items of clothing and stuffing them in his own backpack.

'Called for a bodyguard.'

'What?' I stop where I am and laugh. 'A bodyguard?'

'Two, actually.'

I keep right on laughing. Bodyguards. For us. He has to be joking. 'What's this? An upscale version of the Hofbräu tent save? Do you think I'm going to get my butt pinched *en masse* again?'

He stops then, and comes over to me. 'It's for your own safety, Charlie. There's been a few death threats lately.'

I quit laughing. 'What? Someone's trying to kill you?'

He shrugs. 'Threatening to, anyway.'

I grab one of his arms and shake it hard. 'Jas! You're saying that like it's normal. Like it's an everyday thing!'

'It is in this line of business. Listen, I need you to take this seriously. Here.' He lifts his shirt up his arm and points out a spot that doesn't need to be pointed out. There's a gash that runs about fifteen centimetres straight across, and I can see where the stitches have been. 'That's from one of my little fans. At a concert.'

'But you said you'd cut it surfing.'

Another shrug.

'Holy shit, Jas.'

'Apparently the guy wasn't aiming for my arm. More like my chest. I just happened to move at the last moment.' He pulls his shirt back down then, and reaches out to hold onto both my shoulders. 'So, when we get out of here, you do whatever those bodyguards tell you to do. All right? I'm really not joking. It's one thing for them to go for me, another thing completely if it's you.'

'OK. OK. I will.' I nod.

'Promise?'

Shit, yes, I think. I don't want to get stabbed. I'm not going to martyr myself and die being known as the bride of Satan or something. 'I promise.'

'Good.' Jas gives me a quick hug. 'You'll be fine. Don't worry.' He rushes off into the bathroom.

Don't worry? I watch him go. Um, hello? How can I *not* worry? The question begging to be asked is how Jas was stabbed at a concert with, presumably, security everywhere. But I don't ask it. I don't want to know.

'Where's my damn…?' I hear from the bathroom.

I wake up. 'I've got it. Your toiletry bag. I've got it.'

'Great—thanks.' He comes out of the bathroom zipping up his backpack. 'OK, then. You ready?' Jas says.

I nod.

'Just have to wait for Michael and the other guy,' he says, and sits down on the bed. 'Shouldn't be long. We're lucky we're in town. Come and take a seat.' He pats the mattress.

I go and sit down.

'You're shaking.'

I turn and look at him. 'What do you expect? I'm frigging scared out of my mind! And it's not helping that you're on a first name basis with one of the bodyguards.'

'He's good. I've used him before. You'll be with him— I've arranged it. Don't know the other guy, but I trust Michael…'

…with my life? I finish Jas's sentence in my head. Oh, great. That makes me feel better. And I must look like I'm starting to lose it at this point, because Jas forces me to take a few deep breaths. Then we sit and wait for five or ten minutes in almost complete silence, bar for the noise leaking in from the hallway.

There's a knock on the door after a while. A funny knock.

'That's them.' Jas gives me a hand up. 'Don't worry, it'll be fine. Just do whatever they tell you to do. Without question. And right away.'

Oh, that'll work out swell. Generally, doing what others tell me to do without question and right away isn't one of my fortes. I wish I'd had more practice now.

Jas puts his backpack on and makes sure mine's on too before we go over and stand right beside the door. He opens it a crack and I can just see out. There are two big guys out there. And I mean *big* guys. So big I can't see past them to what's going on.

The flashes start going off again as soon as the door twitches open.

And then, before I can even wonder how all these people got here so fast, I'm being pushed out into the corridor with Jas, the two bodyguards forming a shield around us.

The flashes start up for real then. People begin yelling too. Yelling 'Zamiel!' and 'Jasper!'—whichever will get his attention.

There's a grab here and there. Someone pulling on my jacket. Someone else pulling on my pants.

I hear my name once or twice, but I don't look.

And it's not fun.

Not that I'd thought it would be, but I've seen people do this on TV and never really thought twice about it. No, it's not fun at all.

It's just plain scary.

The bodyguards ferry us down the hall with a lot of pushing and shoving. Finally we get to the end of the corridor. We don't take the stairs as I thought we would. Instead a lift door opens up and we get in. It's not the normal lift; we're down at the wrong end of the corridor for that. It must be the service lift, I think, breathing a sigh of relief as I look around me. And I've never been so grateful to be somewhere so grotty, I decide as I note the padded walls and dirty floor. I'm standing on a lettuce leaf.

Jas is right. It's not exactly the glamorous life people think it is.

He squeezes my hand as he talks to the two bodyguards about our plans. I can't seem to concentrate hard enough to listen, however. My head is making this funny buzzing sound and I start to realise that I might not be feeling quite as well as I thought I was. I start praying that I'm not going to faint and that the fruit toast isn't going to make a star appearance and end up on top of the lettuce leaf.

'You all right?' One of the bodyguards stops talking and grabs one of my arms as I sway a bit. I guess he must be Michael, as he was the one who lifted me off the ground by the seat of my pants when I stumbled upstairs. Not the most ladylike look.

'Charlie?' Jas is looking at me. 'You're a bit pale. You want to sit down?'

Everyone's looking at me now.

'I'm OK,' I say, hoping that I will be.

Jas turns to the bodyguards then. 'She's been sick. She's had cancer,' he whispers.

I give him a punch then, suddenly forgetting that I don't feel so hot. What does he think he's doing? 'Hey, I'm not deaf. And you don't go around telling people that, you idiot!'

'Why not?'

'Because it's private, that's why!'

'Right. Sorry.' He makes his old Bad-Jas face at me.

'You damn well—'

'OK, this is us,' the other bodyguard butts in, holding the doors closed. 'The car's parked right out in front of the lift. You guys'll be in the back.'

I check the lift's display to see what floor we're on. We're in the car park. The second level.

And with that the lift doors open and we're off again.

There are more people down here, even though we're in the car park. They're surrounding the car, and the second bodyguard pushes one or two of them away so he can open the door and let us in the back seat of the black Mercedes.

Michael puts a hand on my head and pushes me in first, then Jas, then clambers in himself. The other guy goes around and gets into the passenger seat. There's already a third guy, a driver, in the car.

The doors slam and lock, and almost instantly the car makes a sharp right and screeches off.

I start to wonder if the screeching thing is really necessary, or if it's just for show, but then remember Jas's stab wound and think better of asking. Instead I put my seat belt on. Something tells me I'm going to need it.

When I've got it safely clicked in place, I start to have a look around as we climb the car park levels. Everyone's wearing black. The bodyguards, the driver, Jas. Not me, however. I have dressed for this experience without much thought, apparently. Instead of wearing the compulsory black, I've donned a fuchsia-pink top, the same old black stretch pants and, of all things, a daffodil-yellow puffy jacket that just screams 'Hey, stab me, baby. I'm over here!' I think of Jas's arm and realise I may as well have a target drawn on my back, displaying each and every vital organ for easy reference.

The car screeches as we go around another bend and I glance from one bodyguard to the other. I don't know about them, but this is hardly my idea of incognito. I mean, if you want people to notice you, probably the best way to go about it is to wear black and dark sunglasses and speed around with two hefty guys and a driver who are wired and wearing black too, in a black Mercedes.

I look at Jas to see if he's enjoying this or not. He doesn't seem to be. But he doesn't seem worried, either. He's leaning forward now with his arms resting on the two front seats, talking to the driver and the other bodyguard. Making plans, I think. It looks like a day at the office more than anything. He turns to me, 'Feeling better? It'll all be over soon.'

Just as he says the words we screech around another corner and my stomach does a little hop sideways. 'Sort of.' I want to nag him to sit back and put his seat belt on, but I don't. If he does this kind of thing all the time and has only got one scar to show for it Jas is probably invincible—he doesn't need my help. I stop worrying about him and lean my head back against the seat so I can concentrate on not needing a sick bag. I'm doubting the three stooges have one. They don't look like the mothering kind.

'We'll be out in just a moment,' the driver says, and Jas sits back in his seat.

'Ready to get down?' he says to me.

'What?' I don't think he wants to boogie.

'Want your auntie Kath to see you in the paper tomorrow?' Jas grins.

This wakes me up. 'No!' Kath would be on the first flight over, the twins strapped to her back, looking forward to throttling me personally with her bare hands if she knew I was speeding around Germany in a black Mercedes with two bodyguards, a driver and a guy with a stab wound.

Michael pulls me down onto Jas's lap, my nose in his crotch, of all places, and I don't protest.

I stay down there for a minute or so, but I can still see the flashes—which makes me think people must be holding their cameras up to the car. We wait for a moment or two. For lights to change? I'm not sure, as I can't see. And then, with another screech of the tyres, we pull out and Michael lifts me up again.

'No wonder you want out,' I say to Jas, glancing out of the window before turning back to him. 'This job must be costing you a fortune in tyres.'

'Funny.'

'Where are we going now?' I try instead.

'Michael's just arranging a car and a hotel for us.'

I look over at Michael, who's on his mobile, but speaking German now. 'Then what?'

'Then,' Jas says, with a sparkle in his eye, 'we're going for a drive.'

A drive sounds fine. It's the sparkle in his eye I'm worried about. 'What kind of a drive?'

'You'll see.' He goes to lean forward again, but I pull him back this time.

'Put your seat belt on,' I say in my best mother voice.

He laughs. 'OK.' And he does as he's told, but then leans forward again anyway.

We go around another corner and I take a deep breath, a gulp, and lean back once more to concentrate on not being sick.

Chapter Twenty

Finally, after what seems like a tyre-screeching eternity, we pull up outside some kind of a car yard.

'Stay here,' Jas says as he and the bodyguard in the front seat get out of the car.

'Yes, sir!' I salute and push the button to wind the window down. It doesn't work. I go to open the door, but the driver tells me not to and turns the air-conditioning up instead.

Usually I'd put up a fight, but I'm starting to feel a whole lot better now the car's stopped moving and I think that, if I'm quiet, my stomach might toughen up and return that bit closer to normal. I pray for Jas to hurry back so we can ditch the guys in black, who are starting to freak me out. I haven't had someone tell me the windows and doors on a car are a no-no since I was a child, and frankly I'm not enjoying their company all that much.

Michael swivels sideways on the back seat to face me. 'So, you had cancer?'

Oh, great. Thanks Jas. 'Mmmm,' I say non-committally.

'My dad's got cancer. Prostate. Pretty nasty.'

That's lovely, I think. What is this? Some kind of a club? I don't even have a prostate.

'What sort did you have?'

'Hodgkin's.'

'That sounds pretty bad.'

No, I think. It was a dream. A piece of cake. I love a good dose of chemo in the morning. 'Mmmm,' I say again, not really wanting to continue the conversation any further, because I know from experience that if I do I'll get all the details of his father's prostate. It's bad enough having cancer yourself without having to hear about everyone else's. Especially when it concerns a prostate that isn't even related to you.

Jas comes back towards the car then and I open my door, grateful for his timing. He swings a key out in front of him. 'No surprise what I've got,' he says, his eyes swivelling past me to Michael.

'What have you got?' I say quickly.

Michael chuckles.

Uh-oh.

I scoot across the seat and get out of the car. 'Why is this worrying me on so many levels?'

'Don't worry. It's just Michael having a bit of fun. Bit of a running joke. And, er, before you see the car, I just want to say I'm not as crap a driver as I used to be. I took some defensive driving lessons a year or so ago.'

'Well, that's something. Hopefully they covered how not to drive off bridges.' Jas had actually done that—written off a car by driving it off a bridge into a creek, *Starsky and Hutch*-style. Not a big bridge, or a river, but still…

'Covered that in the first lesson,' he says sarcastically. 'Guess which car it is?'

Jas swivels me around so I can see a line-up of about twenty vehicles. My eyes search around desperately for a Volvo, but there isn't one. I don't know if any of the others have that side impact protection thing going for them, so I pick out the safest-looking one—the one I'd be happiest to let Jas drive if I was his bodyguard. My choice is a new sedan, a standard sort of family car that looks as if it'd be happy doing quite fast speeds, but not quite as fast as the red Porsche sitting next to it.

'That one?' I try hopefully, but something is telling me it probably isn't.

Jas snorts. 'I wish.'

The rest of the cars are all sporty and reasonably similar. I close my eyes. 'Just tell me it's not the red Porsche.' If there's one thing in this life I hate, it's men in red Porsches.

'It's not the red Porsche,' Jas says, and I open my eyes again. He's grinning. 'It's the *yellow* Porsche. Michael always picks the yellow Porsche.'

I stare at it. 'Why?' After all, it's kind of 'out there', as cars go. It's practically neon.

'Says it'll be easier to keep an eye on me as I float downstream.'

I'd laugh if I thought this wasn't partially the truth. 'Why can't we just have a normal car?' I mean, my retinas practically burned through when I set eyes on the thing.

'That's always my question. But, hey, look on the bright side—it matches your jacket.'

I watch Jas in silence as he walks off to grab our backpacks. The car matches my jacket? What is that about? 'I'm not some floozie who matches her Porsche to her jacket, you know,' I yell.

He just waves a hand at me from the back seat of the Mercedes and I trot over sulkily to join him.

Jas is having a laugh with Michael when I get there. 'I bet James Bond's bodyguard never picks the yellow Porsche,' he says.

Michael guffaws when he hears this. 'James Bond doesn't *need* a bodyguard.'

'Ah. Got me there.' Jas makes a face. 'Thanks, guys. A pleasure, as always.' He shakes their hands.

I smile at the three of them. 'Thanks.'

'Good luck with the cancer.' Michael points a finger at me.

My smile tightens. 'Yeah.'

A few minutes later we're sitting in the Porsche, waiting for Jas to stop stalling it so we can get going. 'I guess they should have thrown in a course on Porsche-driving and maintenance with your recording contract,' I say, just as he finally gets the car moving and we head out onto the street.

'No talking till we get out of the city,' Jas says. 'I hate driving on the right.'

I stop talking immediately, remembering the bridge and noting that my yellow outerwear, while it might resemble a life-jacket, won't help much as a flotation device.

'I was joking. About the not talking,' he says after a while. 'Don't you want to know where we're going?'

'Not if it's going to be underwater.'

'I'm not that bad.'

There's a shocking noise as he changes gear.

'Or up a telephone pole,' I add as we veer a little too close to the side of the road.

'I'm not going to take us up a telephone pole.'

'Promise?'

'Promise.'

That's a relief. I look out of the window and am surprised, once again, at how low I am to the ground. At least if we hit a telephone pole the pole will probably just fall over, I think. The car, being as flat as a pancake, just couldn't pull off a stunt like running halfway up one. 'So, where are we going?'

'We, my friend, are going to hit the castles road.'

'What's that?' I don't like the talk of 'hitting' anything very much.

'A road with castles along it. Know someone who went there on their honeymoon and reckoned it was fantastic. Apparently the castles are dotted all the way along the road—just like McDonald's.'

'What a quaint description.'

'Is for him.'

'I won't ask,' I say with a sigh. It'll be another of the black leather crowd, for sure.

'You'll love where we're staying. I've seen the photos. Amazing. A proper castle. Fortress and everything.'

I pause. 'But can you get a Big Mac and a chocolate sundae with extra topping?'

Jas laughs. 'Probably. They've improved these places since the castles of yore, you know.'

'How so?'

'Let's see. Central heating, indoor plumbing and indoor pools for a start…'

'They didn't have those in the thirteen-hundreds?' I turn to Jas wide-eyed.

'Plenty of boiling oil, though. You notice how you just can't get good boiling oil these days?'

'It's a problem.' I laugh.

We're out of the city soon enough, and I stop being so worried about Jas's driving technique. The traffic on the roads isn't heavy at all, but there are still too many cars for Jas to do whatever speed the car will let him. I start to feel something bordering on comfortable.

And even though we've now finished fleeing, and I desperately want to carry on our conversation from where we were so rudely cut off an hour or two ago, I can't help but start to nod off. There's just something about buses and cars and—oh, anywhere really—that sends me to sleep.

Jas wakes me up a while later.

'Charlie?' He pats me on the shoulder.

I sit straight up on my seat. 'Hands on the wheel! Hands on the wheel!'

'All right, all right.'

I take a look at what Jas is pointing out then. It's a castle. A big one. Quite a long way in the distance, but unmistakable with its high tower. I notice something else then too. The scenery. 'It's so green.' And it is. So very, very green. It's like a postcard—not something you should be seeing in real life. 'I think I should put my dirndl back on,' I say to Jas.

He turns to me for a moment.

'Look at the road! Look at the road!'

He looks at the road. 'You packed your dirndl?'

'Well, no. I was joking about that.'

'Yeah?' He sounds disappointed.

'What's the matter? You didn't get a close enough look at the wood yesterday?'

This is supposed to be funny, but all it does is remind us both of last night. And I don't know quite what to think about that at the moment—what it means, or where we go from here. I feel I should return to my 'we can't just be friends' speech that I was going to hit Jas with after we returned from funky karaoke, but somehow that doesn't seem right now.

He was going to tell me something back there at the hotel, though, before we were so rudely interrupted. Something big. And I want to turn around and ask him what it was, but I know Jas—he'll tell me when he's ready. In his own time. So I lean my head back down against the window and try to fall asleep again, ignoring the butterflies in my stomach that I know aren't from the schnapps episode.

I fall asleep again quite easily. I guess I'm not exactly one of those people who stays up worrying every night. I don't have it in me.

The next time I wake up it's getting dark outside. I lift my head up and peer out of my window. 'Are we almost there?'

'Not far. Next exit, I think.'

'Hungry?' When I'm not sleeping, I'm thinking about my stomach. And right now it seems to be back on track and clamouring for some food.

'Very,' Jas says as we take the exit off the freeway. 'Restaurant's supposed to be great.'

'No comparisons to McDonald's this time, I hope.'

'Don't think so.'

'Then count me in. Entrée, main and dessert.'

'Coffee and port?' He glances over at me.

'I think I might be able to squeeze it in.' I laugh. 'Now that my stomach and I are getting along again.' I check my watch. It's eight-fifteen p.m. 'Do you think the restaurant will be open late enough?'

'We're in Europe now. They eat dinner in the middle of the night, remember? Not like you English.'

'Hey, I never ate my dinner at five-thirty in the afternoon, like my grandparents. It's too weird.'

Jas takes a quick look out of his window. 'OK. From what the guy told me, it should be a left, then second right.'

'I hope he's right. I don't think we have an A-Z. And if we did it'd be in German.'

'I listened carefully, believe me. Don't want to get stuck out in the forest overnight.'

'What—scared of the bears?'

Jas pauses. 'Hell, yes. They're tough, German bears. Do you over for a yellow Porsche and a dirndl soon as look at you.' He takes a left. And then, after a few minutes, the second right. 'Here we…'

The rest of the sentence is lost as we stare in awe at the castle lit up on the hill. It's tall—all stone and red roof with a high, round tower on the right. And it's not one building, as I expected, but three or four.

Granny flats?

I guess you'd pick up a few spare rellies here and there over the centuries. Great-Aunt Gertrudes and the like.

Jas changes gear and we make our way up the hill. I start to see the benefits of the Porsche. It doesn't exactly chug-chug up the incline, if you get what I mean. Maybe I'll pick one up for myself when I buy my first castle.

Jas drops me and our bags off at the front, where the reception sign is, and goes to park the car. Before he comes back I get a moment or two to look around me. It's too beautiful. I had no idea you could stay in places like this—in a real castle. I go over to inspect one of the carved stone walls.

'Ready?' Jas runs over.

I nod, and as we head inside I start to get worried about how much this is going to cost. But all those kinds of thoughts are whisked away as soon as I see the castle interior. The entry's just as stunning as I imagined it to be. All wood panelling with an authentic musty smell.

None of those fake-castle-scented smelly plug-in-the-wall things here. This is the real deal.

We go over to the reception desk, where there's an awkward moment or two as Jas and I have to decide whether to take a double or two singles. But the man on Reception offers a suite with two double beds and we're saved. I start to worry if my credit card can take this kind of damage. I mean, a suite? In this place? I don't think my bank holds me in that kind of esteem.

Jas must see the expression on my face. 'Don't worry about it,' he says, pulling out a different credit card from the one he normally uses. 'This one's on work.'

'How're you going to get away with that?' I ask.

'I'll try smiling sweetly at the accountant.' He smiles in what he must think is a sweet way.

'You look demented.'

'I said I'd *try*. Anyway, don't worry about it. I owe you for getting you messed up in this. Big time,' he says as he hands the card over.

When all the details have been sorted out, a young boy offers to take our bags to our room. It hardly seems worth him carrying the two badly packed backpacks, so we take them ourselves. Niklas—or at least that's what his name badge says—still guides us up to our room, however. It's up quite a number of stone steps, and along a corridor that seems to go on for ever. By the time we actually get there I'm not surprised they have to send someone with you.

Inside, the room is huge, with white walls and wooden beams everywhere. In the middle are two gigantic four-poster beds carved out of wood, complete with curtains surrounding the sides. There's a sofa and, against the stone wall down at the end of the room, a little table and two chairs set up against the window so you can look out at the garden.

It's gorgeous.

Jas closes the door behind us. 'Not bad, huh?' he says. 'Told you it'd be nice.'

I dump my bag on the floor beside one of the beds, too nervous to put it on the bed itself—who knows how old it is?

Jas dumps his bag on the bed, however, ruffling up the counterpane in the process. I give him a withering look.

'What?' he says.

'Nothing.' I sit down carefully on the covers, almost having a heart attack when the bed creaks. It'd be just like me to break something hundreds of years old. Something with a great history, that's been sitting in here for centuries being used by all kinds of famous people, and then Charlie from Australia comes along. And that's it. The end of its working life. I'm going to have to be extra careful, because something tells me that breaking something in here would cost just a fraction more than stealing a ninety-dollar 'it'll turn up on your VISA statement next month' bathrobe from a Hilton.

I lie down on my back. 'So…'

'So…' Jas comes and sit down beside me. 'Guess I have some explaining to do.'

I nod.

He breathes out slowly before he replies. 'Man. I can't believe you spoke to Zed. Can't believe you spoke to Zed and both your eardrums are still intact.'

'Only just.'

'So…er, how did you know? That I'm AWOL, I mean?'

I snort. 'Most people on holiday don't freak out when the phone rings. They don't speak about their job in the past tense. And they don't spend a lot of time talking feverishly in their sleep about their manager coming to—and I quote—"rip their balls off".'

'Ah, you didn't tell me about that.'

'No. So, no more Zamiel?'

Jas nods. 'No more Zamiel.'

'I thought as much. All that moaning and groaning about your job. And when you went psycho about the balloon with Zamiel on it and the plastic figurines, well, things started to fit together a bit.'

'Really?' He looks surprised.

'That and the fact you seemed so weirded out that someone might spot you—like Sharon. It was more than just worrying about the media. People must spot you all the time, after all. So what's the deal? What made you want to pack it all in?'

Jas shrugs. 'Pretty simple, I guess. I hate my job. I hate my life. I'm tired of pretending I'm gay or bisexual or something, when I'm not, that I eat live animals, that I have sex with animals, that I worship the devil and all that kind of…'

I push myself up when I hear this. And then I freeze. My heart stops. I don't breathe. I can't blink. The second half of Jas's sentence passes me by in slow motion and, as if my brain is a VCR, I start rewinding and playing the important bits from the first half of the sentence. Editing here and there as I go.

I'm tired of pretending I'm gay.

I'm tired of pretending I'm bisexual.

I'm tired of pretending I'm gay or bisexual.

'Charlie? What's the matter? You going to be sick again?' I hear Jas say from far, far away.

Things start to go fuzzy around the edges of my vision.

'Charlie?' Jas grabs my arm. 'You sat up too fast. Lie down again.' He pushes me back down on the bed.

I groan after a minute or two.

'You all right? Looked like you were going to faint.'

I'm surprised at this. At almost fainting. I've never done

that before. How…Victorian. I unfreeze. 'What did you just say? About your job?' Maybe I was imagining things.

He looks at me strangely. 'Said I hate my job.'

'What else?'

'Er, and my life. I hate pretending I'm gay or bisexual or something, when I'm not, and I—'

I hold up my hand when he gets to the important bit. 'That's what I thought you said. Don't worry about me. I just need to lie here for a minute or two.'

Jas frowns, worried, but when I've convinced him I'm OK, and that I just need a moment, he walks over to the window and leaves me alone to start some serious internal swearing.

After a few minutes I sit up. 'I think I'll feel better if I get some food into me,' I say. 'How about dinner?'

'Er, you go down. I'd better call Zed first. Guilt's getting to me.'

I make a face. 'Going to get an earful, are you?' Zed had given me one that left my ears ringing.

'Get and give some back, I think.'

This doesn't sound like much fun. 'I'll wait for you down-stairs,' I say, standing up. I'm sure that Jas doesn't want me listening in. 'I'll be at the bar.'

'Have one for me.'

I shudder at the thought of alcohol. 'I think it may just be orange juice.' I'm in the throes of that old 'I'm never drinking again' stage.

'Right. I'll be down soon.'

'Good luck.' I close the door behind me.

I only get lost three times before I find the bar. It's on the same floor as Reception, tucked away in a cosy nook beside the restaurant. I'm soon ensconced by the lovely stone walls and dark beams and sit sipping my orange juice, feeling very, very safe, as if everything will be all right so long as I stay behind the castle's defences.

Which reminds me. I'd better call Kath and Mark later, before they find I'm missing somewhere in Europe and both have aneurysms.

I have to say I'm glad that they gave me this trip. That they knew me well enough to figure out that every time I talked about booking myself a holiday I was a big fat liar and it was never going to happen. Or that Mum knew me well enough. I smile then. Even from the grave she knows what's best for me. That's mothers for you.

Looking back now, I can see I was just plain scared. I'm surprised I even got on the plane, to tell the truth, but Kath and Mark were smart. The whole giving me the ticket the night before the actual trip thing was a stroke of genius— that way I didn't have any time to panic. It was simply a matter of packing, checking and double-checking, and before I could triple-check—or check my glands for the millionth time—I was in London.

I could never have done it myself. Gone into the travel agent, picked a destination, picked a date. It just wasn't on the cards because, like I said before, I was scared. Scared to leave the safety of the hospital that was only ten minutes' drive away. Scared to leave my doctors. Scared that everything would fall apart if I really tried to get on with my life. But now here I am, in Germany, in a castle of all places.

I've been putting off this trip for months for absolutely no reason.

Putting off getting on with my life.

And right now I feel fine. Sort of. Well, close to normal, anyway. I've been stupid—checking my glands every time I cough, every time I get a tiny bit cold. If Jas noticed I was freaking out about getting sick, imagine how many other people in my life had? Kath and Mark must think I'm a complete nutter—no wonder they wanted me to get away from it all. I haven't touched my glands for more than forty-eight hours now, and I'm going to keep it that way. I'm going to set a new record.

It seems I've been learning all kinds of new things on this trip. About me. And, surprisingly, about Jas. I can't believe what I just heard. Jas isn't gay. He isn't bi. For a moment I worry I've missed something, and that there's another option besides him being heterosexual. I don't think so. And, the truth is, knowing this freaks me out. What does the worst sex in my life mean, if this is the case? And what was That Night about?

'I'm done,' a voice says behind me. 'In several senses of the word.'

I swivel around on my bar stool. 'That was quick.'

'Quick. Not painless.'

'Was it that bad?'

'Let's just say I'm glad we're both in different countries.' He takes a seat on the next stool.

'So that's it?'

He nods. 'No more Zamiel. He's dead. Couldn't happen to a nicer person.'

'He's probably pleased.' I pat Jas on the arm. 'Just think about it this way—he's with the devil now.'

Jas laughs.

Watching him, I see that his laugh this time is different. Speaking to Zed has obviously taken a weight off his mind, and for the first time this trip he seems truly relaxed. As I look at him, I'm reminded again of last night. But it's not the worst sex in the world that I recall, but the almost tangible electricity that passed between us even before we grabbed each other in the corridor of Atomika. I remember Jas leaning against my leg. His holding the cherry schnapps to my lips. I think back even further. To Magnolia Lodge. To the boat shed. And I realise the events of the past two years have changed nothing.

I am still completely, desperately, totally, devotedly, idiotically in love with Jasper Ash.

'Charlie?' Jas is shaking my arm gently.

'Leather pants,' I say dreamily.

'What?'

My head jerks back. Oh, no. Did I say that out loud? 'Um...' My fingers grip the bar. 'I was just, um, wondering if you'd have to give all your leather pants back?'

All I get is an odd look in return.

After Jas has a beer we move into the small restaurant, just a few steps away.

There aren't many people in here tonight, and only a few tables are filled out of the twenty or so that are set. Despite this, it's still just as cosy as the bar, and there's a lovely log fire crackling away in the corner that lights up the stained glass windows set in the stonework. As soon as we're left alone I get nervous. The talk's coming—the thing he didn't get to say before. I can feel it.

Thankfully, the waiter brings us two menus. This distracts us and we both open them greedily.

'I think I'm going to be leaving here a lot fatter.' I look up at Jas as I read what's on offer.

'Me too. Good thing those leather pants stretch, huh?' He lifts an eyebrow over the top of his menu.

I raise mine to cover my face. I have *got* to stop with the leather pants thing.

A few minutes later I've got it all worked out. 'I'm going

for the schnitzel with the sunnyside-up egg, gravy, potato salad and salad.'

'Sounds good.' Jas puts his menu down as well. 'Want to share some of the smoked liver pâté to start?'

'Why ever not?' I don't see how I'm going to fit everything in, but I can only try.

The waiter, who I don't think has too much to do at this time of year, is beside us in a matter of seconds.

Jas orders for us both. 'Might get some of those dumplings too,' he adds as the waiter leaves.

'You'll be as big as a house if you eat all that and don't get to jump around on stage any more.'

'Rubbish. I'm a growing lad. Anyway, you *need* fattening up.'

Oh, sure. My jeans have been getting increasingly tighter throughout this trip, and my stretch pants have been stretching in directions they were never designed to.

Jas's eyes narrow. 'You do. You've got little stick arms, Charlie. So, are you going to tell me all about this cancer thing? Or do I have to pry it out of you?'

'What do you want to know?' I toy with my fork. I've been there, done that, and while I didn't get a T-shirt I have the scars to show for it instead.

People don't understand when I tell them I don't feel like discussing my having had cancer in great detail any more, but the fact is I'm trying to stop thinking about it so much. Not in a bad way, I don't want to forget it happened, but it feels like a chapter that's coming to a close in my life. Like when you finish school, or university, and you think things will never be the same again, but finally you move, get a job and start developing new ways, make new friends, and forget about your old life. It's time to move forward. That was part of the reason I was reluctant to tell Jas what I'd been through—because for me it's all finished. I just want to live a normal life again.

'Tell me everything. From the start. When did you find out?'

So I tell the story one more time.

'OK. I first felt the lump on my neck about a year and a half ago, I suppose…' I start. I tell Jas about how, when the lump didn't go away, I went to see my GP. Then I tell him about the tests. *All* the tests—the ultrasound, the chest X-ray, the blood test, the CT scan, the bone marrow biopsy. I also tell him about the new hobby I picked up—collecting doctors. I had a radiation oncologist, a haematologist…the whole bit.

'I liked the radiation oncologist the best, because he was able to explain things so well. It wasn't until I got to him that I really understood what I was in for. He sat me down and told me what I had was around ninety-five per cent curable. But then he told me all the problems that could come with the treatment—that it could make me sterile and I could have a higher risk of developing other cancers and heart disease. He was great, though. I really liked that guy—he didn't sugar-coat things. I knew he was the one for me when he used the "C" word. Everyone else had been too scared to.'

Jas pipes up then. 'The "c" word?'

I see the expression on his face and shake my head. 'Not that "c" word, you dolt. The big C. Cancer. Get your mind out of the gutter for a second.'

'Right. Of course. Sorry. So what happened after that?'

I continue my story, taking him through my first chemo treatment. I tell him how I remember clear as day watching the first syringe of medication being pumped into my arm and wondering if I was doing the right thing.

'And that was the stuff that messed with your hair? Why you had to cut it off?'

I laugh. 'I didn't exactly get it cut. It was the cheapest new do ever. It just fell out. Everywhere. Big handfuls of it—mostly in the shower.'

Our pâté comes then, and we both start digging in ravenously.

'And the drugs?' Jas asks. 'Did they make you really sick?'

'I felt tired, and I desperately wanted to throw up all the time, but with all the anti-nausea medication I'd taken I couldn't. The only way I can describe it is like having every flu you've ever been through at once. I was exhausted even when I was sleeping twenty hours a day, and I completely lost my appetite. Even thinking about food made me want to be sick.'

'That when you lost all the weight?' Jas asks, handing me another piece of bread and pâté.

I take it and nod.

He pauses. 'I can't believe I didn't know. When I saw you on the plane.'

I stop eating. 'Know? That I'd had cancer? Why should you know? I don't have a sign on my back or anything, do I? "Beware of the cancerous girl."'

'Don't joke about it like that.'

'Why not?'

Jas doesn't say anything, but I know what he's on about it. I've recently discovered cancer's some kind of sacred thing in our society. It's taboo. You're not supposed to talk about it, let alone joke about it. 'I'm no different from how I was before, you know.'

He looks at me. 'You are.'

I pause and think about this for a moment or two before I reply. 'I guess from my point of view *things* have changed—

I mean, sometimes the way I do things or approach things is different from before. But I'm still *me*. I feel the same. I still laugh at the same things. I still like the same things. I really don't see things all that differently than I used to, but still, in some ways, I do. It's hard to explain. Maybe it's easier for other people to see.'

'Maybe. I see it. So you finished the chemo and then had the, er, other one. What's it called again?'

'Radiation therapy. It was a breeze. Way easier than I'd thought—though I wasn't so happy about the tatts.'

Jas's eyes almost pop out of their sockets. 'Tatts? As in tattoos?'

'Yep. I had to get little tatts so they'd know where to zap me each time.'

'You still have them?'

I smile, thinking about how I freaked out when they told me I'd be getting a tattoo, and an ugly green-black one, like cats get when they're neutered at the pound, at that—nothing at all like a girly little bluebird or miniature heart. 'No, they've faded.'

'And that was it? The hard part was all over?'

I laugh. 'No way. The hardest part came *after* the treatment. The waiting.'

'Waiting for what?' Jas leans forward, resting his arms on the table.

'Waiting to be told whether I was in remission or not.'

'But you were. You are...right?' Jas butts in.

'Yes. Calm down. They told me in November that I was officially in remission.'

'So you could get on with your life. That was, what, nearly a year ago?'

'Almost.'

'Then why didn't you start sculpting again?'

I pause for a moment as I still don't know the answer to this question. 'I just…couldn't. I'd try, but I couldn't get started. It was kind of like the thing with the food. I wasn't interested. I wasn't able to concentrate for five minutes at a time, either. I'd been so busy up until then, focused on getting through the treatment, but when I was done with that I felt like I had nothing.'

'Nothing? You had your life back!'

I point a finger at him. 'That was exactly the problem. *Exactly* that. Everyone kept telling me that I had my life back and I must be over the moon, but I didn't feel like that. That was just how everyone *else* felt about me having cancer. Not me. You see, after I was declared in remission everyone just expected me to get on with my life. But what I, and they, didn't understand was that my life wasn't the same any more.'

'What do you mean?'

'Well, the thing was, the cancer had gone, but in some ways it was still there. I still felt like me, but it was as if everything I saw around me was different. Like I had someone else's glasses on.'

Jas seems puzzled.

'I just didn't know how to get going again. To start over. I think it's only on this trip that I've realised why—I was trying to make myself go back to doing something I'd already half given up on. I think I've spent my whole life running away from what I really want to do.'

'The sandstone? Like your mum?'

'Yep. Stupid, hey?'

Jas shakes his head. 'No. Not stupid at all.'

The waiter brings our dumplings and we tuck in.

'And now what?' Jas says, mouth full.

I take a deep breath. 'Finish *Sisters*, I guess. I'll have to learn, though. Maybe in Italy.'

'What a drag.'

I smile. 'You could say that. And then there's uni. I want to finish uni.'

'You always wanted to finish uni.'

I roll my eyes. 'This time I might try *passing*.'

There's silence for a second or two before Jas nods. 'Good. I approve.'

'Is that so?' I laugh.

But Jas doesn't join in. He puts down his fork, looking serious.

'What?' I ask.

'Er…' he says, pushing the last dumpling around his plate. 'The sterility thing —like you said before. How do you feel about that? That you mightn't be able to have kids?'

'I'll just have to wait and see what happens. I mean, what was the alternative? Not having the treatment? You can't have kids if you're dead, can you?'

He looks up and laughs then. Really laughs.

'What's so funny?' I say indignantly.

'You sound exactly like your mother.' He bites into his dumpling with gusto, looking altogether too pleased with himself.

Well, I think, I can wipe that expression off his face. 'Now,' I say, lifting my glass to him, 'your turn to spill the beans.'

Chapter Twenty-One

Over our schnitzel, then a shared piece of *apfelstrudel* and two coffees, Jas tells me the whole story.

The whole story from the start—from when he went to Sydney. How the Spawn deal he was offered out of nowhere was too good to pass up. How he knew that even though it wasn't what he really wanted to do it would give him a foot in the door of the music world—a name—something he needed to get where he really wanted to be, which was full-time songwriting. It was the opportunity of a lifetime.

But even though Spawn was hugely successful two years down the track, it wasn't enough for Jas. The in-fighting was hard enough to deal with twenty-four hours a day without hating what he was doing in the first place as well. He said that he knew he sounded ungrateful, talking about it like that, but having three-quarters of the world hate him and want him dead while the other quarter worshipped the ground he walked on was confusing—especially seeing as he himself belonged in the larger group. In the end it was

too much, becoming someone he hated day after day, someone he couldn't bear being.

And then there was the thing with Zed.

Zamiel had been getting death threats all along, but when
one person in particular started to send letters on a regular
basis after the stabbing, Jas decided it was time to up security—Zamiel just wasn't worth dying for. From then on he
stopped going to places his bodyguard didn't want him to go.
It took extra time to do things like check places out from top
to bottom. Zed wasn't happy. Spawn weren't able to meet the
commitments he wanted them to while the security was so
high. The guys in the band got in on the act, thinking Jas was
being over the top about the whole thing. Then suddenly
the letters stopped. Security was relaxed. As the threats became fewer and fewer, Jas even started going out on his own.

'But they were still coming, the threats? Zed was just hid-
ing them from you?' I say, shocked.

Jas nods. 'Coming thick and fast, apparently.'

'While you were going out on your own? And Zed
knew that?'

He shakes his head as if he still doesn't quite believe it
himself. 'Yeah, he knew all right. The guy—the one sending the threats—he knew my real name. He knew where I
stayed in every city. He knew *everything*.'

'How did you find out? That he was still sending the letters, I mean?'

'I overheard Zed last week. On the phone. Boasting how
he'd pulled it all off. The idiot. It's always how they get
caught, isn't it? Guys like him. Can't help but tell someone
how smart they are.'

'And that's when you left?' I ask, pushing my coffee cup
away, silently vowing that I'll never eat again. Or not until
breakfast, anyway.

Jas nods. 'Sounds like I ran away, or something, but it wasn't a planned thing at all. In the end it wasn't really about the death threats. I was just sitting in my hotel room, wondering if this was what I was going to do with the rest of my life, when something made me get up and pack a bag and just…go.' Jas eats the last morsel of *apfelstrudel*, drinks the last drop of his coffee and then leans back in his chair, his hands behind his head. 'It was a completely shitty thing to do to the guys, but it was going to end sooner or later anyway. The fighting was getting worse. Wouldn't have lasted more than another six months at the most.'

'Can they sue you? Did you break a contract or something?'

Jas nods. 'I broke my contract. But after what Zed's done, I don't think they'll be suing. Don't think they have a leg to stand on. Anyway, that's it. I'm done. Back to the old Jas.'

'And now what? What are you going to do job-wise?'

He smiles. 'Think I might take a leaf out of your book and do something just for me.'

'Like?'

'Not write for other people, for a start. Write for me. And see where it goes, I guess. If people like it, great. If they don't, they can bugger off.'

I nod. 'I know what you mean.' But then I pause. 'The thing is, you looked so comfortable up on stage the other night. Like you belonged. Are you sure you're going to be able to give all that away so easily?'

'It's not that I want to give it away. I love performing. It's just that next time I want it to be as me. Doing what I want to do.'

This makes sense. 'Well, I approve too,' I say with a nod, and Jas laughs.

We sit in silence for a while, I think both realising that although we've covered completely different territory since our last parting we're in the same place now, in all kinds of ways.

Basically, at the crossroads.

We look at each other for a moment or two.

I know it's time, then. Time to talk about the one thing we haven't talked about.

Us.

Jas is the one who says it first. 'Let's go back upstairs and talk.'

'Good idea.'

He motions to the waiter, asking for the bill, and the waiter brings it over, already prepared.

I take it from him. 'I'm getting this one.' I give Jas a steely glare. 'I insist.'

'All right, all right.' He looks too tired and overfed to put up much of a fight anyway.

I give the waiter my credit card and prepare to sign my life savings away. After I do, we head back up to our room silently.

When we're inside, Jas goes over and takes a seat at the little table—and, to my horror, puts his feet up on the other chair. He's taken off his shoes, but still...And he must see the look on my face, because he laughs. 'It's OK. Don't think it's thirteenth-century or anything. Probably from the late IKEA dynasty.'

I don't think so, but can't be bothered to argue. Instead, I pace around the room, inspecting something here, touching something there, not being able to keep still in my highly caffeinated, anticipatory state.

'So how do you think you'll get started? With the song-writing thing, I mean.' I say to Jas after a while.

Jas stretches and yawns. 'Already started, really.'

'What do you mean?'

'Been songwriting the whole time I've been doing the Spawn thing. Selling the odd thing here and there.'

I stop fidgeting and turn to look at him. 'Anything I'd know?'

He names four or five songs and I'm blown away. They've all been really big hits in the last year or so. Especially the last one, which has been a gigantic success for one of the boy bands.

'No way! You wrote that?' I say, going and perching near the window, only a few metres away from Jas. 'That makes me feel a whole lot better.'

'Better? Why?'

'I had it stuck in my head for about a month. It almost sent me insane.' Remembering it, I can't help but start humming a few bars of the song.

Jas joins in and starts singing the words, picking up his feet and moving them in the air—the accompanying boy band dance moves, I realise, and laugh. As he keeps on going I look at him and remember how things used to be. How things have been again during the past few days. I always feel so *good* around Jas. With his last note, I clap. Well, at least I know why I was so addicted to the song now. It was the boat shed all over again. How could I not have known he'd written it?

He takes a mock bow when I finish my round of applause. 'Hideous, isn't it?'

I shake my head. 'It's one of the better ones. That's why I liked it. It's not all that "girl, I really love you, you're the only one for me, I'd die for you" load of crap. That stuff doesn't work when it's belting out of a seventeen-year-old, does it? Not for me, anyway. I just don't buy it.'

'That's what I think too,' Jas says, sitting up a bit.

'Maybe you should try something along the lines of "girl, I really love you, or at least I'll tell you I do to get you into bed, because I'm seventeen and completely oversexed". It'd be closer to the truth.'

Jas smiles. 'Probably a whole lot closer. Something tells me I wouldn't be selling many songs like that, though. Guess I can come out of the closet about it all now, hey?'

'Oh, God.' I look away, the reference making me remember how wrong I've been about him. I feel my face turning red again.

'What?'

'I didn't say anything,' I say, a bit too fast.

'Yes, you did. You said, "Oh, God". I heard you.'

I examine the wall, tracing the grains in one of the beams with one finger. My cheeks are burning. I hate being a blusher.

There's a very long silence.

When I check back, Jas is staring straight at me. And, try as I might, I can't look away. Because I know that this is it. The thing he didn't get to say before.

'You know what?' Jas says, getting up from his chair. 'I'm tired of pretending about us. Tired of skirting around everything.' He blurts the words out.

I'd been about to say something—a nice little conversation-filler, perhaps. But this stops me in my tracks. It stops Jas too. He seems surprised he's said what he's said.

'What do you, um, mean?' I say quietly.

He gets a bit more animated then, and starts walking around the room, stopping here and there to look at me. 'Let me ask you something,' he says. 'If we're getting everything out in the open.'

Are we? I don't like the sound of this much. 'Ask me what?'

'When we met up. On the plane. When you asked me about piglet-face. There was something going on, wasn't there? Did you think…?' He stops moving now, 'Did you think I was bi or something? Did you really believe that media stuff?'

Shit. Am I *that* transparent? But then I think about what he's just asked me. He asked me if I thought he was bi. I perk up at that. 'No,' I say truthfully. After all, I thought he was gay, didn't I? Score one, Charlie!

He reads my expression. 'How about gay, then?'

Double shit.

'Ah!' He points at me and comes closer. 'I knew it. I knew it! I thought you were joking on the plane, about piglet-face, but you weren't, were you? And when you got me to repeat all that stuff before, it kinda clicked. You thought I was gay! How could you think that, Charlie?' He starts laughing.

I get defensive then. I unfreeze. 'Well, hello?' I stop holding onto the beam next to me and become more agitated, trying to get him to see my point. I think then that if someone were to see us we'd look like a couple of Mexican jumping beans, the way we're carrying on. 'How was I supposed to know you weren't gay? I mean, the pieces all fit together that way. One minute you're pushing me off you in the apartment, and the next minute I'm hearing ten different reports in the media that you're gay and seeing some guy's tongue shoved down your throat. What am I supposed to think?'

Jas just looks at me.

'Well?' I try again.

'Well, what?'

I don't know, I think, throwing my hands up in the air. 'Well, and how about all those other things you said?'

'Like what? I never said anything. Certainly never said I'm gay. Because *I'm not!*' Jas is flinging his arms around now too, trying to make his point.

'Like the thing with the gingerbread heart. You said that all the men would beat you up, or something, but then you said all the homophobes would as well.'

'What? I meant they'd *think* I was gay. Wearing a gingerbread heart and all.'

What? 'Because all gay men wear gingerbread hearts, do they?'

I get the same look back. 'Yes. With blue ribbons. It's a sign they're available. Some of them even ice on their phone numbers. Are you insane? It was a throwaway line, that's all. Now, what else? What else did you think I said?'

I pause for a moment and think back.

'OK. At funky karaoke the other night. The thing about Sharon. You said something about her not getting it. That she was thick.'

His forehead wrinkles in concentration as he thinks back. 'At funky karaoke? That? Just meant I was never going to be interested in her. And why are we calling it funky karaoke now?'

I huff. 'I don't know!' Another instance springs to mind then—one that Jas has already brought up. 'OK, and on the plane I distinctly remember you saying, "I do have *some* taste, you know. I wouldn't go out with a guy like him." Those were your *exact* words.'

Jas pauses. 'Ah. I guess that one's a little bit ambiguous.'

'Is it ever!'

'But, still, Charlie…'

'Don't say it!' As if I don't feel like an idiot enough already, now he's going to point it out to me. I take a deep breath, trying to stop feeling so tense. I feel as if I've been gripping onto something for dear life for hours. With my fingernails. I try to get a hold of myself while Jas waits for me. One more breath. 'Right. Let's just get this straight, then, shall we? Get it sorted. I didn't think I could ask, but now it seems I can, so I will. You're not gay? You're not bi? You've never been gay? You've never been bi? You never will be gay? You never will be bi?' I tick the choices off on my fingers as I go.

'OK, OK.' Jas lifts his hands in mock surrender. 'I agree. To all those things. Anything else we should get straightened out while we're at it?'

There's a long pause. Um, last night might be a good start, I think. And the other thing—the skirting around thing. The pretending about us. I wouldn't mind getting that cleared up, either. I shrug. May as well go for broke. 'What did you mean before?' I take the second option. 'About the pretending? The skirting?'

'You know.'

'No, I don't know.'

This leads into a stare-off, which Jas breaks. 'What did you think last night was about?' he says.

Triple shit. I don't know the correct answer to this one, and I can't seem to come up with a decent half-truth, so I try the real truth for once, 'I thought it was—you know— a "one show only" kind of thing. That you were just, um...drunk.'

'Jesus, Charlie!' Jas runs his hands through his hair. 'I would never do that to you. All this trip I've been wanting to...ever since I saw you on the plane. But I held off. I thought you weren't interested. You said you weren't. At Brown's. You told me you didn't feel that way about me any more.'

Oh. Whoops. 'That was just, um, something to say.'

'Something to say?'

'You kind of caught me by surprise. I didn't know how to answer!'

There's another silence. Where do we go from here? But then, from somewhere, I get an ounce of courage. All I know is I have to ask him the big question. The question I've been wanting to ask since I first saw him on the plane.

The question about That Night.

I have to ask it because I still don't know the answer to this one, do I? I mean, at first I thought I'd been rejected because Jas was gay, and I figured that those girls in the apartment had just been sexuality-testers. He'd been putting out feelers, for want of a better term.

So much for that theory.

Then, after last night and the bad sex, I figured...oh, who knows what I figured? Over the last twenty-four hours my brain hasn't been in much of a condition to figure anything. So, I come right out and say it. Blazing guns. 'The night before you left the apartment. I need you to explain...'

'I know. I know I owe you an explanation about that.' He pauses then. 'I was hoping you might have forgotten.'

'Forgotten! Not likely! You don't forget that kind of thing. It's burned on my memory. Branded. I can still hear the sizzle.'

'Yeah. I'm kinda the same on that score,' he says as he slumps down into the chair he'd been sitting in before.

He seems really embarrassed, I think, watching him. All of a sudden he can't meet my eyes. And is that...? I look more closely. I think his cheeks are turning red.

'I don't know if I can say it. It's so...'

'Embarrassing?' I finish off the sentence for him. 'Don't worry. It can't be any worse than me thinking you were gay.'

I've got dibs on embarrassment this whole trip. You're not going to come close. You couldn't even if you tried.'

'But it's a guy thing.'

A guy thing? Oh, now I get it—why he's so coy. It's a thing he shouldn't be disclosing to me, being of the opposite sex. 'Come on. You're going to have to tell me sooner or later. I promise I won't laugh.'

'OK. OK.' He sits there for a bit.

'Well?'

'Don't rush me.' He's so serious I have to try not to laugh right then and there. 'I know you're going to laugh, Charlie.' He looks up, pointing at me.

'I'm not going to laugh.'

'You are.'

I sigh.

'Just remember I was young. And impressionable.'

'All right. I'll remember you were young and impressionable. Now, out with it.'

'OK. Those girls. The ones at the apartment. I never slept with them.'

'What?' He must be joking to think I'd believe this. No wonder he thought I'd laugh. 'You are such a bad liar, Jas.'

'It's true. I never slept with any of them. When I left that apartment I was basically, you know…' he lowers his voice to a whisper '…still a virgin.'

'Oh, come on…' I'm not that gullible. There were scores of those girls. They seemed happy enough. They smiled in the morning like a litter of Cheshire cats. I look at Jas, trying to see if he's lying or not. I've lived with him long enough to know when he is and when he isn't. I realise he's not. He's not lying at all. 'Then what…?'

'…were they doing there?' Jas finishes off my sentence this time.

I nod.

'I meant to sleep with them. It just never happened.'

'But why not?'

He pauses. 'That's the embarrassing bit.'

'Sounds like it.'

Jas frowns.

'Sorry,' I say. 'Carry on.'

'Goes back quite a few years before that. To my last year of high school.'

'Right.' I urge him on, take a step closer.

'At the end of the year we'd arranged to go away. On a holiday. A week in an apartment at the beach. Schoolies week and all that.'

I nod.

'All the guys I went with—they weren't…you know…'

'Virgins?' I try. Obviously this is not a thing a guy can ever own up to, even if he's only sixteen.

Jas nods. 'I'd met this group of girls, at schoolies week, you see. Was inevitable that something would happen with one of them. But the guys I was sharing with—one night, before I went out to meet the girls, they told me something.'

'Told you something?' Where the hell is he going with this?

I get a deeper frown.

'Sorry.'

Jas takes a breath. 'They told me to watch out because sometimes it just wouldn't work…'

'What wouldn't work?'

Frown three.

'Oh. Oh!'

Jas nods. 'They sat around the living room and gave me this whole big talk about it. How it won't work and then you think about it and that makes it worse. A vicious circle. I didn't know it then, but it was essentially a practical joke.'

'And what happened? When you went out?'

'It didn't work.'

'No. God, that's a bit cruel!'

'You're telling me. Just kept right on happening after that. They completely messed with my head.'

I stand there, shocked. The kitchen girls flit into my head again. 'But those girls. They seemed pretty happy in the morning.'

Jas looks up at me and grins. 'Ah, they *were* happy.'

What?

'Could still do *other* things, you know. In fact I became a bit of an expert.'

My mouth falls open. Other things…

'I'm all right now. I, er, I saw a professional. After I moved out.'

'A sex doctor?'

Jas shakes his head slyly.

'What…?' I start. Oh. That kind of professional. As in the oldest kind of profession. And that's when I start laughing. Pissing myself laughing.

'You said you wouldn't laugh,' Jas says. 'You promised!'

'I lied!'

'It's not funny. Cherelle was very helpful.'

'Cherelle! *Cherelle!* I'll bet she was!' I keep right on laughing until I run out of breath. 'Why didn't you—you know—with me—that night in the apartment? Why didn't I get the special treatment, like the girls in the kitchen?'

Jas groans. 'I was embarrassed! I knew you. I had to see you again.'

'So you gave me the "it's not you, it's me" speech. Nice

one. I guess that all worked out like you wanted it to, didn't it?' I think of the two years we never saw each other.

'Yeah. Not exactly.'

'Still, it's nice to know it *wasn't* me.' I smirk.

'Told you it wasn't!'

I roll my eyes. 'And of course I was going to believe you.'

There's a pause as, That Night covered, I remember something else. Something almost, if not quite as bad. Last Night.

And Jas must know what I'm thinking, because he gets up and comes over towards me. 'Last night. That was me too. I was drunk. Sorry. But I was thinking…'

'Mmmm?' I say as he comes closer.

'I was thinking maybe I could make it up to you.'

Make it up to me? My heart stops beating when I hear that.

The next thing I know Jas has taken me by the hand and is leading me over to the bed.

Then, slowly but surely, my heart kicks back in…

…and I have the best sex of my life.

Chapter Twenty-Two

When I wake up, it takes me a minute or two to remember where I am and what I've been doing. When I do, I can't help but smile. I roll over and put my arm out, ready for it to land somewhere on top of Jas, but he's not there.

I sit up. 'Jas?'

A voice comes straight back. 'Hang on. I'm in here.'

I let my breath out again. He's in the bathroom.

He comes out with a toothbrush stuck in his mouth, making a 'be there in a sec' sign with one finger.

I get up then and, my nightie never having made it out of Jas's backpack, grab a sheet and wrap it around me toga-style. It trails on the floor like a train as I make my way to the bathroom.

'Thought you'd never wake up,' Jas says when I stick my head around the door, his mouth full of frothy toothpaste.

'You tired me out with your slick moves,' I joke as he rinses.

'Come here,' he orders when he's done, turning back around and leaning on the basin. Willingly, I pad on over, tripping over my sheet as I go. When I reach him, Jas pulls the fabric away from me and brings it up to let it fall back down over us, like a tent. I tilt my head up to his face and he kisses me.

'Delicious. Minty-fresh,' I say when I pull away.

'Unlike some.' He laughs. 'What's with the sheet?'

'What's wrong with it?' I glance down.

'It's on, for a start. Take it off. Immediately.'

I let it fall to the bathroom floor. It's only fair. After all, Jas isn't wearing a stitch…

'That's more like it,' he says with authority.

This makes me laugh. 'Think you're in control here, do you?' I bring up one hand and point downwards. Something's giving him away. 'You're easily pleased.'

'You call *us* easy?'

Hmmm. I guess he has me on that one. I yawn now. 'I don't know about you, but I'm very, very tired. I think we should go back to bed.' By the time I've finished my sentence I've already led him back over there.

'Can't argue with that. But wait a second. I've got a present for you…' Jas says, before I can throw him down on the bed and ravish him.

'Not another dirndl?' I sit down, wary.

'Nope. Found it this morning. Didn't even know it was in there.' He goes across the room to rummage in his backpack, bringing back something plastic with a cord on it. He places it over my head.

I bring the object up to read what it says. '"Backstage pass. Access all areas."' I frown. 'I don't get it.'

'I just thought you might like to, er, access *all* areas, you know?'

'Is that right?' I raise an eyebrow.

Jas holds out a hand and I take it. He grabs my arm and

pulls me up off the bed dramatically. 'There's just one thing. One thing I have to be sure of,' he says seriously, giving me the stare—the one that makes my knees weak.

'What?'

'The leather pants. What's that all about?'

I laugh, and tell him if he'd bothered to bring any I could have shown him, but now he'll just have to wait. Then I finally drag him down onto the bed and demand some of what was making those girls at the apartment so happy. After all—as we discussed last night and, more heatedly, two years ago—it wasn't me, it was him. Now I figure it should be all about *me*.

And Jas…

Well, he does what he's told.

He is, after all, the kind of guy who looks after his fans.

A good hour or so later—he really does look after his fans; I wasn't joking about that—we order up some breakfast: some toast and coffee to throw down before we have to be on our way.

'Do we have to go?' I moan as Jas passes me a second cup. 'I love it here.'

'If we want the rest of our luggage we have to go.'

'Bugger the luggage.'

'My thoughts exactly. But we've got to take the car back.'

'We could keep the car,' I say hopefully.

'Ah, so now the car's OK? Now you're siding with Michael?'

'It might come in handy for doing the groceries.' I try to keep a straight face, but can't.

'You'll be a kept woman in no time.'

I put down my cup. 'I'll never be a kept woman, and don't

you forget it. I can write my own pop songs and sell them to boy bands if I want a yellow Porsche.'

'Maybe I should move on too. Sculpt things out of cow dung, or something. Call it modern art and sell each installation to stupid rich people at ridiculous prices.'

'Go on, then.'

'Just get a move on, Notting.'

Down in the reception area, Jas charges the room, breakfast and our few phone calls to his work account while I flip through the papers. After I've seen them all, I go over to him and place them on the counter. 'Look, look and look.' I point.

He looks.

It's us, us and us.

Three pictures. One as we're leaving the hotel room, with Michael towering by my side, and two different but similar ones of the getaway car, with my face hidden on Jas's lap. I take a closer look—there's no way anyone who didn't know it was me would be able to tell, but it's more than enough for Kath to set off on the warpath if she puts two and two together. Which wouldn't be hard. I have to call her.

Jas sees my face and hands me his mobile.

I dial the number and head outside. It's a good fifteen minutes before I walk back over to Jas, waiting by the front door.

'How was it?' he asks.

'Exactly like I expected. I should be more careful. Do I really know this guy? Strange men and boiled lollies—the whole deal. You're going to have a lot of explaining to do when you meet up with them.'

'I can't wait.'

'You'd better start doing some good deeds. Donating large wads of cash to charity and so on.'

'Already do,' he says smugly. 'Only I don't talk about it.'

'Well, you'd better *start* talking about it.'

We make our way out to the car, which has been brought around to the portico.

'I'm going to have to do that anyway.' Jas looks over at me. 'Start talking and fast, I mean. Have to spend a few days giving interviews. I didn't tell you last night, but I'm supposed to be in New York in two days. I'm leaving from Munich.'

I glance up at him in surprise as I get in the car. 'You're not coming back to London? Not coming on the bus?'

He shakes his head. 'No time.'

'You don't want to go to New York, do you?' It's written all over his face.

'Nope. But it's only fair if I want out.'

I nod on the outside, but my insides twist. Being separated from Jas now, after all we've been through, seems like relationship suicide. 'And then what? After New York?' I say quietly.

'Depends if you want to stick around for a bit or not. I could meet you back at home. Or in London. In a month.'

'A month? It'll take that long?'

'Yeah, I know. And it's not that I don't want you to come, believe me, but it's not fair. I won't have any time, and I can't guarantee how safe it's going to be. Kath's going to kill me as it is.'

I pause. 'But what about when you're done? What are you going to do after that?'

Jas grins. 'I might take a few months' holiday. Or a few years'. Let things die down a bit.'

'Anywhere in mind?' I ask as he starts up the car.

'Maybe somewhere warm. Or a white Christmas.'

I give him a look before we speed off, my head hitting the back of the seat. 'I wish you wouldn't do that.' I reach up with one hand. 'I'm getting whiplash.'

'Sorry.' He laughs. 'It's the boy in me. So, what about you?'

'I might stay in London for a bit.' There's silence for a moment. 'You will really come back, won't you?' I know I sound needy, but I can't help myself.

Jas slows down. Right down. And then he reaches over to grab one of my hands.

'You don't need to worry about that. You go wherever you want, and this time I'll track you down. Like a bloodhound.'

We drive most of the way back to Munich in silence.

As we get into the city and start to navigate our way to the car rental place, I bring up New York again. 'So when are you going? To New York, I mean?'

'Tomorrow morning.'

We drive into the car yard and pull up in a spare space. I grab our backpacks while Jas goes inside to drop the keys off and call us a cab.

Minutes later we're on our way to the hotel. Everything seems to be moving so fast. This morning, the drive back, even the cab seems to be travelling faster than all the other cars on the road. I look over at Jas and try to guess what he's thinking. When he sees me watching him he gives me a quick smile and squeezes my knee.

We're at the hotel in no time. As we pull up we both see the tour bus at the same time, parked up near the corner. 'Just in time, huh?' Jas says to me.

'Mmmm,' is all I answer.

We're unloading the boot of the cab when Jas spots Sharon. 'Look who's here to greet us.' He swivels me around by the waist so I can see her standing in the lobby.

'I was wondering about that before. I meant to ask what you're going to do.'

Jas goes to pick up our bags from the footpath, but I stop him.

'Wait a second.'

'I don't know. Nothing, I guess. Don't care.'

'You do so care. Just don't…be too hard on her. She was excited, you know? I doubt she had any idea what would actually happen.'

'Yeah, I know.' He exhales.

However, when we get inside Sharon's nowhere to be seen. Shane is, though, running around trying to get the Beer-drinking Society organised. When we spot him, we go over.

'If it isn't you two, eh? I was wondering where you'd vanished to. Great exit, by the way.'

'Thanks,' Jas says.

'Bodyguards were a nice touch. Let the cat out of the bag a bit, but.'

'One of the last times. Had to make it good.'

I smile. 'I guess we'd better go pack.'

Shane checks his watch. 'Leaving in fifteen minutes and counting.'

Hearing this, I do a runner for the lift. 'Come on.' I beckon Jas. 'I need to get changed as well as pack.'

Ten minutes later I'm packed, and am pulling on my jacket over a fresh set of clothes. 'You'd better hurry.' I look up from my jacket's zipper to see Jas hasn't packed anything at all but has spent most of his time in the room texting.

'I'm staying here tonight. Thought I may as well, rather than move somewhere else.'

I stop in my tracks. 'But is it safe?'

'Don't really think it's necessary, but Michael's coming.'

'Oh.'

'Charlie…' Jas comes over.

I struggle, still trying to do myself up. 'Here.' He reaches out to help me.

'It's OK, I've got it.' I give it one final tug.

'Great.'

I look around the room. Anywhere but at Jas, really. 'Well, that's it, then. I'd better go. Are you coming down?'

'Course.' He goes over and opens the door so I can wheel my suitcase out. 'Want me to take it?'

I shake my head. 'It's OK.' Down the end of the hall, the lift doors are just opening. I make a run for it again. 'Quick!'

We both race down and cram into the already full lift. There's silence as it descends the two floors to the lobby.

In the lobby itself, all of the bags piled everywhere only a few minutes ago are gone. Only a few people are left standing around now, and I realise the others must all be on the bus. Everything's still moving in double-quick time, and I feel as if my life's an hourglass, with about five grains of sand left before my time runs out. I make my way over to Shane, who's standing with his back to us, talking to some-one.

'I'm ready,' I say, and he turns.

He's been talking to Sharon.

'Fantastic,' he says, taking my bag. 'This is the last one.' He heads out to the bus with it.

Which leaves Jas and I with Sharon.

The three of us stare at each other silently. Finally, Sharon speaks up. 'I'm, um, sorry…about yesterday. I didn't know it would be like that.'

'What did you think it would be like?' Jas asks, sounding more than slightly pissed off. I nudge him on the arm.

Sharon shakes her head. 'I don't know. I thought maybe

a paper would come and take a photo of the two of us or something. I didn't think…' She looks miserable. As if she really is sorry.

There's a pause before Jas speaks again. 'Look. Don't worry about it. Not your fault.'

But Sharon just hunches over even further. 'So, are you guys, like, breaking up?'

'I'd, er, say so—yeah.'

'Can you sign something for me, then?' she says, and rummages around in her bag for a bit, eventually finding what she's looking for—a Spawn CD.

'Sure.' Jas takes the CD from her, as well as the pen she's offering. He wiggles the cover out, signs it, and hands everything back to her.

'Jas Ash?' she says. 'Shouldn't Zamiel sign it?'

'There's no more Zamiel,' he says, and Sharon's expression becomes almost distraught. 'Look,' he adds quickly, seeing this, 'why don't you give me your name and address? I'll send you something when it's all over. One of his jackets or something.'

'Really? That would be great!' Sharon seems far more animated after hearing this. She writes down her name and address on a piece of paper for Jas and gives it to him. 'Thanks, um, Jas.'

Jas gives me a sideways wink. 'I'd send you a pair of his leather pants, but they're spoken for.'

I roll my eyes. Oh, great. Tell the whole world, why don't you?

'Hey, hadn't you guys better get on the bus?' Jas glances outside as we hear the motor start up.

Sharon starts off, but then turns back for a second. 'Aren't you coming?'

Jas shakes his head. 'Got to go to New York.'

She makes a face. 'Sorry.'

'It's OK. Go on—go. I'll send you something.'

'Thanks.' She waves and heads outside. Jas and I follow slowly.

'That was nice. Offering her the jacket,' I say.

'She looked like her bloody budgie had died.'

'I told you she didn't mean it to happen. She was probably just as freaked out by the whole thing as I was.'

'I know.' Jas nods. We make our way to the side of the bus and stop on the footpath, opposite the bus steps.

'So…' I say.

'So…' Jas repeats. 'You've got all my numbers? I'll call you. Every day. And you know you can call me any time, yeah?'

'OK.'

'And we'll meet in London. In less than a month. Promise.'

Shane herds the last few stragglers onto the bus.

'Ready, Miss Charlotte?' Shane calls out, now he's on the bus himself.

I look up at him, then turn to Jas, and do what I have to do before my brain kicks in—I reach out, grab his jacket and pull him towards me…

'I'm coming to New York.'

'Come to New York.'

We both laugh and take a moment or two to get ourselves together again. That is, before we go and do the speaking at the same time thing all over again…

'I didn't want to impose.'

'Didn't want to ask.'

Jas grabs me then, and hugs me long and hard before he pulls back. 'Let's get your bag,' he says.

We call Shane back down off the bus and he obligingly

fishes out my bag from the bus's storage space. While he's doing this Jas sneaks up and puts a large wad of money into his tip jar. He deserves it.

'Thanks for everything, Shane,' I say, giving him a quick hug and a kiss on the cheek after he puts my bag down on the footpath. 'You've been great.'

'Stellar,' Jas adds, shaking his hand.

'Least I could do,' Shane says with a smile.

'I hope the trip back's OK,' I tell him.

He groans. 'Me too. There's one more after this, and that's it.'

Jas and I stare at him, unbelieving. 'You're coming back?' I ask the question for both of us.

'Two tours. Back to back. I'm sure you understand.' He punches Jas on the arm and laughs before he heads back inside the bus. 'You crazy kids have some fun for me. And don't forget you have to name your firstborn after me now. It was the champagne that got you together in the end; I'm sure of it.'

'What's he talking about?' Jas looks at me.

'I'll tell you later,' I say, before turning my attention back to Shane. 'We will have a good time—thanks. And good luck with uni,' I call out. Shane sticks his head out. Puts his finger to his lips. 'Oops. Sorry.'

He waves a hand and then grins evilly. 'And we're off— like a raped ape!' he belts out, then sticks his head back in- side the bus quick-smart.

'That's disgusting!' I yell, pointing at him.

There's another grin from Shane. This time from inside the bus, where he's safe.

'That's *disgusting*!' I turn to Jas, still pointing at Shane.

'Especially if you're the ape,' Jas says.

We both watch as the bus pulls out and drives off down

the street to the faint strains of 'Aussie, Aussie, Aussie, oi, oi, oi!', which makes us laugh.

It's a while before I look up at Jas. 'So, what're we going to do after New York?'

He claps his hands together and grins. 'How about Italy? Hear you have some business to attend to.'

I size him up. 'You'll have to stay in hostels and stuff, though. No more Brown's. I'm on a budget, remember?'

'I remember.'

'And no sneaking around paying for things.'

'My line of credit will be seriously diminished after New York, don't worry.'

'And more talking. There has to be more talking.'

'Yeah, definitely more talking. Between, er, other things, of course.'

'Of course.' I laugh.

'Now. That bottle of champagne?' Jas says. 'The one I think might have been from Shane?'

'Mmmm?'

'It's upstairs, isn't it?'

I nod.

'It's unopened, isn't it?'

I finally get where he's going with this and grab his hand, dragging him back inside the hotel. 'Not for long,' I say, with a smile that almost cracks my face. 'Not for long.'

When your current life just isn't doing it for you,
you might have to go halfway across the world
to find out what makes you tick. Check out these
books to discover what else is out there.

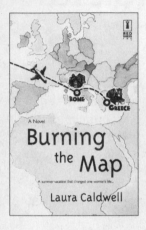

With all these options we might just
keep you up all night!

Pick up your favorite titles
at your local bookseller.
For more info on our titles and authors
check out reddressink.com.

RED
DRESS
I N K
™